BRAVELANDS

BLOOD AND BONE

BRAVELANDS

ALSO BY ERIN HUNTER

WARRIORS

WARRIORS
SUPER EDITIONS

EXPLORE THE
WARRIORS
WORLD

FIELD GUIDES

NOVELLAS

NOVELLA COLLECTIONS

MANGA

SEEKERS

SURVIVORS

BRAVELANDS

BLOOD AND BONE

ERIN HUNTER

HARPER

An Imprint of HarperCollinsPublishers

Special thanks to Gillian Philip

Bravelands: Blood and Bone

Copyright © 2018 by Working Partners Limited

Series created by Working Partners Limited

Map art © 2018 by Virginia Allyn

Interior art © 2018 by Owen Richardson

Library of Congress Cataloging-in-Publication Data

Names: Hunter, Erin, author.

Title: Blood and bone / Erin Hunter.

Description: First edition. | New York, NY : Harper, an imprint of HarperCollins Publishers, [2018] | Series: Bravelands ; #3 | Summary: "A new Great Father now rules over the animals of Bravelands, but he is not what he seems, and unless the elephant Sky, the baboon Thorn, and the lion Fearless can fight his lies and unite the animals of the plains, the balance of Bravelands may be destroyed forever"-- Provided by publisher.

Identifiers: LCCN 2018013362|

ISBN 978-0-06-264210-3 (hardback) | ISBN 978-0-06-264211-0 (library)

Subjects: | CYAC: Baboons--Fiction. | Lion--Fiction. | Elephants--Fiction. | Adventure and adventurers--Fiction. | Africa--Fiction. | BISAC: JUVENILE FICTION / Animals / General. | JUVENILE FICTION / Action & Adventure / General. | JUVENILE FICTION / Fantasy & Magic.

Classification: LCC PZ7.H916625 Blo 2018 | DDC [Fic]--dc23 LC record available at https://lccn.loc.gov/2018013362

Typography by Ellice M. Lee

18 19 20 21 22   CG/LSCH   10 9 8 7 6 5 4 3 2 1

❖

First Edition

BRAVELANDS

BLOOD AND BONE

PROLOGUE

The currents beneath Windrider's broad black wings surged, flinging her off-balance. Creasing her eyes against the driving rain, she tilted her wingtips and banked into the chaos and fury of the wind.

"We should find shelter," cried Blackwing at her side. Lightning exploded in a white blast, its long forked claws flashing into the savannah far below the flock of white-backed vultures.

"We cannot," rasped Windrider. "We must reach the swallows in time!"

Lightning dazzled the sky again, and Windrider could not tell if Blackwing heard her words against the crash of thunder and rain. How the swallows were fighting the storm, she did not know; it was hard enough for her own flock with their massive, powerful wings. But there the small birds were—not

far ahead, their flight path heading north. They were struggling to keep their pointed formation, but their leader battled
on against the violence of the storm.

"Quickwing!" screeched Windrider. "Quickwing, wait!"

There was hesitation in his tiny wingbeats, until he
swooped, rising to meet her. His bright eyes were hard and
determined.

"What is there to wait for?" he chirruped. "Let us be,
Windrider!"

"The Great Spirit has returned, Quickwing, I promise you," cried Windrider. The great bird and the small one
soared around each other, the rain lashing them. "You must
not abandon Bravelands!"

"The Great Spirit has abandoned *us*," the swallows' leader
retorted. "Why should we stay? The Northlands grow balmy
and serene once more. We long for them. Summer flies north,
Windrider, and we fly with it!"

A second swallow broke formation to circle them. "This is
no place for us!" she chirped. "The Great Spirit does not bring
such storms in this season, so the Great Spirit is truly gone! In
the Northlands the sun is gentle, and we can raise our chicks
in peace."

"You are nomads, I know," rasped Windrider, "but you
have always waited for the sign from Great Mother." As the
swallows swooped back into line and headed once more into
the teeth of the storm, she adjusted her path to soar alongside
them. "This year has been strange and terrible, but Bravelands
is still Bravelands."

"Yes, Great Mother always told us when we should migrate," replied Quickwing. "But this new Great Father? He has said *nothing*."

"He has given us no sign," put in another swallow. "So we leave while we still can. This is no place for us."

"And who knows if we will ever come back?" added Quickwing bitterly. "Look at this storm, Windrider! Can you truly claim balance has returned? Why should we not give up on the Great Spirit? It has given up on us!"

Twitching her wingtips, Windrider hovered and banked, then swooped downward in a broad spiral. The wind tore at her feathers, the torrents of rain lashed her eyes, but she could make out beneath her a lone, lightning-ruined tree. Far worse than the unnatural weather, a great wave of sorrow and defeat buffeted her.

We must rest, at least. Blackwing was right about that.

She heard his harsh croak behind her as the flock followed her down through the raging weather. "You did all you could, Windrider."

"Did I?" She felt desolate, and unusually powerless. "Yet I could not stop them. Quickwing and his flock will leave. I have failed the Great Spirit."

The splintered trunk of the Lightning Tree glistened black with rain, its three crooked shards clawing skyward. Suddenly she longed to feel the tree beneath her talons, to cling to its branches and hunch her head into her shoulders and rest her weary muscles. Windrider stretched her wings and angled them, slowing her flight.

And then the sky exploded in a blaze of white-hot brilliance, each cloud and blade of grass momentarily etched in stark silver.

The blast flung Windrider back; the wing of another vulture caught hers, and for a moment the flock was thrown into chaos, flapping desperately, their voices raised in a discordant tumult of shrieks and caws. As Windrider righted herself, the rank stench of burning seeped into her nostrils. Black smoke and bright ash mingled with the rain. The Lightning Tree had erupted in sparks and flame.

The fire was close enough to singe my wings. And my flock . . .

"To the land!" Her cry was raucous with fear.

One by one the vultures stooped to the ground, folding and flapping their wings, taking running hops to gain clawholds on the sodden earth and slippery rock. Windrider realized she was breathing hard.

Rain ran in streams from their singed feathers as the vultures huddled close and watched the Lightning Tree burn.

"It is an omen," whispered Blackwing.

"Yes," croaked Windrider. A sense of doom clutched her heart as she watched the flames roar. "Yes, Blackwing. Great danger lies ahead."

"Again," he murmured, closing his eyes.

"We must take shelter in the forest," she told them all, her voice dull with shock. "Come, my flock."

She stretched her wings once more and lurched into the sky, Blackwing at her side. It was a low and short flight to the canopy of the trees, yet it exhausted her. Landing unsteadily, clutching a high branch with her talons, she turned her head to gaze back at the Lightning Tree, its flames still leaping high into the rain-drenched sky.

Great Spirit, I know you are with us. I know it.

Desolate, she hunched her head into her wings and closed her eyes.

I trust in you still. Whatever danger approaches, protect us. Protect Bravelands. . . .

CHAPTER 1

Sky Strider's lungs ached, and her hide was soaked to a gray that was almost black. Her legs felt weak, and her feet, usually so powerful and steady, slithered wildly in the mud as she thundered through the forest. She feared that at any moment she might slip and crash to the ground.

Yet she could not stop. Branches whipped her eyes, ears, and trunk, and she almost stumbled on a newly fallen kigelia branch, but she blundered on, driven by a force inside her that she couldn't explain.

I must get there.

Where?

I don't know but I must!

The thick vegetation opened up very suddenly, and Sky stumbled to the edge of a small clearing. Lightning flashed above the canopy, illuminating the whole scene before her, and the young elephant choked on a cry of horror.

A group of baboons stood there, tails stiff, their muzzles peeled back in rage. With them was a young maneless lion, who crouched menacingly over something in the center of the circle. The sight of a lion in the company of baboons no longer shocked Sky—not after all that had happened in the last seasons—but the expression on the lion's face did.

It's Fearless! Cub of the Stars! But I hardly recognize him.

He loomed over another baboon, this one sprawled on the ground, bleeding and terrified. The lion's jaws were open, slaver dripping, his long teeth bared and his amber eyes alight with a killing rage.

"You betrayed us!" Fearless roared at the baboon. With a jolt, Sky saw who it was—Thorn Middleleaf of the Brightforest Troop.

She felt something wrench within her. These two, lion and baboon, had been so close. And now Thorn lay sprawled in the mud beneath Fearless's jaws.

Everything in Bravelands seems broken, Sky thought. She raised her trunk.

"*Stop!*" Her cry resounded through the clearing.

The baboons turned to her as one, tense with shock, but Fearless didn't even look up. He only glared at his captive with determined fury. "Die, traitor!"

Sky knew she had no choice. She charged.

Before her the baboons scattered in a panic, whooping and hollering the alarm—and clearing her way. Fearless was already lunging for Thorn's throat, but before his lethal fangs could close and kill, Sky smashed into him, her head colliding with his shoulder.

Fearless was flung across the clearing. He slammed into the twisted trunk of a fig tree and collapsed to the ground, limp.

Sky stared at him for a moment, gasping with relief even as the shock of what she had done chilled her blood. At her feet, Thorn Middleleaf gave a whimper and staggered to his paws.

"Sky! *Thank you,*" he said hoarsely.

Sky couldn't reply. Drained by her fierce burst of energy, she shambled across the clearing to where Fearless Gallantpride lay unmoving in the rain.

Oh, Great Spirit, let him be alive!

She put her trunk to his tawny flank—and suddenly she was no longer Sky Strider, granddaughter of the last Great Mother: she was a tiny lion cub, prancing across the plains, tail held high as she followed a beautiful lioness. *My name is Swiftcub. My father is Gallant of Gallantpride.*

Startled, Sky yanked her trunk away, her heart pounding painfully in her chest. She stood very still for a moment until the dizziness of the vision passed. She was still getting used to her new gift—the ability to see into the memories of any creature she touched. It was unnerving, but at least it meant Fearless was still alive.

Thorn was beside her. He crouched on his stocky haunches, peering anxiously at the lion who had once been his friend. Blood streaked the young baboon's fur; he looked bedraggled and wretched in the lashing rain. *But his wounds aren't deadly either*, thought Sky with relief: Fearless had not had time to do him mortal damage.

"Oh, Fearless," Thorn murmured, closing his eyes. "It's not his fault, Sky."

"What happened?" she asked. "Why did Fearless attack you?"

"Stinger Crownleaf." Agony contorted Thorn's features. "He's calling himself Great Father now."

A wave of desolation engulfed Sky. She couldn't move for a moment: the sense of sheer *wrongness* left her breathless and disoriented.

Thorn's expression became bitter. "Stinger turned Fearless against me. And all the others, too. I can't blame Fearless, or my troop. Stinger can be very convincing."

Sky couldn't believe Thorn's words. *Stinger Crownleaf is Great Father? It makes no sense. The Great Spirit is still within me!*

Determination filled her. Damage had been done; it was her job to undo it.

"Thorn, we need to get out of here," she told him grimly. "Fearless will be all right, don't worry. A few cracked ribs, I think, but he'll heal. *We* won't be all right, Thorn—not if we don't leave this place. Those baboons will find their nerve again soon, and they'll be back."

With a shudder, Thorn rose to all fours. Before he could argue, Sky was curling her trunk around his body and lifting him onto her shoulders.

And suddenly there was no rain.

Dappled sunlight filtered through the canopy, warming her fur as she sat on her favorite jackalberry branch. She sank her fangs into a mango, delicious and fragrant. She wished Berry could be with her to share it.

Sky shook herself briskly to chase the vision away. "Hold on tight, Thorn!"

As soon as she felt his paws clutch the edge of her ears, she set off in a trot through the trees. Twigs snapped and leaves pattered down around them. It was impossible to avoid leaving a trail, but the storm was still wild, and with luck the rain would give them enough cover. Filled with urgency, Sky picked up as much speed as she could on the treacherous ground.

But however fast she ran, there was no escaping the memories that passed to her through Thorn's grasp. *A baboon with large, liquid eyes and gold-streaked fur sat close by on the jackalberry branch, smiling shyly when Thorn offered her half the mango.*

"We'll be together," Berry said softly. "I know we'll end up in the same rank, Thorn; I know it in my bones. We're meant to be, you and I."

Thorn's heart felt almost too full of love. "I know it, too, Berry. . . ."

Sky took a sharp gasp of air. *That memory is private!* Clenching her jaws, she plowed on through the teeming rain, trying to think only of the next footfall, and the next.

By the time she felt it was safe to stop, a gray and miserable dawn was paling the sky. Thorn, exhausted, was half dozing against her neck, but she nudged him awake with the tip of her trunk.

The young baboon clambered down to the muddy ground, swiping rain from his eyes, and blinking at the shadowy clearing. "Where are we?"

"We're safe. For now." Sky sank to the ground, flanks heaving. "And we can talk here. Tell me everything, Thorn. I can't believe Fearless tried to kill you."

"And he would have succeeded, if not for you." Thorn shivered. "But I still don't blame him."

"Your own Crownleaf told him to do it?" Sky shook her head, bewildered.

"It's a long, awful story, Sky. But he's got everyone fooled. You know how he got to be Crownleaf? By killing the last two. Bark and Grub."

She stared, stunned. "Surely not—"

"Yes," said Thorn. "I found him out and confronted him; he's been looking for a way to get rid of me ever since. Last night, I was afraid he'd finally found it."

Sky could barely believe it. "And now he's saying he's Great Father? What about Stronghide?"

"Gone," said Thorn. "Stinger didn't need him anymore, so he turned the animals against him. And Sky, that isn't all Stinger's done." He was watching her, his eyes full of sadness and sympathy. "Stronghide killed your grandmother so he could become Great Father—all Bravelands knows it now. But he didn't come up with his plan by himself. It was—"

"Stinger," she said hoarsely.

Thorn was silent for a second. Then he nodded. "He's like a spider, Sky, spinning webs to trap us all."

Sky shook her ears, but not from denial. Aching, helpless anger raced through her blood. *"Stinger Crownleaf had Great Mother killed."*

"He did. I'm sorry, Sky. So sorry." Thorn reached for her foreleg. Sky wanted his comfort, but she drew aside to avoid his touch. "Great Mother is a terrible loss to all of us. But especially to you. And to do such a thing before she had the chance to pass on the Great Spirit? It's evil, Sky."

"Oh, it is." Sky felt the hot fury intensify. "He can't get away with this, Thorn. We can't let him. What Stinger did—it didn't just break the Code. I think it's broken all of Bravelands."

"That's why we have to get rid of him," growled Thorn.

"Yes." Her rage turned to fierce determination. "Stinger must be exiled, far away from Bravelands."

Thorn peeled back his lips. He looked straight into Sky's eyes. "I didn't mean we should exile him," he said carefully.

His words cooled her raging blood. Returning his stare, Sky felt a sudden, calm certainty that stilled her trembling limbs.

"No, Thorn. *Only kill to survive*, remember? We'll deal with Stinger according to the Code of Bravelands."

"He doesn't respect the Code!" said Thorn bitterly. "He's broken it already, countless times! How do you think you can just make him leave?"

Sky lowered her trunk and blew at the ground between her feet. "The thing is, Thorn . . . I need to tell you. Something happened to me. I have a mission."

"What kind of mission?"

She took a deep breath and looked up. "The Great Spirit," she told him gravely. "I'm carrying it. It's with me, inside me."

Thorn's eyes were wide, and for a moment he looked stunned. "You mean you're . . . you're the new Great Mother?"

"No!" said Sky hastily. "No, I'm not. My mission is to find the new Great Parent and pass the Spirit to them." She glanced away. "I know it sounds crazy."

Thorn wrinkled his muzzle in deep thought. At last, he nodded slowly.

"I think I understand, Sky. The Great Spirit has to be somewhere, doesn't it? And it certainly isn't with Stinger."

Sky's voice grew grim. "He's got the animals fooled for now, but that will change when the true Great Parent arrives. The animals will drive him into exile as he deserves, and no one will have to break the Code."

The young baboon was watching her with fascination, picking at a wound on his snout. For a few heartbeats, he looked as if he was lost for the right words. At last he asked, "What does it feel like, Sky? The Great Spirit, I mean."

"I can hardly explain it." Sky felt suddenly shy. "It's like a—a force, in my bones and my hide and my blood. But it's separate from me. I think . . ." She recalled the desperate run that had spurred her into the forest, though she hadn't known what she would find. "I think the Great Spirit brought me to you just now. It must have known the Code was about to be broken."

Thorn sat back on his haunches, still staring at her. "Then I'm as grateful to the Great Spirit as I am to you," he said softly. "It really does know everything."

She nodded, silent, and stirred the mud with her trunk.

At last she looked up again.

"But Thorn . . . Bravelands is so vast. Somewhere out there is an animal who'll be our new Great Parent—I must find them, and I don't even know where to start."

"Sky, don't worry. If the Great Spirit brought you to me, it will guide you to the new Great Parent, too. You'll see."

His words made Sky feel lighter. The Great Spirit had trust in her; now she had to return that trust.

From somewhere among the trees, a branch snapped. She started, her ears tilted toward it. "We've been here too long already," she told Thorn. "You should run. Stinger will be looking for you."

"Oh, I know it," he muttered. "He won't give up easily. When Stinger knows what he wants, he just reaches out and takes it." He shook himself, sending rain showering from his fur, then gave her a grin. "But I'll miss your company. Thank you again, Sky Strider. I owe you my life. Good luck."

She watched him turn and lope away into the trees. He moved slowly at first, then abruptly leaped up onto a low branch, scrambled higher, and was gone from sight.

Sky stood still, listening to the fading rustle and crackle of leaves until she was sure he'd finally gone. She shook her ears and blew out a breath through her trunk. At least Thorn was safe for now.

And it's time for me to leave, too—before Stinger strikes again.

CHAPTER 2

Thorn hadn't realized it was possible to miss the heavy downpours. The air felt hot as he sucked it into his lungs, and his fur was clammy with the oppressive heat. All the same he ran and ran, bounding over hollows and fallen branches, gasping for breath, not daring to slow down. The Strongbranches would be coming for him; he needed to put all the distance he could between himself and his murderous pursuers.

He didn't want to think about Fearless. But unwanted memories of those terrible moments flashed through his head: gaping jaws, long lethal fangs, hot slaver dripping onto his face, reeking of the blood of prey.

There had been a time when he'd ridden happily on Fearless's back, when they'd played and planned and hunted together. *How did it all go so wrong?*

Stupid question, he told himself, his breath rasping hot in his throat. *I believed all Stinger's lies. How can I blame anyone else for being just as gullible?*

Despair wrenched at Thorn; he could see no way to convince anyone of the truth. Fearless idolized Stinger so much that he would kill Thorn on his orders. Even worse was the memory of Berry's expression when Thorn had been blamed for her father's crimes. There had been disgust in her eyes, and loathing.

I'd give anything to show her the truth, to win her back. But I don't know how.

"Don't waste energy, you idiot!" he gasped to himself, out loud. There was one thing he had to do before he could fix any of the disasters Stinger had brought on Bravelands: stay alive.

At last he burst into a glade and saw a familiar patch of croton bushes. There beyond it was the huge kigelia tree with the hollow at the top where Nut had hidden after his exile from Brightforest Troop.

But his relief was short-lived. What did he expect to find, after all? His pace slowed and he glanced warily around as he approached the tree.

There was a smear of blood on the grass beside the trunk, and tufts of fur were caught on twigs and burrs. That blood had to be Starleaf's: Stinger's guards, the Strongbranches, must have dragged the old baboon violently from the hollow near the top of the trunk. Nut's hideout had not been secret enough to save her.

Thorn's heart turned over. Starleaf had always been kind to him; her son, Mud, was his best friend in the world. And now

Mud believed that Thorn had killed his mother. *Stinger is taking everyone from me.*

He couldn't dwell on that now. Thorn scrambled up the trunk, feeling bits of thick scabby bark flaking under his claws. He fought a sense of dread as he neared the hollow and clenched his jaws, certain that inside he would find Nut's mangled body.

He puffed out a breath of relief. The hollow was empty. Perhaps Nut had escaped after all? He had always been Thorn's enemy when they were young baboons together in Brightforest Troop, but Thorn did not want to see him dead. Nut, too, was a victim of Stinger's lies and machinations, shamed and driven out of the troop.

Thorn had no idea what to do now, though. Clambering down the trunk, he dropped lightly to the bloodstained grass and peered around. Nut was nowhere to be seen and he daren't call out. Who knew how close the Strongbranches might be?

The foliage around him dripped and rustled, still soaked by the rains, but Thorn stayed very still, listening. A prickly bush at the edge of the glade looked more broken than the others, and the ground beside it was scraped and scuffed. Faintly, Thorn heard a low moan.

He scrambled across to the bush and crouched to part the branches. "Nut!"

He'd never thought he could be so glad to see the mean-spirited baboon. But Thorn's breath caught in his throat when he saw the state of him; his own wounds and bruises were light in comparison. Nut's matted hide was covered in bloody bites

and scratches, and his broad snout looked misshapen and
bruised. One of his eyes was swollen shut. His ribs rose and
fell faintly.

Thorn squirmed in beside him and gently shook his shoulders. Nut gave a petrified whimper, flinching away.

"Nut, it's me. Thorn! We have to go!"

Nut's head lolled around, and he squeezed his good eye,
trying to focus. He gave a groan of pain. "Th-Thorn?"

"Yes. Nut, can you move? We have to leave *now*, the Strongbranches will be coming!"

Nut chittered in terror. When Thorn gripped his shoulders, he tried valiantly to sit up.

"They took Starleaf," he croaked. "I tried to stop them,
Thorn, I did try. But there were so many of them."

"I know. There was nothing you could have done, Nut."

"They beat me, told me they'd leave me here to die. That
nobody cared enough to bother dragging me back . . ."

"You're not going to die," Thorn told him firmly. *At least I
hope you're not.* Nut looked dreadful.

"What . . . what happened to Starleaf? Is she . . . is she all
right?"

"I'm sorry." Thorn squeezed his shoulder very gently, but
even that light touch made Nut wince. "The Strongbranches
killed her."

"No," whispered Nut. "They . . . Oh no, poor Mud."

Thorn couldn't bear to think about his best friend and
what he was going through. "Come on, Nut, you've got to try
to get up. Soon it'll be too late."

The glade was shattered by a sudden, resounding baboon-screech. Thorn froze. His fur stood up all over his body.

"Did you hear that, Nut?" he whispered. "That was Grass's voice!"

With Thorn's help, Nut managed to stagger to his paws, panting with effort and pain. The two of them crawled out from beneath the bush. Supporting Nut with an arm around his back, Thorn glanced around the clearing and sniffed the air. Piled beside a broken trunk was some almost-fresh hyena dung.

"I've got an idea," he murmured, "though you might not like it."

Leaving Nut leaning against a rock, he scooped up pawfuls of the dung and smeared it on his fur, rubbing it thoroughly into his hide. It reeked, rank and disgusting, but he was pretty sure he didn't smell like a baboon anymore. Rising up on his hind legs, he turned to Nut with two more pawfuls of the stuff.

"Oh no." Nut shook his head slowly and peeled his lips back from his teeth. "You can't be serious. No! Get your filthy paws off me!"

Thorn ignored him; it wasn't as if Nut could struggle. He couldn't deny there was a certain satisfaction in covering his old enemy with dung. "It'll cover our scent," he told him firmly. Trying to stifle a grin, he added, "And it's the best kind. Even Strongbranches won't want to take on a hyena."

"It's revolting!" spat Nut.

"Shut up." Thorn yanked him to his feet. "Let's go."

It was slow going; Nut was limping badly, his breath coming in hoarse rasps, and the forest was dense and tangled. The damp heat seemed more oppressive than ever. As Thorn wrenched aside a low-hanging bough, it sprang back, catching his flank and knocking off a clump of drying dung.

Ahead the undergrowth looked even more impenetrable, but Thorn knew they had no choice but to forge on. Gripping Nut firmly, he pushed aside thorny branches with his free paw and forced a way through for both of them. Close by in the bushes, some small creature scuttled away at their approach; birds erupted in a flurry of wings from the canopy overhead, squawking in alarm.

I hope the Strongbranches didn't hear that, he thought anxiously.

When they wriggled out of tangled branches and into a cramped clearing, Thorn eyed his exhausted companion with misgiving. Nut's eyes were closed and his shallow breath was rasping. But worse, Nut's coating of dung looked as patchy as his own; they were losing their scent cover.

"Hurry!" He seized Nut's forearm and helped him scramble over a fallen log. It took some effort: Nut might be badly injured, but he was still a big, lanky creature.

Through the trees came a whoop from another baboon, and then the forest was alive with excited hoots and screams.

"The Strongbranches—they're right behind us!" gasped Nut. "Your stupid dung-trick didn't work! We're going to *die*."

Thorn took no notice; he could barely contemplate how awful their position was. *Think, Thorn!* There had to be a way out of this. There *had* to!

"I smell the traitors!" Grass's shout was hideously loud and close. "Come on!"

For a horrible instant, Thorn couldn't move. Desperately, he looked above and around him. What now? They would never outrun the Strongbranches. *Climb a tree?*

That was the only option, bad as it was. Hauling the wretched Nut to his feet, Thorn half urged, half shoved him up the nearest mahogany trunk. In their clumsy haste, strips and chunks of its bark peeled away beneath their claws and pattered to the ground. *They'll know where we are in moments.* Thorn's heart was heavy with dread, but he scrambled on, tugging Nut with him. He couldn't despair yet.

His muscles aching, Thorn clambered up through the lowest branches, and with a final effort he dragged Nut onto a thick bough. The abundant, dark green leaves drooped around them. Thorn was sure they couldn't be seen—but they would certainly be smelled. *They'll find us soon. Then we're dead.*

It was so hard to think clearly when time was running out. Thorn got to his paws and peered desperately through the leaves. He stifled a gasp of fear. Far below him, the Strongbranches were loping into the glade. Chittering in anger, sniffing the air, they rose onto their hind legs.

"Find them!" barked Grass.

Thorn shrank back into the cover of the leaves, his insides shriveling. Then, as he looked wildly around the foliage, something caught his eye. There was an odd, bulging growth on one of the mahogany branches, just above and to the side. He took a breath as hope sparked.

"Nut, get ready to run!"

"We can't! They'll catch us, there's no hope—"

"There's a bees' nest up here," he hissed. "I need something to throw!"

Nut's eyes widened and his gaze darted frantically. "There—that branch?"

It was a stunted outgrowth from the trunk, rotten and dead. Thorn grabbed it and snapped it off. It was just about big enough. He drew back his paw and narrowed his eyes at the nest.

"They're in the trees!" came Grass's triumphant yell from below.

No more time. Thorn clenched his jaws and flung the branch.

It shot straight and true, crashing hard into the top of the nest with a dull *thwap*. The nest's fixing broke and plummeted down through the foliage, exploding into a black, buzzing, enraged swarm.

"Run!" screamed Thorn.

Grabbing Nut, he sprinted along the branches of the mahogany trees, leaping through the forest canopy and away from the furious bees that swirled in a violent cloud.

Shrieks and wails erupted from the Strongbranches far below. They were thrown into panicked terror, slapping at their fur, tearing at their muzzles. Thorn did not wait to watch, but urged Nut on from tree to tree. Something hot and sharp pierced Thorn's flank, and then his neck, but he slapped the stray bees away and kept running and leaping.

As their pursuers' cries and shrieks of pain receded, Thorn

didn't slacken his pace. He urged Nut on, keeping as high as he could above the ground. After what felt like half the length of Bravelands, with Nut lagging farther and farther behind, Thorn was glad to see the trees thinning out. Stopping yet again, balanced on a branch, he waited for Nut to catch up. The broad-faced baboon looked worse than ever, but he clearly had no energy to object when Thorn forced him on.

"At least the trees aren't as thick here," Thorn consoled him. "But we can't risk stopping yet."

He felt safe to come to a final halt only when night was falling. Nut staggered to his side, gasping raggedly on his haunches, without even breath enough left to curse Thorn. Tree frogs and crickets were beginning to pipe and whistle in the undergrowth. Thorn stood in silence, listening, his chest and muscles aching.

"I think we've lost them," he panted at last. He rubbed at the sting on his neck. It had been worth it.

"But where do we go now?" asked Nut plaintively, wincing at his own stings. Tentatively he bent to pull a stinger out of his shoulder with his teeth, and his head remained hanging as if he couldn't raise it again. "Nowhere's safe."

"Well," began Thorn, wrinkling his muzzle, "I've been trying to think about that. I've got an idea."

"It'll be a terrible one," whined Nut. "*All* your ideas are terrible."

Thorn had a feeling Nut was going to consider this the worst idea of all. He slumped back against the crook of a thick branch. The place he'd thought of was not too far away—assuming the sun had gone down in its usual place, and they'd traveled as far as he reckoned they had. But distance wasn't the problem. . . .

Spit it out, Thorn. It wasn't as if Nut was capable of fighting him over it.

"Leopard Forest," said Thorn grimly.

Nut's eyes widened. He shook his head and rubbed his ears, as if he couldn't believe what Thorn had suggested.

"I'm serious," Thorn added.

Nut finally managed a hoarse screech of protest. "No way!" He tried to rise, and fell back. "That's the most dangerous place in Bravelands—everyone knows it!"

"Exactly," said Thorn. He patted Nut's filthy shoulder, hoping he could reassure himself, too. "The Strongbranches will never look for us there."

CHAPTER 3

"I like rain," grumbled *Silverhorn.* "I like the way it makes the savannah green. But if it doesn't stop soon, I swear grass is going to start growing out of my hide."

Sky and Rock, on either side of the young rhino, rumbled with laughter. "I know how you feel," said Rock. "I'm looking forward to seeing the sun again. And not being *wet.*"

Sky gave the young bull elephant an affectionate glance over Silverhorn's shoulders. Rock's deep-set green eyes met hers, filled with amusement, and Sky realized again how happy she was to be back in his company. Her friends had been waiting for her, near the forest, and it had given her a warm glow of gratitude to see those familiar, solid silhouettes on the grassland. They must have stood for a long time, patiently enduring the rain.

The sky had turned from clear blue to a low, heavy sheet

of dark gray; somewhere above the cloud layer, lightning still flashed from time to time. Distant thunder rolled menacingly, and Sky knew that at any moment the constant drizzle would burst into another lashing torrent. She ached to return to the watering hole, to be back in the comforting embrace of her aunts. It had been so long since she'd left them and journeyed to the mountains, seeking answers to the turmoil in her mind.

"Are you sure you want us to come with you?" asked Rock. Silverhorn paused to graze on a thorny shrub, and the two elephants stood together, letting her eat.

Sky tugged on a clump of bedraggled grass. "I'm sure," she said, more confidently than she felt. Poor little Moon had joined her on her journey, and now she was returning without him. Instead, she was coming home with—of all creatures—a bull elephant and a *rhinoceros*.

Rock studied her as she chewed listlessly on her mouthful of grass. "It's just . . ." he said, and hesitated. "I'm not supposed to hang around family herds, you know that. And as for Silverhorn . . ." He flapped his ears in a gesture of mock horror.

"No, it'll be fine," said Sky. "You're both my friends, and I want my family to meet you."

"Then we'll come," he told her, extending his trunk to twine with hers.

She flinched away before he could touch her. Rock gave a slight frown, but nodded and turned away to pick at the shoots of a stunted shrub.

Sky had the horrible feeling she'd hurt him, but she couldn't help it. Perhaps it was a fine and useful gift to see the past of others, but it felt wrong somehow: like trampling on the most secret parts of their lives.

Silverhorn was trotting toward Sky and Rock, looking cheerfully well fed. "Have you two eaten?" she asked, swiveling her tiny ears. "Good. Let's go!"

Sky had swallowed barely a mouthful of grass, but she wasn't hungry anyway. As the three paced on across the plains, a gloomy sense of foreboding weighted her stomach, more heavily with every step. More than anything she wanted to see her family.

But I have so much to explain. . . .

"Sky! Sky, is that you?" One by one, the small group of elephants lifted their heads, flapping their huge ears forward and raising their trunks to taste the scents of the new arrivals. Behind them the surface of the watering hole was dull in the gray light and pockmarked with rain; the trees surrounding it hung heavy, drenched by the storm. Rock and Silverhorn waited beneath them at a respectful distance from the herd.

Comet came trotting toward Sky, her eyes shining. "It *is* you! Oh, Sky, we've missed you. Where have you been?"

In moments, Sky was surrounded by her beloved aunts, crooning and blowing and stroking her hide with their trunks. She felt so safe and loved, she did not even mind their touches; indeed, their memories felt like a secure, happy place to be. *Browsing the trees for green leaves; suckling tiny new calves; trekking across the savannah behind Great Mother.* Sky basked in the familiarity of every image.

"Sky, we were so worried!" cried the matriarch, Rain.

It was so good to see her face again, Sky thought, with its crisscrossing of heavy wrinkles that spoke of age and wisdom and experience. She nestled close to the matriarch's side, letting Rain caress her head with her white-patched trunk. "And who are these two?" Rain was looking toward Rock and Silverhorn.

As the powerful young bull and the rhino emerged from the trees, Sky introduced them. "They've been traveling with me," she explained.

"But where's Moon?" Star, his mother, peered eagerly past them, blinking her long lashes. "Moon?" she trumpeted. "He went with you, Sky, didn't he? The little mischief. Moon!"

Sky's gut twisted sickeningly. It was the moment she'd been dreading more than any other.

"He did," she whispered. "I couldn't send him back, it's my fault. I . . ." Her words stuck in her throat.

"Sky?" Rain stroked her head, an edge of terrible fear in her voice. "What is it?"

"Titanpride," blurted Sky at last, misery overcoming her. "Moon was . . . he . . . Titanpride k-killed him."

For a moment, no elephant could speak. Then Star's cry shattered the silence. She raised her head and gave a wild trumpet of awful grief. Her body swayed, and it seemed to be only the support of the others that kept her from stumbling to her knees. As the other elephants took up her keening cry,

Sky huddled between Rain and Comet, hardly able to bear the sound of Star's mourning.

"This is what we feared," groaned Comet. "The Cub of the Stars warned us about Titanpride."

"But how?" Rain murmured, her brow wrinkling into even deeper furrows. "How did it happen, Sky?"

"They came after him—they could see he was little. The cowards!" Sky blinked back angry tears and stretched her trunk toward the rhino. "Silverhorn tried to fight them off, but there was nothing she could do."

"And I heard Sky's distress call." Rock came forward humbly, Silverhorn behind him. "Between us we finally drove the lions off, but it was too late."

"They both stayed with me after that," whispered Sky. "I told . . . I told Moon a story. He wasn't alone. . . ."

"Oh, young one." Comet nudged her gently with her head.

"Silverhorn. Rock." Rain nodded to the rhino and the young bull. If she was surprised by the odd pair, she kept it well hidden. "You've protected Sky, and you tried to protect Moon. You are good friends to her, and you are welcome."

Sky could feel only a vague, leaden relief that Rain wasn't sending her friends away.

"Moon can't lie out there all alone," said a hoarse voice. Star nudged the other elephants away and walked more steadily toward Sky and the matriarch. "We can't leave him, Rain. We can't!"

"Of course we won't." Rain stroked the bereaved mother with her trunk. "We'll collect his bones, Star, I promise, and we'll take him to the Plain of Our Ancestors."

"He will be with his family," murmured Comet, hooking her trunk over Star's neck.

"Yes," said Star, her face desolate. "Yes."

"Rain," said Sky hesitantly, "there's more. I have more to tell you."

Rain turned to her, her eyes dark and serious. "Go on, Sky."

Sky took a deep breath. "I know how Great Mother died. I know what happened."

"Oh, young one." Rain stroked Sky's neck. "We have heard about Stronghide's villainy. And news has come that he is now dead. You don't need to worry about him anymore."

"No, no. You don't understand—I mean, I know what *really* happened." Sky gazed around at her aunts, meeting their concerned eyes. "It was Stinger Crownleaf who did it."

"What?" they all spoke as one.

"The False Parent?" said Rain. "But how could he have done it? A baboon wouldn't be able to murder an elephant."

"Stronghide and his crash of rhinos, they were the ones who forced Great Mother into the water." Sky's voice trembled and faltered. "But the plan was Stinger's!"

Rain's eyes grew dark and angry in her furrowed face. "You're sure of this?"

Sky nodded, miserable and shivering. Saying it all out loud made it somehow even worse. "I'm sure."

The herd was quiet for a moment, exchanging glances of horror.

"How could any animal believe he possesses the Great Spirit?" There was a tremor of anger growing in Rain's voice.

"And where *is* the Great Spirit?" Cloud demanded. "Has it abandoned us?"

Sky swallowed hard. "It's right here. It's in me."

In silence, the elephants stared at her, then at one another.

"Sky," said Rain slowly. "Are you our Great Mother?"

"No! No, I'm not. But . . ." She dipped her head shyly. "I'm carrying the Great Spirit."

Sky closed her eyes, trying to order her thoughts. "When Titanpride attacked . . . before Moon died . . . we were going somewhere." She told them about the journey into the mountains, and the vulture she had met there. "He was old. So very old . . ." She sucked in a breath. "And I could understand what he was saying to me."

The elephants' eyes were wide with wonder. Not one of them contradicted her.

"He told me that I have to find the new Great Parent and pass the Great Spirit on to them. Because Great Mother never got the chance."

"Sky," Rain said in a hushed tone, "I have never heard of such a thing before. But I don't doubt that the Great Spirit is with you. We all knew, all of us, that you were very special. This proves it."

Awkwardly, Sky stared at the ground. She did feel special, but it was none of her doing. *It's the Great Spirit. It's the one with power, not me.*

Rain turned to face the others. "We will confront the False Parent with what he has done. Let's see if he will do the right thing—admit his guilt and go."

As the herd trumpeted their approval, hope thrilled in Sky's chest. Was it really possible that Stinger would be dealt with today? She wished she could tell Thorn. *He'll be gone*, she thought, *and we won't have to break the Code to do it.*

One after another the elephants fell in behind Rain as she turned and marched along the water's edge. Sky set out after the herd, with Rock and Silverhorn at her side. She could see where the herd was heading. The shore of the watering hole curved into a broad, sweeping bay, at the far end of which jutted a long spit of land—like a vast trunk stretching out over the water. It was dark green, thick with forest, and its far end gave way to a perilous, red-rocked cliff.

"That is where Stinger has set up his new camp," cried Rain up ahead. "Baboon Island, he calls it—but maybe not for much longer. Come, sisters!"

They reached the spit and strode onto it, past several animals milling on the shore—zebras, kudu, and wildebeests, all hoping, Sky realized with dismay, to speak to Stinger—and under the dense trees. Baboons moved busily around them, darting here and there on errands and chores. Among them all, directing, stood Stinger Crownleaf; just the sight of his cunning eyes sent a shiver through Sky's bones. He was big— bigger than most of the other baboons—and a thin white scar ran above his nostrils. As the elephant herd approached he bounded forward and rose onto his hind legs, his eyes bright and sharp. A formation of guard baboons drew close around him, their faces hard and wary.

Sky hurried up the line of elephants to speak to the matriarch. "Rain," she said anxiously, "we'll have to be careful. . . ."

"Careful? He's just a baboon!" Rain snorted her disdain.

Just a baboon. Sky felt a shiver of unease. "He's cunning, Aunt Rain. Thorn says he'll do anything, say anything; he can convince a bird that the sky is red."

Rain blew out through her trunk. "What chance does one baboon have against the Strider family?"

"My friends!" Stinger called, as the thunder of the elephants' feet slowed and halted, and a hush fell. "Welcome to Baboon Island! Draw nearer, and tell me how I can be of help to the elephants of Bravelands."

"Help?" Rain stepped forward, her strong voice echoing around the tree canopy. "You can help no creature, False Parent!"

There were shocked gasps from the baboon troop and the animals on the shore. Every pair of eyes turned to stare incredulously at Rain.

"This creature—this impostor—killed Great Mother!" trumpeted Rain, as the family drew up protectively at her side. "Stinger Crownleaf, you are no Great Father of Bravelands. You have no right to that name!"

Stinger's dark eyes widened with shock—and hurt. For an instant he swayed, and almost dropped back onto all fours. "What are you saying, Rain Strider?"

Animals were drawing closer now, hanging onto Rain's

words. A hippo gasped; impalas exchanged apprehensive glances. But Stinger had recovered himself and stood firm. Unease gnawed in Sky's gut.

Rain narrowed her eyes. "Leave now, Stinger Crownleaf."

"Leave? What—I—" Stinger's eyes closed, an expression of deepest pain on his face. "Rain, your grief has turned your mind. This is . . . this is nonsense. Stronghide's crime was shocking, and I feel deeply, so deeply, for your loss. Believe me, I do." He turned to the largest group of zebras and wildebeests clustered at the shore, whose perplexed stares shifted between Stinger and the Striders. "I, the Great Father of the Bravelands, feel each animal's pain as my own. But such accusations—they are madness! Grieve as you need to. But peace, dear sister!"

Sky's heart thudded. So Stinger was going to try to brazen it out.

"Do you deny your crimes, Stinger Crownleaf?" blared Rain. "Leave Bravelands of your own free will—or we, the Strider family, will make you go!"

The elephants were shifting now, lining up in a single rank to face Stinger. Rock moved forward to stand stalwart at Sky's side. Pale, watery sunlight gleamed from his fearsome tusks. She looked wildly around at the herd. They tossed their tusks, and the ground seemed to shake with the violence of their stamping feet. Sky's heart was galloping in her chest. Everything suddenly felt stretched taut, like the muscles of a predator ready to spring—unstoppable and deadly.

Stinger drew himself up again, that expression of pain

mixed now with a sad determination. "Surely you will not break the Code, my sisters? Not even in your terrible grief."

"This is your last chance, False Parent," growled Rain.

Stinger set his jaws. "I am going nowhere, Rain Strider. I am the Great Father of Bravelands, and I will not abandon my children."

"Liar! Killer!" Rain gave a bellow of pure rage. *"Charge!"*

For a moment, Sky stood rooted to the ground in horror. *No, this is wrong!* But the herd was already thundering forward, tusks lowered for battle. Sky ran behind them. "The Code!" she cried. "We mustn't break it!" But the elephants didn't hear her over their trumpeting bellows and pounding feet. The baboons around Stinger fell back in panic.

For all his bravado, Stinger was quick to run. He spun with astonishing speed, springing from tussock to tussock until he reached the trunk of a stinkwood tree. Paw over paw he scrambled up, leaping high into the thick spreading branches.

Rock was first to reach him. He did not slow his pace, but lowered his head and slammed his skull hard into the stinkwood's trunk. The whole tree shuddered, and leaves fluttered to the ground.

"Coward!" trumpeted Rain, joining Rock to crash her head into the tree.

"My children, do you hear what they call your Great Father?" Stinger bellowed to the animals below. Wildebeests, kudu, and zebras gazed up at him, awestruck, and across the water even a leopard paused in its drinking to blink up at the defiant baboon. "This herd of elephants attacks one lone baboon, yet they say I'm the coward? It is an insult to the Great Spirit!" Edging along the longest branch, he sprang to the next tree.

The elephants turned toward it, enraged, but Stinger took firm hold of a branch and rose onto his hind legs.

"See how the Great Spirit protects me?" he called down, even as the sturdy mahogany trembled. "Are you watching, my children? Do you see how the Spirit grants your Great Father strong trees and good branches?"

A tremendous blow to the mahogany rocked him back. Catching his balance, he ran again, leaping for another tree. This one was a colossal kigelia, and as the elephants slammed heads and tusks against it, there was the thump and thud of its massive long fruits hitting the hard ground.

"Rain, the Code!" cried Sky again. But the matriarch was crashing farther up the island.

"He's retreating," trumpeted Rain. "After him! Trap him!"

Even the huge kigelia was creaking and groaning under the battering of the elephant herd. It swayed and shuddered, its fruit crashing down now in a constant hideous battering. Rain slammed her head into it, again and again.

Sky could almost see Stinger counting the beats as he poised himself for another leap. He sprang suddenly over her head for the ground, racing across a clearing to the next patch of forest. The elephants swung as one to face their enemy.

"We have him!" cried Rain. "Take our revenge, sisters!"

Sky felt a cold wrench in her gut. The Code was sure to be broken, she realized. Brutally, savagely, it was going to be shattered into a thousand fragments. *And I can't stop it. . . .*

The herd advanced slowly now, their feet shaking the earth. Rain's face was alive with anger as she lurched past the kigelia tree toward Stinger. Sky stared at her, terrified of what the matriarch might do.

And then the thunder crashed again.

No. It wasn't thunder, Sky realized, but the noise of it was even louder than the roar of the storm. A crack shivered up the trunk of the mighty kigelia tree, splitting it in two. Wood splintered and ripped, with a sound like the shriek of an animal in unbearable pain. One whole side of the trunk peeled away, taking the biggest branches with it. For a moment it seemed to pause, held in midair by a few last shreds of its own timber. Then, abruptly, it collapsed.

Rain was right in its path. Sky gave a gasping squeal as the massive trunk and branches slammed onto the back of the matriarch's neck.

The great elephant was flung forward onto her knees, shaking the earth with her impact. For a wild moment Sky thought her aunt would recover her footing, but then realization and horror flooded through her: Rain's head lolled at an impossible angle to her collapsing body. With an echoing, horrible crash and rumble, the matriarch was slammed to the earth and buried beneath a chaos of leaf, branch, and wood.

The cries of the Strider herd were awful. When Sky's panicked eyes flickered to Stinger Crownleaf, she saw him gazing down on the scene from a tree branch, his expression unnaturally cool and calm. Trembling, she stared at her family once again; the elephants raced to pull the tree from Rain, tugging and straining, shoving with their tusks. But Sky was too frozen with horror to help. She stood there stunned, empty and helpless, as though the tree had crushed her too.

Sky had seen the shape of Rain's twisted backbone as she fell. The matriarch's neck was broken.

She was already dead.

CHAPTER 4

Fearless started awake, and immediately wished he hadn't. Grogginess and pain swam over him, and he collapsed back down, groaning. The murky twilight told him night was falling, but that was all he knew; he could hardly think straight. A long-fingered paw clutched his shoulder, shaking him gently. *How long have I been here?*

"Cub of the Stars, wake up!"

It felt like a huge effort to roll over and open his eyes, but he managed it, blinking. Everything hurt: his ribs, his head, his neck muscles. "Stinger?"

The baboon crouched over him, a frown of worry on his intelligent face. "Yes, Fearless, it's me. You must get up!"

"Yes. Yes, let me just . . ." Fearless propped himself up on his forepaws, but his head sagged. There seemed to be an entire troop of monkeys inside his skull, hammering on it with rocks.

"Take it slowly, my friend. I'm just glad you're alive. You were brutally attacked."

Now it was coming back to him. He remembered cornering the traitor Thorn in the glade—Thorn, once his beloved friend, who had turned out to be so evil he had killed Mud's mother. Fearless remembered the anger coursing through him, the sense of awful betrayal, as he glared down at the treacherous baboon. He remembered lunging to finish him off.

And suddenly, thundering feet, and an explosion of pain, and then—nothing.

"The Strongbranches reported back to me," said Great Father gravely. "They said you'd been attacked by Sky Strider—that crazy renegade elephant. I knew something must have happened. When you didn't return from the forest, I was worried."

"Thank you," mumbled Fearless. *I failed. I failed in my duty to Great Father; I didn't kill Thorn Middleleaf.* "I'm sorry, Stinger. I let you down. And now you've saved me again. Just like when I was a cub."

"You haven't let me down, Cub of the Stars." Stinger gave him a fond smile.

Fearless gave a morose growl. "You asked me for one thing, and I failed." It had been a hard thing to be asked, a dreadful thing—but he'd owed it to Stinger. Now the debt wasn't paid after all.

He staggered up, swaying only slightly, as Stinger patted his flank in reassurance. The forest wasn't spinning so fast now, and the ground beneath his paws felt almost steady. Fearless clenched his jaws.

"There's more bad news, I'm afraid," Stinger murmured. "More chaos in Bravelands, more hatred and rebellion. Sky's herd launched a surprise attack on me today."

Fearless stared at his friend and mentor, horrified. "They *attacked* you? You, the Great Father?"

Stinger nodded. "They did their best to kill me. I only just managed to escape through the trees." He closed his eyes and gave a sad sigh.

"How dare they!" Fearless could feel his strength returning with his anger. "They're jealous, that has to be it. They wanted the Great Parent to be an elephant again. They can't stand that the Great Spirit chose you!"

"I think so," agreed Stinger softly. "Thorn has corrupted Sky Strider, I fear, and that corruption has spread—to her herd, and who knows how much further? These are dangerous times, Fearless. We need to stick together, look out for each other more than ever."

"Yes," snarled Fearless. "I won't let you down again, Stinger, I promise."

"Don't worry. We'll find Thorn, I'm sure of it." Stinger gave him a smile. "And then you can make it up to me—by finishing what you've started."

"You can rely on me." Along with the frustration, Fearless was aware of a sneaking relief at his failure. However evil and treacherous Thorn had become, it would be grim work to kill his former friend. But it had to be done. Lashing his tail, he growled: "Next time I have Thorn Middleleaf's throat between my jaws, I'll make him pay for what he's done. No elephant will stop me!"

"I trust you, my good friend." Stinger rubbed his neck. "Come on, we must return to the camp. I want the Goodleaves to check you over, make sure you're all right."

"I'm fine, Stinger. I'll be fighting fit again soon."

"No, Fearless, you must let me take care of you. The Goodleaves will soothe that sore head, and they'll tend to any cracked bones. I wouldn't have it any other way." Stinger leaned his head into Fearless's neck. "I can't leave your health to chance. You're too important to me."

Fearless found himself hoarse with gratitude and affection. "Thank you, Great Father."

"Much too important," Stinger murmured as he led the lion from the glade. "I won't ever risk losing you, my Cub of the Stars."

The baboon guarding the entrance to Baboon Island had been strengthened by the presence of several Strongbranches, Fearless noticed. They looked wary and aggressive, scowling and baring their fangs at any animal that ventured too close. But when Stinger walked toward them with Fearless, they drew back deferentially, bowing their heads.

"You can't be too careful after what happened," remarked Fearless.

"I agree," said Stinger gravely. "My Strongbranches can be trusted to keep me safe—at least until you are fully recovered, Fearless. You are the one I rely on most."

Fearless's heart felt warm and huge inside him as Stinger led him toward the gathering place of the Goodleaves. It felt good to be needed, to be trusted—and to be cared for. *Perhaps I really am as much Baboon as Lion.*

Since the day Stinger had rescued Fearless as a tiny cub from an eagle's nest, the baboon had always treated him with respect and affection. Fearless wished he could say the same for the lions he'd lived with since his father's death.

He closed his eyes as Blossom and Petal Goodleaf bounded toward him, chittering with concern, and submitted meekly to their probing paws. He winced as Blossom stroked his flank firmly, but he resisted snapping or growling.

A small, familiar voice made him blink his eyes open. "Fearless!" said Mud. "I'm so glad you're all right. He is all right, isn't he?" He glanced anxiously at Blossom Goodleaf.

The old baboon smiled and nodded. "As far as we can tell, there's no real damage, Mud Lowleaf. A few cracked ribs, but those will mend in time, and your friend is strong."

Mud blew out a breath of relief and laid a paw on Fearless's shoulder. "I'm glad," he said softly.

Fearless lashed him gently with his tongue. There was such awful sadness in the scrawny little baboon's eyes, and a miserable slump to his shoulders. "I'm so sorry about your mother," growled Fearless gently. "And Thorn. He was your friend."

"And yours." Mud blinked rapidly. "I don't understand it, Fearless." His voice was agonized. "How could he do something so terrible?"

"I don't know." Fearless nuzzled him comfortingly, though his heart beat hard with anger. "Thorn had us all fooled, Mud. He betrayed the whole troop."

"Off you go, Fearless," announced Blossom. "You'll heal fine, but take care for a while. Don't go fighting any elephants!"

"Not elephants, certainly," murmured Fearless darkly. "Thank you, Blossom."

Together, he and Mud made their way to a dappled glade near the point of the peninsula; Stinger had chosen it as the gathering place when Brightforest Troop had moved here from the abandoned hyena den. It had a different atmosphere from their old Council Glade at Tall Trees, sunnier and airier—and that was fitting now that Stinger had dissolved the Council. It felt more open and less formal, Fearless thought approvingly. *A baboon could speak freely here.*

In the center of the clearing was a huge, flat-topped sandstone boulder that gleamed pale in the starlight; on it sat Stinger Crownleaf, looking solemn and wise as he surveyed his troop. Fearless came to a halt and gazed proudly at his mentor. *Crownleaf, and Great Father! He deserves this. I hope every animal in Bravelands comes to realize that.*

Birds were flapping around Stinger; that was to be expected, since one of the Great Parent's gifts was the ability to speak and understand Skytongue. It was odd that they flew in such tight circles, though, and one bird even pecked sharply at his fur when it swooped close enough.

"It's strange." A little way in front of Fearless, a baboon was muttering to her companion. "The birds revered Great Mother! They were her messengers."

"Even that fraudulent rhino had his oxpeckers." Her companion shrugged. "Why don't these birds like Stinger? They should show him more respect, surely?"

Stinger's gaze flitted to the two gossiping baboons, and an expression of irritation crossed his face. Then he glanced at Fearless, right behind them. "Cub of the Stars!" he cried in a commanding voice. "Come forward!"

He heard them, thought Fearless, flicking his tail disdainfully as he strutted past the two females, now shifting uneasily on their haunches. That would teach them to show some respect of their own.

Stinger waited patiently until Fearless was standing beside the Crown Stone. Fearless raised his head and stared at the circle of baboons.

"Look, my troop." Stinger gestured at his friend. "What leader needs birds when he has a lion? In the wake of the recent turmoil and uncertainty, the Spirit has raised me above the old Great Mother, and far above that disgraced rhino impostor. A clear sign of the true Great Parent was needed, and our Cub of the Stars is that sign: a proof of the Great Spirit's blessing. Do you not agree?"

The chorus of baboon voices was immediate and enthusiastic—and loudest of all, thought Fearless with amusement, were the two gossipers. "Yes, Stinger Crownleaf!"

"Long live the Great Father!" cried a baboon from the far side of the glade.

"May he rule and guide Bravelands in peace and justice!" hooted another.

Stinger slanted his gaze sideways, and one of his paws shot out, almost too fast to see. One of the harrying birds gave a squawk of shock as he snatched it from the air.

Stinger did not hesitate. He gripped the bird's head and body and twisted sharply. Then he flung it to the ground before the Crown Stone, a limp and lifeless mess of feathers.

"There," declared Stinger, as the other birds swerved and shot into the trees, screeching. "This is the Spirit's power, and it does not take lightly such disrespect to the Great Parent."

The assembled baboons nodded and whooped, each trying to outdo the others in their eagerness. Fearless gazed at his Crownleaf, brimming with renewed admiration. He reminded him of a lion, in complete authority over his pride.

"Now: Titan," Stinger mused at last, when the troop was fully silent and attentive. "He is becoming ever more of a problem for my Bravelands. I have received word that Titan-pride has taken over Steadfastpride, and is already scouting for more prides to conquer."

Fearless started, his breath catching.

"We all know that lions have no respect for the Great Parent," Stinger went on, "but this arrogant Titan goes too far, my friends. Too far! It seems to me that he is setting himself up as an opposing power to the Great Spirit itself."

There were cries of disapproval from the troop. "Shame on him!" cried one baboon.

"Wise Stinger!" hooted another. "Tell us what to do."

"When you chose me as your Crownleaf," Stinger went on, hushing them with a regal paw, "I was humbled by the trust you placed in me. I promised you then that I would respect tradition—but that I would also think new thoughts, adapt to new circumstances. You gave me this great honor, this weighty responsibility, because you saw in me—if I may say so—a fresh and creative way of thinking, a willingness to change."

Baboons turned to one another, nodding in approval.

Stinger looked around at them all, thoughtful and solemn. "What you recognized as my wisdom and creativity—I propose to use them for the good of all Bravelands. There must be a new way of living together, prosperous and peaceful and just. I wish to change Bravelands forever."

They were all hanging on his words now, breathlessly curious. Fearless felt his heart swell with pride at the Great Father's calm authority. He'd been right about the glade; this gathering felt so much less quarrelsome and fractious than the old Council meetings.

"Both grass-eaters and flesh-eaters will henceforth be contained within strict boundaries," declared Stinger. "This will make food distribution fair. All shall have enough to eat, and none shall deprive others through their greed and power-lust."

Murmured approval rippled around the glade. "But how will you enforce the new rule?" called out Grass Strongbranch, his eyes wide and inquisitive. "The other creatures of Brave-lands can be rebellious, Great Father. We've seen that already."

Stinger inclined his head. "That is an excellent question, Grass," he said, making the burly Strongbranch grin in plea-sure as he chewed on his usual grass stalk. "Let me explain. A baboon envoy will live with each group of animals. These envoys will be called *Driftleaves*, and they will enforce the boundaries I set. What's more, the Driftleaves will report back to me if there is any sign of rule-flouting, or rabble-rousing, or any suspicious behavior. This is how we, the baboons, will make Bravelands safe and peaceful once more!"

Baboons pummeled the ground and bounced, screeching with approval.

"There has been such turmoil lately." Stinger shook his head sadly. "We have a duty, I believe, to do this. And the responsibility falls on us, uniquely! Who but baboons have the cleverness, the wisdom, the skill? We alone can stabilize our beloved Bravelands and put a stop to Titan's aggressive, fearmongering ways!"

Brightforest Troop was at a pitch of excitement by now. The baboons whooped and hollered and stamped their delight, calling out the name of Stinger Crownleaf until the leaves of the canopy shook.

Fearless was happy too, but he was not quite able to roar his unqualified delight. Something Stinger had said was tighten-ing into a knot of anxiety in his stomach.

Steadfastpride. His mother had once told him about them—a pride that lived in the west of Bravelands. *She said Steadfast was devoted to the safety of his pride. That he would defend them against all threats, to the death.*

If Titanpride had attacked them, the battle would have been bitter. He hoped his sister, Valor, hadn't been hurt in the fighting.

Stinger was already busy with his new scheme, appointing Driftleaves from among the eager baboons and assigning them to various herds and families. "Splinter: the meerkats of Sand Hill, I believe. That would suit you very well. Fang . . . let's see . . . you can keep the warthogs in order. Twig: you go to Rockslide's rhinoceros crash; they're a docile bunch, for rhinos, and they shouldn't give you any trouble. Mud?"

Mud bounded forward, his eyes shining.

"Let me see." Stinger seemed to study him for a very long time. "I want to honor your dear mother with your assignment. She made us all proud, and her son should have a post befitting her status."

Mud lowered his eyes. "Thank you, Great Father." His voice was hoarse with gratitude. "That means so much to me. It would mean a lot to my mother, too."

"My most dangerous enemies," went on Stinger thoughtfully, "are the elephants. And that is why I am sending you to them."

Mud looked up, startled. His face was pinched with anxiety. "Yes, Stinger," he said a little shakily.

"You, I think, should deal very well with the elephants. You're small, and you won't make them suspicious. Yet you have sharp eyes and your patience is renowned. You will observe my enemies closely, just as I need you to."

Mud still looked uncertain, but he managed to stutter, "I—I'm honored, Great Father."

"And so you should be, my good baboon. Now, as for you, Bug . . ."

Fearless drew Mud aside, licking his head. "Be careful, Mud," he murmured. "I understand Stinger's reasoning, but take care all the same. I hear the elephants have become very treacherous."

"Oh, I can deal with them," Mud told him, clenching his paws. "They can't be worse than Thorn, can they?"

"Fearless!" Stinger's cry made him turn sharply. The Crownleaf had finished his assignments; baboons were already dispersing through the trees toward their new details. "Fearless, you have a job, too."

"What can I do, Stinger?" Fearless swiveled his ears forward, keen to serve his leader.

Stinger sauntered over to him, rising onto his hind legs so that he could hook an arm over Fearless's tawny back.

"We have delayed enough, Cub of the Stars; it's time to find your destiny! You remember I suggested you start a new pride? With the lions who escaped Titan's takeover of Dauntlesspride?" Stinger leaned his head closer. "Well, it's time. With your own pride, you'll be ready to take on Titan when you're fully grown. By the time you have your mane, you'll be well placed to defeat him. And frankly"—the baboon lowered his voice and ruffled Fearless's shoulder fur—"I'll rest easier knowing you have a pride to rely on. I've been watching Titan closely, Cub of the Stars, and it's time this rampage of his was curbed."

A glow of excitement raced through Fearless's belly and hide. This was what he had wanted: what Stinger had always planned for him. "I'll do it, Stinger Crownleaf!"

"Good!" Stinger clapped his paws together. "Now, one of my scouts has brought me a report of a group of young lions. They're hiding out at a waterfall south of the Lightning Tree."

"I know the place." Fearless stretched his haunches and lashed his tail.

"They must be the exiled lions of Dauntlesspride. Go and claim your pride, Cub of the Stars!"

Fearless set off through the trees. There was no hiding his pride at being set such a solemn and challenging task, and he called a cheerful farewell to the guards as he passed them. He might still be young—a lion without his mane—but already it felt as if he had waited a lifetime for this chance. And how could it be clearer? *Finally! It's my time. The Great Father himself knows it!*

There was just one thing he must do before he could set out on the path of his destiny: go back to Titanpride. He had to rescue his sister from Titan. When that was done, every tie to the brute's dreadful pride would be broken. And instead he would build Fearlesspride; he would make it strong and respected throughout Bravelands. He would create a family of his own—lions that protected and defended one another, and lived without fear. And all the while, he would grow stronger, and bigger, and heavier. He would grow his mane—a fine, flowing mane worthy of Gallant's son.

And then he would return to Titanpride for the final time.

On that day, I will fulfill the oath I made to myself. I will avenge my father.

I will kill Titan.

CHAPTER 5

The heat bore down on Sky as if a great boulder rested upon her back: the ferocious pressure of an impending storm that wouldn't break. *A bit like the grief inside me*, she thought.

Great Mother, Moon, and now Rain: would the Strider herd ever be safe and secure and happy again?

A good distance across the sunbaked plains, she could make out the shapes of Rock and Silverhorn, distorted by the shimmering heat. Their tails flicked constantly at flies; oxpeckers rode on their backs, pecking at parasites on their hides. Sky's friends had withdrawn discreetly after the attack on Baboon Island, leaving the elephant herd to mourn their matriarch.

"Rain led us for such a short time," lamented Twilight, tears brimming in her eyes. "How could the Great Spirit let this happen?"

"It makes no sense," moaned Star. "First my little Moon, and now Rain. So soon."

"What do we do now?" Her voice plaintive, Cloud swung her trunk. "Comet?"

The new matriarch could only shake her head dumbly. She looked weighted down by both sorrow and an unexpected, unwelcome responsibility.

Comet might be the next oldest in the herd, thought Sky, but she was far, far younger than Rain had been. She didn't have nearly as much experience or wisdom. *I don't think she was ready for this. But then, none of us were.*

"Everything will be all right," Comet told them, but there was no conviction in her voice. "The Great Spirit will never abandon us."

Comet was doing her best, Sky realized, but she still missed Great Mother so much. The old matriarch had been so wise, and she had wielded such gentle authority. She would have known exactly what to do now. *She would have guided us.*

The elephants butted and stroked one another with their trunks, desperate to share comfort and consolation, but when Twilight reached out to caress Sky's ear, the younger elephant couldn't help flinching. She knew they were only trying to help, but every touch sent a memory flying through Sky that did not belong to her. For an instant, as Twilight made contact, Sky was a bigger, older elephant, trudging valiantly through a rainstorm as wildebeests stamped and shook water from their hides and horns.

She was relieved when a gaggle of warthogs trotted over to the elephant herd, their broad flat faces curious and concerned. "Comet Strider!" grunted their leader.

Comet, too, looked glad of a distraction. "Snuffle," she greeted him. "How can we help you?"

The warthogs exchanged glances, a little taken aback. "It's not so much what you can help us with," muttered Snuffle. "We just . . . We were wondering . . . We've heard rumors."

"It can't be true," put in another. "Can it? We heard the Strider family attacked Great Father!"

Comet sighed, her trunk drooping. Then she raised her head in defiance. "Yes. It's true. We had good reason, Snuffle."

He gaped at her, shaking his stubby tusks.

"You must understand, Snuffle—all of you—Stinger Crownleaf is not the true Great Father. He was responsible for Great Mother's death."

The warthogs muttered together in shock. "I don't understand!" exclaimed Snuffle. "*Stronghide* killed Great Mother; we *know* that."

"It's all a bit far-fetched," put in his friend. "A baboon killing an elephant? Whoever heard of such a thing?"

"That's just it," said Comet. "Who would have thought it possible—before Stinger came along?"

The warthogs exchanged confused glances. "I don't know who to believe," muttered Snuffle.

"We just want everything to go back to normal!" squealed a young female.

"That's what we want, too," Comet told them.

The warthogs eyed her warily. A couple of them grumbled mutinously at the back.

I don't like this. Uneasily, Sky stirred the damp dust with her foot. Stinger would be telling a different story, she knew. And so many animals had seen how close the elephants had come to breaking the Code. He could use it to turn all of Bravelands against them. *If only I could have stopped it!*

Her fears only grew stronger over the next few days. The elephants remained close to the watering hole, spraying their hides and rolling in the shallows in an effort to combat the heat, but the other herds gave them a wide berth. It was noticeable that no animals wandered toward them to sympathize with their losses, or simply to chat and gossip. Sky was aware of stolen glances, of suspicious stares, of animals who turned rapidly away when she raised her trunk to greet them. And it was impossible not to hear the mutters of the herds as they passed the elephants on their way to the water's edge.

" . . . the Strider family, they just took it upon themselves . . ."

"No explanation, no discussion . . ."

" . . . They've always been far too sure of themselves, those elephants. Arrogant, you might say . . ."

"The nerve of them, really!"

Sky did her best to tune out the grumbling gossip, but the stares were unavoidable. And making it all so much worse was the weather, which refused to break; the surface of the lake shimmered and wobbled, and the vegetation sagged and drooped beneath the broiling heat. Only the crocodiles seemed happy, thought Sky, as she watched one drift close to the shoreline, smirking. Just yesterday she'd seen one grab a weary gazelle and drag it down; it had reminded her horribly of Great Mother's fate.

What was more, she could see the shoreline itself withdrawing every day, leaving a wasteland of cracked mud and wilted weeds. Murky clouds darkened the sky from time to time, but no rain fell.

It's as if the Great Spirit is punishing us.

"Sky, I'm worried," Comet confided in her, a few days after the warthogs' visit. They stood together on the cracked mudflats; as Comet nudged her head, Sky had a flash of another watering hole, where a younger Comet drank happily with a handsome bull elephant. Trying not to wince, she drew away from the new matriarch.

"The other animals have always respected the elephants," Comet went on. "And not just because of Great Mother. But that's all gone, and I don't know what to do. We can't let Stinger go on claiming to be the Great Father! It's *wrong.* But how can we get rid of him? All of Bravelands seems to be on his side." She took a deep breath. "Can the Great Spirit guide us, Sky? Because I can't."

Sky stared at the mud beneath her feet. "I think it already has," she said in a small voice.

"What?" Comet flapped her ears forward.

"Comet, I've been thinking about what happened. That

day when we attacked Stinger—we were trying to break the Code. I think we all knew it, deep down. We wanted to kill him."

"If I'm honest . . ." Comet closed her eyes. "It's true. We did want him dead. We were too furious, too reckless."

Sky gave a small, reluctant nod. "I think what we did . . . It angered the Great Spirit."

Comet stood silent, looking out over the shrunken watering hole. "Maybe you're right, Sky."

"That's why attacking Stinger physically won't do any good. There's only one way we can get rid of him."

"Tell me." Comet stroked her ear with the tip of her trunk.

A memory of that same bull elephant. He was protecting Comet from an angry hippo, tossing his tusks furiously and scaring it off.

Sky shook herself. She met Comet's eyes. "I have to find the true Great Parent. That's when we'll defeat Stinger. Only then."

"But that might well take . . . What's happening?" Comet turned sharply toward the rest of the herd, raising her trunk and cocking her ears forward.

For the first time in days, animals were approaching the elephants—but not for a pleasant conversation, Sky feared. A large group was heading for their herd: zebras, wildebeests, antelopes, hippos. A family of meerkats scampered at their side. The warthogs were trotting to keep up, their ears pricked.

Comet marched toward them, coming to a halt beside the

rest of the elephants. She stood proudly, head high. "What brings you here, friends?"

A powerful-looking wildebeest stepped forward. "You have angered the Great Spirit, Comet. All of you! You attacked the Great Father."

Sky swallowed hard. It was the truth, but this was the wrong moment to admit it.

Indeed, Comet snapped back angrily, "I told you before. We had good reason!"

"Did you?" The wildebeest tilted his head. "The Great Spirit doesn't seem to agree. Look at what happened to Rain. Look at the watering hole! Can you feel the heat on your hide? These storms, this weather, it isn't natural. The Great Spirit is angry with you, Comet Strider. Great Mother would have been ashamed of you all!"

Sky gasped, hurt, but she couldn't protest. She had a sick feeling in her gut. *Maybe she would.*

"You have to leave the watering hole," the wildebeest demanded. "Now!"

A chorus of neighs, snorts, and squeals rose in agreement. All the animals were glaring at the elephants in hostility. It struck Sky that they must have been planning this confrontation for a long time.

"Wait!" said Comet, swinging her trunk. "Don't you understand? Stinger is not the true Great Father!"

"How dare you!" whinnied a zebra. "That is an insult to the Great Spirit itself."

"We all know you're jealous," grunted a hippo as his friends nodded vigorously. "You want an elephant to be Great Parent —so you tried to kill him to get your way."

"*He's* the killer," trumpeted Comet furiously. "He murdered our own Great Mother!"

"What proof do you have? None!" A kudu stamped the ground, making meerkats scurry out of danger. "But we saw you try to kill *him*! We saw it with our own eyes! How dare you accuse the Great Father of your own sins!" He lowered his spiraling horns.

The zebra reared up, then pawed the mud. "Go away from here!"

Two hippos shambled forward, jaws gaping to show their brutal teeth. "What the zebra said."

Twilight and Cloud flapped their ears angrily and swung their tusks, but Comet was quiet. Her eyes were full of turmoil. She lowered her head to Sky.

"What should we do? There will be a bloody fight if we stay!"

"We must go, Comet," Sky whispered. "They're right, aren't they? We have angered the Great Spirit. Let's go before the Code really is broken."

Comet raised her trunk. There was anger in her voice, but defeat and sadness too. "Come, my herd. We will leave this place."

"What?" Cloud turned to her in shock.

Twilight swung her head. "Maybe you're right, Comet." She

sounded bitter. "We have Rain's tusk. And Star needs to col-lect poor Moon's bones; we promised we would go with her."

"Yes," said Star softly, the pain audible in her voice. "We should go to the Plain of Our Ancestors. It's been too long already."

Cloud caressed her shoulder gently. "Star's right."

"We will leave," declared Comet. She turned and began to stride away from the lake, toward the savannah and the hills beyond. Over her shoulder she trumpeted to the herds: "You'll see the truth about Stinger one day, friends. But clearly not today."

The elephants urged Star and Sky protectively into the center of the group. Glancing back, Sky could see the other animals lined up, watching them go. Their eyes and lowered horns were so hostile, she stared up at the sky instead. Against the looming gray clouds, huge birds soared on broad black wings.

Vultures.

The great birds banked and turned, then swooped down to circle the watering hole.

The vultures had always been Great Mother's messengers. There was often a purpose to their flight, as Sky had discov-ered for herself; now she had the sense they were searching for something. She halted. Suddenly, she knew.

They're searching for the same thing I am. The Great Parent.

"Comet!"

The matriarch turned, flapping her ears forward in ques-tion.

"Comet, I can't come with you."

"What?" Twilight's ears flapped forward. Slowly, Sky backed away from the herd as their surprised faces turned to her.

"You go on without me," said Sky. "I have to stay here. I know it."

Comet stared at her. "Sky, you can't leave us!"

"I have to." Sky's ears drooped in sadness, but determination had taken root within her. "I know the Great Parent is somewhere in Bravelands. Right here. I have to find them."

"But Sky," said Cloud, "if you stay with us, we'll help you search—we'll look after you. . . ."

Her voice faded into silence. Every elephant was gazing at Sky now in hurt and confusion. She backed farther away, shaking her head slowly.

Comet opened her mouth as if to speak, then closed it again. It was Star who took a step forward.

"Oh, Sky," she pleaded. "We can't lose you too. Please come with us."

"I can't," said Sky, her voice breaking. "The Great Spirit gave me this task. It's the only way all this will end—when the true Great Parent is with us."

Comet sighed in sorrow, but she nodded. "I think Great Mother will watch over you, Sky. May she and the Great Spirit keep you safe on your quest."

One by one, their eyes dark and sad, the Strider family turned reluctantly away and marched on once more.

Sky watched them trudge across the savannah, their shapes

fading and trembling in the silver heat. The smaller they became, the farther they went from her, the more her heart ached.

"I can do this," she said out loud, a little shakily. "I have to."

"And you won't be alone." A deep voice made her turn sharply.

A warm flood of gratitude rushed through her as she watched her friends approach. "Rock! Silverhorn! Aren't you—I mean, don't you want to go back to your own herds?"

"No," Rock told her firmly.

Silverhorn trotted to a halt at her side, her deep-set eyes warm with affection. "We want to help you, Sky."

"We saw what happened." Rock sounded angry. "Those grass-eaters are fools."

"And we have good news," put in the rhinoceros, rubbing her horn against her foreleg.

"Yes," said Rock. "And you look like you need a little of that."

Brightening, Sky looked from one to the other. *They're on my side, both of them.* That felt good, especially now.

"We've been asking around at the watering hole," Rock explained. "There are all sorts of rumors about new Great Parents."

"Yes," put in Silverhorn. A chuckle rumbled in her throat. "Like a crazy old hyrax who claimed to be the Great *Grandfather*. And a giraffe who swore blind he'd seen the Great Spirit enter a scorpion!"

"But we thought you'd be interested in this one," Rock

went on. "It sounds a bit more serious. There's a buffalo who's claiming to be the true Great Father."

"He's in one of the big herds south of here," added Silverhorn. "And it sounds like they all believe him."

Sky's heart soared, her sadness abruptly lifting. Perhaps she would complete her task and be back with her herd sooner than anyone thought. She blinked happily at her two friends.

"Then let's go to him right now!"

CHAPTER 6

An unforgiving sun blazed white and intense. There was no breeze to stir the long grass where Fearless crouched motionless on his belly. He couldn't even move to ease the heat on his hide; he must not be seen. His skin felt damp with the humidity, his fur prickly, but he must not squirm. He opened his jaws, panting as quietly as he could. *Stay still*, he reminded himself: *your life might depend on it.*

This was the very edge of Titanpride territory. Across the plain he could see the lions sprawled out, basking in the heat. The pride seemed a good deal bigger than he remembered. He could make out Resolute, and Honor, and a few more familiar lions, but there were many he did not recognize. *The conquered lions of Steadfastpride*, he guessed.

Fearless let his gaze drift over each lion, hoping to spot his sister, but suddenly his chest clenched with fear. Right in the center, his head up as he surveyed his pride, lay the huge, black-maned Titan. His plump-bellied mate, Artful, was beside him as usual; their little cub, Ruthless, sat quietly near them. *That's not like Ruthless*, thought Fearless. *That cub could play from dawn until dusk, and then some.*

Fearless creased his eyes against the glare, searching the pride once more. He could see no sign of Valor; perhaps she was hunting.

There was no point rushing in, then, and he was glad. His best and safest plan would be to wait for his sister to return, then intercept her before she reached the pride. Best for them to slip away secretly together.

Fearless sank his body deeper into the grass, preparing himself to endure the heat until Valor's return. He could tolerate the discomfort if it meant avoiding Titan's wrath. Then a sudden sharp movement in the grass caught his attention. He glanced toward it, and his heart plummeted.

Ruthless's small head had jerked up.

The little cub looked alert and eager now, as he sniffed the air and flicked his ears. Abruptly he leaped to his paws and scampered straight toward Fearless.

The other lions raised their heads in astonishment, and Titan swung his huge-maned head to stare. "What is it, Ruthless?"

"It's Fearless, I can smell him!" cried the cub in delight.

Dread tightened Fearless's chest, and he gave an inward groan. For a moment he clung to the hope that he could simply lie still, that Ruthless would fail to spot him.

But the whole pride was alert now; some were standing up and sniffing the hot air, and every one of them was looking in his direction. They knew where he was.

Fearless knew he had no choice but to bluff it out. Rising stiffly to his paws, trying to still his trembling tail, he paced through the grass toward them.

Titan was on his feet now, stalking to meet him with a twisted snarl on his features. "Where have you been?" he roared. "I'm sick of you disappearing all the time!"

Fearless swallowed hard, half thinking he was already as good as dead, but he kept walking. When he was close to the lions he picked up his pace and trotted in among the pride, trying to look as if he was glad to be back.

"I've been hunting for days," he lied. "But the prey was scarce."

"Liar," growled Artful. "You *never* bring back any food. Where do you go? What are you up to?"

"Leave him alone, Mother," cried Ruthless. "Fearless hasn't done anything wrong."

Titan swung a huge paw at his son, swatting him hard to the ground. Fearless flinched, shocked. He'd witnessed Titan bullying his son before, but this was the first time he'd seen him strike the cub in anger.

"Look at what you're doing, Fearless!" roared Titan, turning on him. Fearless couldn't help but wince as slaver flew from the snarling jaws and spattered his face. "You're corrupting my son. *My own son!* The future of Titanpride!"

Ruthless rolled over, looking shocked and hurt, and

stumbled to his paws. "Father—"

"I won't have it!" Titan ignored the cub. "Do you hear me, Fearless? You are never to speak to my son again. He is nothing to do with you, and I've had enough of Gallant's litter-runt lying and plotting against me. Lying to *my own cub!*"

"I don't, Titan!" protested Fearless. "I never—Ruthless isn't—"

"Silence!" Titan's roar shook the grass. "You've pushed me too far, son of Gallant. You're not going to run off again, I'll make sure of it."

"What do you mean?" Fearless did not like the thoughtful, cruel light in Titan's eye. He backed away nervously.

"One of your hind legs, that should do it." Titan eyed his flank. "I'll snap a bone. You can always help the lionesses by dragging the game back for them, so you'll still be useful, in a pathetic way. And I won't even be breaking my oath." He stalked forward, his muzzle wrinkling back from his long yellow fangs.

Fearless scrabbled back, panicking. How could this have happened so fast? "No, Titan!"

"Yes, Gallantbrat. Oh yes."

Titan drew himself back for the strike, his shoulder muscles bunching under his scarred hide. Fearless shot panicked looks left and right, but the whole pride had come forward to surround him, blocking his escape. Their yellow eyes burned, hostile and pitiless. There was nowhere to run.

Fearless wanted to shut his eyes, but he found he couldn't. Titan was taking his time, enjoying his victim's fear, and his face was twisted with sadistic hate. Fearless could only stare, frozen with helpless horror, as Titan finally sprang, jaws open and dripping.

Then, out of nowhere, a golden blur hurtled through the air, slamming into Titan's flank. The huge lion gave a grunt of shock and staggered sideways, his wide fangs just grazing Fearless's hide.

"Run, Fearless!" A powerful, ferocious lioness was clinging to Titan's flank with her claws, raking him.

Fearless's terror and confusion cleared in an instant. "Valor!"

No! He'll kill her!

"You won't hurt my brother, brute," snarled Valor, tearing at the pride leader with her teeth.

Titan was recovering fast, bunching his muscles, shaking his whole body violently to fling her off. She thudded onto the grass, and he gave a deep-throated roar of rage.

But Valor was back on her paws in an instant, bounding lightly toward Fearless. "Come on!"

He needed no second telling. He bolted with her through the narrow gap she had created with her assault. Brother and sister darted through the furious pride, now ducking to dodge an attack, now swerving when their way was blocked. Jaws lunged and claws slashed; Fearless felt a sharp, hot pain in his shoulder as one claw caught him, but he was running as fast as he ever had and swerving nimbly. He had to, he knew it, or he'd die here.

"Get after them!" howled Titan. "Kill them!"

Fearless and Valor were smaller and lighter than most of their pursuers; in this chaos of enraged, full-grown lions, it was their only advantage. Valor flattened herself suddenly and veered aside to avoid Resolute's pounce, then cried, "This way!"

Fearless ducked, leaped, and followed her, his heart racing and his lungs straining. Ahead, Valor hurtled for the long grass, plunging in, and he sprinted after her. The grass grew thicker and longer, but Fearless knew its cover wouldn't save them for long. They ran for their lives, not daring to slow, their breath rasping in harsh, heavy pants. All too soon the grass thinned and they were exposed on open ground once more.

Fearless threw a glance behind them, and his guts flipped over. Titanpride was just thirty paces away, spilling out of the grass, paws pounding the scrubby earth.

His lungs and muscles burned painfully and his vision was blurred, but he could make out a darker, rougher line on their restricted horizon.

"There!" he bellowed. "Hurry!" With a huge effort he put on a burst of speed and raced ahead of Valor, leading the way toward a long, thick line of spiky scrub. Together they dived into it, ignoring the scratch and rip of thorns.

"They're close," panted Valor, pawing away a viciously sharp branch.

"Not close enough," gasped Fearless. "Titan and his big cronies can't fight their way through this. Not fast."

Leading the way, Fearless fought and struggled through the

tangled undergrowth, driven by the knowledge that this was going to be a lot harder for Titan. The very thought of his enemy's furious frustration gave him a new spurt of energy.

Just when he was beginning to think they would be caught in these thorns forever, he burst from the undergrowth onto a stretch of flat plain, Valor so close behind him that she almost collided with his rump. They shook leaves and twigs from their fur.

"We can slow down a bit," panted Valor, and nodded. "Go that way."

A distant strip of acacia woodland quivered in the heat. As they set off briskly toward it, Fearless peered nervously over his shoulder once more.

The big lions behind them were still fighting their way through the scrub; Fearless could hear snarls, occasional yelps, and the smash and clatter of branches. He allowed himself a twinge of satisfaction.

"I hope Titan spears a paw on one of those thorns," growled Valor.

"We're not that lucky." Fearless gave a breathless laugh.

The noise of pursuit was fading rapidly as they trotted away. But a roar of fury followed them through the oppressive heat, making the air around them tremble.

"I'll track you down, Gallantbrats! Run all you like, I'll find you! *You will never be safe!*"

The two siblings did not even pause; instead they picked up their pace again, loping grimly across the red earth. They kept running until their lungs could take no more, then trotted to a halt, flanks heaving, ears pricked.

"They gave up," panted Valor. "Thank the stars." She looked at her brother. "So what do we do now?"

Fearless's chest ached. He shook his head.

"We could find Loyal," suggested Valor, baring her teeth in disgust, as if the name tasted bad in her mouth. "Team up with him."

"No way!" exclaimed Fearless, curling his muzzle. "We're not that desperate. I want nothing to do with that oath-breaker."

"That's easy to say," she told him dryly. "We *are* pretty desperate. What other options do we have?"

"Plenty," growled Fearless. "I'm not answering to Titan, Loyal, or any other lion from now on. Not ever."

He stood tall, his claws extending to dig possessively into the earth of Bravelands. He bared his fangs.

"I'm going to find what's left of Dauntlesspride, Valor. And I'm going to lead them. This is where Fearlesspride begins!"

CHAPTER 7

At least it was a little cooler in Leopard Forest. Energetic climbing was easier beneath the shady canopy, and Thorn was rather enjoying scrambling high into the massive fig tree. There was even a touch of breeze here that did not reach the dank, humid forest floor.

Thorn plucked the ripe fruits, eating some and tossing most down to Nut. He didn't mind how many Nut ate; there were plenty to go around, and his former enemy's injuries meant he couldn't climb yet.

Pausing, Thorn glanced across at the jackfruit tree he'd spotted. The enormous fruits would be more awkward to gather, but he'd work that out when he got to it. So long as he didn't yield to temptation and let a small-to-middling one drop on Nut's head, it would be fine. Nut was certainly a big eater, but it looked as if Leopard Forest could feed them for moons, if not forever.

This place was an even more perfect hideout than he'd expected. Sinking his teeth into yet another fig, Thorn tugged a couple from their stem and dropped them down to the other baboon.

"Thanks," called Nut, a little moodily.

Stretching toward another branch, Thorn groaned. *I'm stuffed*, he realized. He couldn't resist snatching up a passing caterpillar and popping it into his mouth, but the rest of the figs he cradled in an arm as he swung back down the tree.

Even Nut hadn't been able to eat the entire crop; he sat beside scattered, untouched figs, peering around the clearing. "It's nothing like Tall Trees," he mumbled.

"But the fruits! There's loads," Thorn reminded him.

He knew what Nut meant, though. The vegetation beyond this small clearing was very dense; they had battled their way in through thick, tangled undergrowth and dense fronds of lichen and creepers. The scents of the forest were hard to distinguish; they were such a chaos of leaf and dung and insects and rotting loam.

"There's plenty to eat, but nothing tastes as good as a Tall Trees mango." Nut shot a furtive glance at the shadows as a branch creaked and snapped. "I'm still not sure about this. . . ."

"I know it feels strange, but it's our best chance of hiding out. I don't think Stinger and his Strongbranches will dare come in here."

"But the leopards might kill us," pointed out Nut.

"They *might*, but the Strongbranches definitely *will*. Come on, let's go farther and find ourselves a good camp." *It's taking up all my energy to keep Nut cheerful*, Thorn thought with a roll of his eyes. "We'll store the figs where we can find them again. I shouldn't have picked so many, but I couldn't resist." He gestured between the twisted trunks of the fig trees, to another sturdy trunk in the shadows. "And look, there's a jackfruit tree!"

Nut's eyes brightened at that, and Thorn managed to cajole him to his feet. The two young baboons crept on through the thick forest, ears straining for any threatening sound.

The limping Nut fell behind quickly, and Thorn turned to help him clamber over a rotten log. *We'd better find a good camp soon*, he realized. *I'm not sure how much farther Nut can travel. But the deeper into this forest we go, the safer we'll be. . . .*

The shadows ahead of him moved and shifted. Thorn froze.

Nut clutched his arm. "What is it?" he hissed.

"Shh!" Thorn held his breath. *Oh, please. Not leopards. Please.*

The shadow moved again. Somewhere in its darkness, a pair of sinister yellow orbs glowed abruptly into life.

Thorn jumped, stifling a yelp. "Leopard!"

Nut's grip tightened painfully; Thorn could feel him shaking. "Thorn, there's *more of them!*"

It was true. All around, eyes blinked menacingly in the shadows. "It's all right, Nut," squeaked Thorn hoarsely.

"Leopards," moaned Nut. "Lots of leopards. I told you we shouldn't have come here!"

He's right. We're surrounded! Thorn gulped, trying to keep calm and think straight. Surely Mud had told him about leopards once? He'd told him about so many other creatures. Oh, how he wished his loyal, knowledgeable friend was here with him. Something was nibbling at the back of his mind; he couldn't quite put his paw on it. *Leopards. I* know *Mud told me something. . . .* If only he could think properly, he might—

It hit him in a flash. "Wait—leopards hunt alone! I don't think—"

His words ended in a yelp of terror as something sprang from the trees. Thorn just had time to realize it was no leopard—and then powerful, long-fingered paws seized him in a savage grip. Lips peeled back from vicious fangs, and angry hoots screeched all around him.

Baboons!

There must be a dozen of them at least. He'd had no idea there was a troop living here. And he knew exactly how Brightforest would have responded to baboons from a rival troop invading their territory—they'd have driven them off, beaten them violently, maybe even killed them. . . .

Thorn struggled, writhing to escape, but the paws that held him were too strong, their claws digging sharply into his hide.

"Wait," he babbled. "We don't mean any harm. Let us go!"

"No chance," snarled a burly baboon, pacing forward between his companions. "We are Crookedtree Troop, and this is our territory. You're strangers. And you are *not welcome here!*"

"Then we'll go! We didn't know—"

"That's your bad luck," growled one of the baboons holding

him. "If you're even telling the truth, invaders!"

The new and terrifying baboons said not another word, but set off through the forest at a brisk run, dragging Thorn and Nut with them. Nut was squealing and squirming, but in his wounded state he had even less chance of escaping than Thorn did. There was a cold lump of fear in Thorn's gut.

"Let me go! Let me go!" hollered Nut.

"Please don't hurt him," Thorn gasped to his captor. "He's already injured and—"

"Shut your snouts! Both of you!" The lead baboon swept aside a screen of thick gray lichen, and Thorn and Nut were thrust savagely forward into a broad glade.

Thorn staggered and blinked, waiting for his eyes to adjust. Right in the center of the clearing, a thick-trunked tree grew high up to where its wildly crooked and bent branches tangled with the canopy. At its roots was a vast mound of black feathers, the lowest ones tattered and faded, the newest fresh and glossy. *That must be their idea of a Crown Stone.*

And sitting on top of it, with a silent and steady gaze, was the Crookedtree Crownleaf.

She was a slender, pale-furred female, all skinny muscle and long-fingered, elegant paws; her eyes looked huge and very dark gold in her hollow face. Yet she obviously wasn't short of food; she was surrounded by female baboons who selected fresh fruits from a pile by the tree and handed them reverently up to her. Thorn thought they looked like submissive, timid young things—until they all turned as one and looked at him. Their yellow eyes were cold with menace.

The baboon on the Crown Stone of feathers, by contrast, had a blank, mild gaze. With an air of indifference, she watched the approach of her patrol and their captives.

"Tendril Crownleaf!" barked the leader, and bowed. "We found two trespassers on our territory. Shall we kill them for you?"

"Whoa!" Thorn wrenched himself free from their grip. "Crownleaf, this was an accident! We didn't know!"

"Nobody told us there was another troop living here," babbled Nut. "We'll go away. We'll never come back!"

Slowly, elegantly, Tendril Crownleaf raised a paw. Thorn opened his mouth, ready to apologize, plead, defend himself— but all his words dried in his throat. His jaws clamped shut again. Stunned, he realized that even Nut's vociferous complaints had died to silence.

How did she do that? he wondered.

"Greetings, strangers," said Tendril in a polite, level tone. "You have wandered into Crookedtree territory. I am sure this was a mistake on your part."

Thorn nodded eagerly. "Yes, it was."

"What a pity. You are, after all, strangers. And Crookedtree has learned the trouble that strangers can bring."

Thorn opened his mouth to protest, but at a single piercing gaze from the Crownleaf, he closed it again.

"Nonetheless," she went on in that flat, calm voice, "I shall see that you are treated fairly." She gave them a smile that was both entrancing and cold. "Highleaf councilors: please join me."

Baboons bounded forward, taking up positions to the right and left of their Crownleaf, facing the newcomers. They all looked darkly hostile. When they had taken their places, Tendril simply sighed and turned her gaze once more on Thorn and Nut. There was the hint of a smile at the corner of her mouth, but it wasn't a friendly one.

"Where are you from, strangers?" barked one of the Highleaves.

Thorn and Nut exchanged a glance.

"You may not confer," said the Crownleaf, with her first hint of sharpness. "Answer honestly, and all will be well."

Nut was glaring a warning at him, but Thorn took a small step forward. "Tendril Crownleaf, we are baboons of Brightforest Troop. Our home was in the forest near the watering hole—the forest known as Tall Trees."

"Then why aren't you there?" demanded a big Highleaf.

"Well, Brightforest Troop had left there; we'd moved on. . . ." Thorn licked his jaws; it was awkward to explain, especially under the glares of Tendril's council. He certainly wasn't going to mention Nut's earlier exile. "The whole troop had moved to an abandoned hyena den on the plains and—"

"But not you two," interrupted a cold-eyed councilor. "What did you do to be driven out?"

Thorn swallowed, preparing to answer calmly, but beside him Nut was suddenly gripped by panic. "Let us go! We won't come back!" The injured baboon struggled and wriggled feebly, chittering in terror. His guards had no problem subduing him; one of them clamped a paw across his snout.

The Crookedtree baboons exchanged suspicious looks.

"Let me explain," gasped Thorn. He knew his voice was shaking, but he couldn't help it. He didn't like to think what would happen if he couldn't win these baboons over, and Nut was *not* helping. "We had a bad Crownleaf," he confessed to the Highleaves before him. "His name is Stinger. He ruled through guile and violence and threats, and he blamed both of us for crimes he had committed himself. We were going to be killed—we had no choice but to run away. But coming here was an accident!"

Tendril looked distant and thoughtful. She touched her chin lightly.

"This I understand," she said at last. "In the past, a stranger brought terrible trouble to Crookedtree Troop. Since that . . . incident . . . we have kept ourselves isolated, hidden from the other baboons of Bravelands. No one comes to Crookedtree Troop." She gazed skyward. "Most certainly, no one leaves."

Thorn swallowed hard.

"So you must understand that you have given me a dilemma," she went on, still calm. "Should I risk the safety of my troop again, harboring disruptive strangers?" She paused and tilted her head. "Or should I not?"

There was a churning apprehension in Thorn's gut. *I wonder what will happen if she decides not.*

"Highleaves." She turned to them briskly. "Do you believe this baboon's tale of woe?"

Thoughtfully, one of them shut an eye. "It sounds plausible, Tendril Crownleaf."

"I'm not so sure," growled another.

An elderly baboon scratched at his armpit. "They look like troublemakers to me."

"Please, Crownleaf." Thorn strained desperately forward. "If you let us stay, we can be useful to you. We're good hunters, and hard workers! Nut's injured right now, but he'll soon heal. Please, will you let us stay a few days, and we'll prove our worth?" His heart was in his throat. "If you're displeased with us, you can throw us out."

Tendril's smile curled up until it almost looked real.

"I don't think you've been listening," she said with dry amusement.

Thorn's throat was too tight to reply.

"Very well, strangers," she went on. "You have my permission to stay. But you may not leave. Not ever. You will stay, not for a few days or a few moons, but forever. The Shadow Forest is your home now. No other ever will be."

Abruptly, the guards released Thorn and Nut. Nut stumbled a little, rubbing his muzzle, then grabbed Thorn's arm and hissed in his ear. "Coming here was another of your terrible ideas. These baboons are crazy!"

"It'll be fine," muttered Thorn, wishing he could be sure. "We're safe from Stinger, aren't we? No one even knows this troop exists."

"But we're prisoners! We can never leave!"

"When we want to leave," whispered Thorn grimly, "we'll find a way."

Tendril Crownleaf had stopped murmuring to her

Highleaves and had risen up on her hind legs, frowning at something beyond the trees. As she raised a paw to hush everyone, a baboon burst into the clearing, his eyes wide with shock and anger.

"Crownleaf, an attack! We're under assault! Everyone must take to the trees!"

Tendril spun on her Crown Stone of feathers. Her eyes, fixed on Thorn and Nut, burned cold yellow with fury. "Hold them, Creeper! These strangers are liars. They are enemies after all. They have led an attack here!"

"No," gasped Thorn. "No, that's not true! We didn't know—"

"Shut up!" snarled the burly Creeper, as the Crookedtree baboons surrounded the pair once more. A horrible silence fell, broken only by the rasping, terrified breaths of Thorn and Nut.

"The Code is clear," declared Tendril in a ringing voice. *"Only kill to survive."*

For a fleeting moment, Thorn felt a surge of hope.

"These strangers have endangered all our lives, Creeper." The Crownleaf turned her back. "Kill them both."

CHAPTER 8

"This death broke the Code," murmured Sky. "I don't even have to touch it to know that."

The three friends stood on the lowest slope of a foothill, staring aghast at the remains of a male buffalo. He had been strong, with broad, brutal horns and a thickly muscled neck. Usually there would not be much left to lie rotting in the sun. But except for some jackal damage and raw strips torn off by the rot-eater birds, who had flown away as they approached, the hulking corpse was intact.

"Why would he have been killed and not eaten?" Rock frowned.

Silverhorn shuddered as she snuffled at the flesh. "The body smells of lion."

"It has to be the work of Titanpride," said Sky. "Remember when they killed Moon? Titan said he wanted to display his power to all of Bravelands. And that was *all* he wanted. Not a meal, not to feed the cubs of his pride." Anger kindled inside her. "And this is how he's doing it."

"So he's trying to strike fear into all the animals, every herd." Rock recoiled from the buffalo's lifeless body. "Titan is a threat to all of us."

Gently, Sky touched her trunk to the buffalo's bloodied head. No memory reached her; the creature's spirit must have already returned to the stars, as she knew all spirits would. She hoped this one had made a quick journey.

The words of the grass-eaters came back to her, words she'd heard when Great Mother had reconciled a dispute between two herds. "May your spirit run free in the savannah of the stars," she murmured, "and may the Great Spirit repay your sacrifice with sweet grass that grows fresh forever."

"Let's hope so," rumbled Rock. "Because otherwise this poor creature's sacrifice means nothing."

Below them, farther down the slope, the buffalo herd was spread out across the grassland in a great black horde. Grass-eaters they might be, but they were powerful, aggressive, and thoroughly dangerous. Sky swallowed hard.

"Don't worry," murmured Rock beside her. "Silverhorn and I will be at your side."

Summoning all her courage, Sky set off down the shallow slope. The grassland before her thrummed in the relentless heat; above them the sky was a roiling mass of cloud that refused to burst. Clammy heat clung to them like a living thing. Beneath a line of wilting trees there was a smear of glittering silver, and as they drew closer Sky saw it was a small watering hole. *Smaller than it used to be, that's obvious.* The water had withdrawn into little more than a puddle in a patch of dry, cracked mud.

Before any buffalo could even turn and challenge the three friends, a baboon bounded toward them, his tail high and his teeth bared. Sky hesitated and flapped her ears forward in surprise.

"You!" the baboon cried. "You're the ones who tried to kill Great Father! Get out of here before I make you go!"

Rock gave a gruff laugh and marched forward. "You and whose herd? We're not going anywhere."

The baboon looked taken aback, but he wrinkled his snout and chittered in annoyance. "You've *got* to go," he insisted. "I've got enough problems to deal with as it is."

"What's wrong?" Sky lowered her head to him. "Maybe we can help?"

"Hah!" scoffed the baboon. "I doubt it."

"Who *are* you, anyway?" Silverhorn peered at him. "What are you doing here?"

"I'm the Driftleaf for this herd," he said, puffing out his chest.

"Driftleaf?" Sky asked.

"We've been appointed by the Great Father himself, to keep an eye on the herds." His expression grew even surlier. "Not that these buffalo show me any respect *at all*."

Rock blinked at him. The big bull elephant gazed out at the herd, then back at the baboon once more. "Are you surprised?" he said. "Seriously?"

"They're not even supposed to be in this part of the plains!" snapped the Driftleaf. "They're way past the boundary decided by Great Father."

Sky wrinkled her trunk. *So Stinger has his spies everywhere.*

"And to top it all," the baboon grumbled, "one of these brutes has decided *he's* the Great Father. How do these idiots get these things into their heads?"

Sky exchanged a dry glance with Rock, but managed not to say anything.

"What's Stinger Crownleaf going to say when he hears about this?" muttered the baboon. "It's me that'll get the blame. But you tell me! How am I supposed to keep an enormous buffalo herd in line? Why couldn't I have been Driftleaf for the meerkats?"

He looked as if he might go on grumbling until sunset, so Sky interrupted him. "Then we might be able to help you after all," she told him brightly. "That's why we're here—to find out if this buffalo is telling the truth or not."

"He's not," snapped the Driftleaf.

" . . . So if you could point us toward him?" Sky finished. "If you please, Driftleaf?"

He narrowed his yellow eyes, and his lip curled. "I'm not helping Great Father's enemies. It's bad enough having Titan-pride sniffing around."

Rock rolled his eyes and took a single, menacing stride toward the baboon.

"All right, all right!" The Driftleaf threw up his paws in quick surrender. "But don't come running to me saying he's the Great Father, because he *isn't.* There. Right there, see? Between those two young bulls. By the little kopje."

Why does he have to be the biggest buffalo in the herd? thought Sky with an inward sigh. He looked enormous even at a distance: his chest broad and thickly muscled, his head more than chunky enough to support his colossal horns.

Huge, brooding heads rose to stare at them as they walked forward, but the buffalo made no attempt to clear a path for them. The three friends had to shoulder and shove their way through the milling beasts, and even with Rock at her side, Sky couldn't help quailing. The full-grown buffalo were easily as big as her and Silverhorn, and their horns looked almost too heavy for their heads: chunky, massive, and lethal. Many of them jostled her deliberately, and mutters and bellows rose around her.

"You shouldn't be here."

"You don't belong."

"Intruders!"

"Even worse than that wretched Driftleaf."

The grumbles didn't bother her as much as their constant shoving. Over and over again, Sky found herself in a buffalo-memory—charging a leopard to scare it away from calves, snorting through broad nostrils as she drank thirstily from a shrinking waterhole, stampeding with her comrades across the plains.

She squeezed her eyes tight, trying to shut the memories out, and felt herself shunted hard by a buffalo's shoulder. Her heart beat thunderously. *They're so big, and there are so many of them. They could crush us easily.*

At her side, Rock halted and nudged her, and she blinked her eyes open.

She'd been right: the buffalo claiming to be Great Father was the biggest of them all. His brutish head was held low beneath the weight of his colossal horns, but his black gaze was steady on her, and hostile. He sucked in a breath through his flaring red nostrils, his huge chest swelling; then he blew out a challenging snort.

At his side, his advisers—who were only slightly smaller— shambled around in surprise to face her.

"Who are you and what do you want?" growled one of them. "We're discussing Titanpride and we don't have time for this."

Sky swallowed and drew herself up. "I am Sky Strider, and these are my friends Rock and Silverhorn." She nodded at her companions.

"What of it?" rumbled the buffalo leader. "I am Thud."

"But *you* will address him as Great Father," snapped one of the others.

"That's why I came here," said Sky, gathering her nerve. "I'm the envoy of the Great Spirit, and I'm here to confirm whether you are indeed the one true Great Father."

"What?" Thud looked startled. "Why?"

"Never heard of such a process," grumbled one of his advisers.

"It hasn't happened before," admitted Sky. "It's never had to."

"This is nonsense," rumbled the other adviser, but he turned to mutter urgently in Thud's ear.

"I am chosen," declared Thud. He angled his head to listen once more to his adviser, then added, "There's no doubt. No question at all."

The second buffalo was whispering to him now. Thud's eyes darkened in concentration. At last he looked again at Sky. "It's Stinger Crownleaf who is the fraud," he announced firmly.

They're feeding him lines, she realized. *I don't think Thud's very bright.*

He couldn't be the Great Parent; that much was obvious. But Sky had a duty to know for certain, so she dipped her head humbly and said in a small voice, "May I, if you please?"

"Um . . ." began Thud. "I suppose you may. Whatever it—"

Sky did not wait for his advisers to protest. She reached out with her trunk and touched Thud's rock-hard brow.

The familiar, rushing sensation swept over her. Disoriented, she blinked hard.

She was thundering over the plains, not fast enough. Some distance away a smaller, female buffalo galloped frantically, separated from the herd, a pride of lions in pursuit. My sister!

Sky-Thud's head was too heavy, her feet too slow. She couldn't reach them in time! Titanpride would kill her sister!

The lions sprang, and more of them sprinted from the side, ambushing the young female. A lioness clung to her rump, biting. Another sank greedy jaws into her throat. The young buffalo squealed, stumbled, fell.

I'm too late.

Another buffalo galloped hard at her side—it's Stamp, he's my adviser now—fierce and furious as Thud was. But they both knew they would not be in time to drive Titanpride away. "This would not happen," *grunted Stamp, panting,* "if a buffalo was Great Father!"

Sky-Thud's mind was slow, and confused by grief and anger. What did he mean? "Great Father . . . ?"

"You could do it, Thud. You could be Great Father. You're big and strong, you could teach the prides respect! You could rule Bravelands. . . ."

Gasping, Sky tore her mind free of Thud's memories. It was the same as always; only a moment had passed, and Thud was still gaping at her in open-mouthed disbelief. His advisers were bellowing in furious offense.

"How dare you touch the Great Father!"

"He isn't," declared Sky faintly. "He isn't the Great Father."

"*What?*" Stamp squared up to Sky, his head lowered, his black eyes glittering.

Rock and Silverhorn moved fast, pushing their way between Sky and the buffalo. "That's enough," rumbled Rock threateningly.

"I'm sorry." Sky had recovered her breath, and her courage. "Thud, I can tell that you want the best for your herd. You're a fine, brave leader. But you're not the Great Father."

Thud just stared at her, blinking in confusion. "I'm not?"

"Don't listen to her, Thud!" bellowed Stamp. "Tell him, Crash!"

"Thud, you led us over that stupid boundary, remember?" demanded the one called Crash. "You defied the usurper Stinger! You're the strongest of all buffalo!"

"You are certainly the Great Father!" roared Stamp. "Don't lose faith in yourself! In us!"

"Actually," muttered Thud, "I'm not *completely* sure. . . ."

A much smaller shape was pushing his way through the thronging buffalo, smacking flanks aside bad-temperedly and very ineffectually. The Driftleaf squirmed between two sturdy rumps and dusted off his fur.

"We can sort this out right now," he declared, with a savage glare at Sky. "Come with me to see Stinger, Thud. You can decide this between yourselves, once and for all."

"That's a very good idea." Crash nodded.

"I think that would sort it out," agreed Stamp.

Oh, night and morning, these two are no smarter than Thud! Sky shook her head vehemently, her short tusks swinging. "No, Thud, you mustn't! Stinger's dangerous—he kills his friends and allies without a thought, never mind y—"

"Shut up, you!" snapped Crash imperiously. "A baboon? Kill Thud? Don't be ridiculous."

"Ridiculous!" echoed Stamp. He bellowed a summons to the herd.

Sky looked desperately from one buffalo to another. It had been her news that had driven Rain to confront Stinger. Would Thud have any better luck? If he didn't, it would be her fault. "He gets rid of all his rivals, don't you understand? He won't stand for any threat to his power. This is a mistake, Thud!"

But around her, the herd was already moving. The deep lowing message was passing from ear to ear. The vast throng of buffalo was turning with astonishing speed, lurching into motion, plodding due west along the valley. Dust rose up as a multitude of hooves struck the ground, and the noise was soon deafening. Sky's pleas and warnings were nothing against the din of the moving herd, and as she cantered frantically after Thud, the racket swelled and drowned her out altogether.

"Thud!" all the buffalo bellowed, his name echoing and rebounding across the plains. "Long live Thud! Great Father Thud!"

In what seemed like only moments, Sky, Rock, and Silverhorn stood alone on the churned, empty grassland. They could only watch, helpless, as the dark mass of the buffalo herd shrank and vanished into the trembling heat haze, the dust of their hooves billowing into the sky.

CHAPTER 9

Creeper's arms, long and powerfully muscled, locked around Thorn's throat. However hard Thorn fought, he could not escape his thuggish captor. Another big Crookedtree baboon seized the trembling Nut, whose eyes were rolling with terror. Thorn found himself shoved to the ground, choking, his snout ground into the soil. His head swam with the thick forest scents. Even the heat was against him: it was so intense now, he felt drained and weak. His muscles were limp, and his blood was like thick, sluggish water. *I'm doomed. We both are.*

"Hold them down," snapped Creeper.

In the moment of silence as they waited, Thorn wrenched his head around. Creeper was crouching, prizing a big, rough rock from the ground. When he rose to his feet, he tossed it easily from paw to paw.

"It'll be quick," he sneered. "Quicker than you deserve, spies."

A recent memory flashed into Thorn's head: Fearless, pinning him down, his jaws open for the kill. Only now, it was even more hopeless. *There's no Sky here to save me.*

"Please don't kill us," babbled Nut. "We didn't mean any harm. We'll go."

Thorn stayed tight-lipped; he'd tried saying all that already, and it had made no difference. He didn't want to give these brutes the satisfaction of hearing him beg again. He breathed hard through his nostrils, trying to steady his heart, waiting for the rock to come smashing down on his skull.

I just wish I could see Berry. One last time . . .

"Yeow! Ahhh!"

For a moment Thorn thought it was Nut who had hollered. But it was Creeper who was squealing in pain, and no wonder; a second stone flew through the air and hit the big baboon with a loud crack. As the stone bounced and rolled on the ground, Thorn was abruptly released. He lurched to his feet as Creeper rubbed his bleeding skull.

Branches were cracking, leaves scattering and fluttering down to the floor of the glade. Around them, the foliage swayed wildly. And then a whole troop of green vervet monkeys burst into the clearing, fangs exposed, yammering in challenge.

"Take them!" squealed the monkeys' leader, pointing at the baboons. "Take this forest!"

"We'll deal with you strangers later," Creeper hissed in

Thorn's ear. "Comrades! Time to fight!"

He and his cohort spun and ran to meet the monkeys' charge, hooting and shrieking with rage. Tendril Crownleaf bounded to the head of her troops.

"Cut them off!" she whooped in fury. "Lichen, maneuver to the right! Stick, protect the young!"

"This is our chance!" Thorn grabbed Nut's arm. Then he hesitated, peering at the monkeys. A thrill of angry recognition went through his spine, and he tightened his grip on Nut. "It's the same troop that attacked Tall Trees!" he whispered. "The ones who wounded Berry on the plain!"

He stared at the leader: yes, it was that same mean-faced monkey with the vicious twist to his mouth. Spite Cleanfur had not only bitten off Berry's beautiful tail—he'd gloated about doing it. He had a cruel savagery about him that Thorn loathed.

"They must have picked up on our scent and followed us here," he growled to Nut. "I told you what they did, remember?"

"So?" spat Nut. "We can escape, like you said. Let's get out of here!"

Breathing hard, torn by conflicting impulses, Thorn blinked at the battle that raged in the clearing. There had to be thirty or forty monkeys, though it was hard to count in the shrieking chaos. They flung themselves on the baboons in knots of three or four, overwhelming them by sheer numbers; fur flew and blood spattered as the baboons fell back, fighting desperately. A female baboon screamed in pain as two vervets tore at her ears with their vicious fangs. A vision of Berry flashed into his mind, lying barely alive, her tail-stump raw.

"No." Anger kindled inside Thorn, bringing him to a decision. "We can't leave! We owe these monkeys a beating."

"You said the Strongbranches already got revenge!"

"On monkeys who might have had nothing to do with it," growled Thorn, remembering the lethal trickery of weakening the branches in the acacia woodland. He'd hated doing it, but he'd had to pretend to be a willing member of the Strongbranches—and this, in contrast, was an honest battle. "Spite Cleanfur was never punished for what he did. And what if Tendril's right and this attack really is our fault? These monkeys probably followed us here."

"Yes, to baboons who want to *kill us*," Nut pointed out. "Let's leave the monkeys to it. I don't care which of this lot ends up dead."

"No, listen," said Thorn, tugging Nut's shoulder fur. "If we run, the Crookedtree baboons will come looking for us. And these monkeys are our enemies too! If we help Crookedtree fight, they'll know we're on their side. They'll let us stay. Where else are we going to go?"

"Anywhere!" muttered Nut.

"If we leave now, we'll be hunted down by the Strongbranches," insisted Thorn. "Our best chance is to stay here for long enough that they'll think we're never coming back."

"Oh, sky and stone," groaned Nut. "You're crazy."

All the same, when Thorn turned and sprang to join the fight, he heard Nut lurching at his heels.

The melee was intense and bloody. Thorn felt his insides go cold when the sheer number of monkeys, far more than the baboons, became brutally clear. Claws raked, jaws snarled and snapped, and blood droplets flew from bites and scratches. Two baboons shrieked in fear and leaped for the safety of a branch, but they were grabbed by monkeys and dragged back to earth with a horrible thud. Thorn darted across to help them, seizing long monkey tails and tearing them away from the baboons.

Three small baboons were under assault from a mass of monkeys at the edge of the glade. Thorn slashed his claws at the skinny vervet who was attacking him, then turned and bounded to their aid.

Seizing a monkey's neck, he dragged it off a bleeding female. She scrambled out from under the fight, panting in terror, and Thorn sank his fangs into her attacker's shoulder. The monkey screamed, wriggled from his grip, and sprang away, but as Thorn lunged for him, he heard a familiar voice scream in agony.

"Nut!"

He's already injured! How will he defend himself? Desperately Thorn craned around, rubbing his eyes and trying to peer through the noise and chaos of the battle.

Creeper's broad back was blocking most of his view. Only moments ago the big patrol leader had been ready to smash both Thorn's skull and Nut's; now he had turned his savage rage on three monkeys at once, ripping at them with his long claws and powerful jaws. Thorn ducked and crawled past him, and finally saw Nut: a big male monkey had him on the ground, raining blows on his injured body. Thorn scrambled past Creeper, then sprang at Nut's attacker.

He dragged at the creature, hauling it off Nut even as he tried to dodge its claws. Fiery pain raked his ear, but that only made him angrier. Baring his teeth in an enraged snarl, he slashed at the monkey's eyes, then tumbled back as it scampered away, screeching.

"Nut, are you all right?" His fellow Brightforest exile was streaked with blood, his fur was torn, and his chest heaved.

But Nut only stared back at him, panting. "Are *you*?"

Thorn felt a hot trickle of blood running down his jaw, and he put a paw to his ear. It had been badly ripped. He clenched his teeth. "I'm fine."

"And I'm useless," growled Nut bitterly. "Look at Tendril!"

The Crookedtree Crownleaf was balanced high on a branch, glancing one way and then another, her eyes wide and alarmed. Spite was up there too—he and another monkey had her cornered, and now they were creeping toward her from two sides. The rotten branch she stood on was swaying, creaking, sagging. There was a screech of ripping timber.

She was too high up, Thorn realized with a shiver of dread. *If she falls, she'll die!*

Thorn bounded for the tree, scrambling rapidly up through the branches. Spite's tail dangled and twitched in front of him as the vicious monkey focused all his attention on Tendril.

"We'll be taking your forest, Baboon," Spite jeered. "You won't need it when you're dead!"

Tendril just glared at him with hatred.

"Nothing to say, Tendril Crownleaf?" taunted Spite. "Oh well. Did you know baboons can fly? We'll show you!"

Thorn had heard more than enough. "Hey, Spite!" he hooted. "Remember me?"

Startled, Spite twisted and peered down at him. The monkey's eyes widened and his muzzle peeled back. "You!"

"Yes," yelled Thorn. "I beat your champion Sneer, and now I'm here for you!"

"Ah, of course, you're the one with the pretty golden friend." Spite curled his lip mockingly. "The one with no tail. Tell her she should have been more careful with it!" He turned back to Tendril, flicking a dismissive paw at Thorn.

"Look who's talking." Spite's tail still dangled close to him; Thorn took his chance, lunging with both paws and grabbing it.

Spite jerked his head around, and Thorn saw the shock in his black eyes, but he didn't hesitate. He yanked hard, pulling the monkey off-balance, then gave his tail another violent tug.

Caught off guard, Spite tumbled backward. He snatched desperately at a branch, missed, and fell; he plummeted down with an echoing crash of foliage and hit the earth with a sickening crack.

"Monkeys can't fly, I guess!" yelled Thorn.

In the sudden silence, Thorn peered down, heart in his mouth. Spite's paw twitched and he gave a groan. His hind leg thrashed as if he were trying to stand.

And then, far below, Nut lurched to his feet and lunged

at the stunned monkey. Thorn gaped as the injured baboon sank his fangs into Spite's neck. Blood spurted, and Spite's eyes started wide. As a dark pool spread beneath him, his body went limp.

Thorn pounded the branch beneath him and hooted. *Not so useless after all, Nut!*

Their leader dead, the effect on the monkey troop was immediate; they gave hoots and shrieks of terror, hurtling around and fleeing into the trees. Once again the foliage bounced and swayed as they rapidly vanished into it. Thorn heard the crash and rustle of branches, and the monkeys' screeches as they retreated, but the racket soon faded, and the forest was silent once more.

One by one, baboons limped into the clearing around Spite's corpse, muttering with fury and triumph. Stick chittered with angry concern as he checked a female's bites, then gently took her arm and led her limping off. Some baboons sprawled on the ground, badly wounded; others gathered to lift them carefully and carry them away through the trees.

Tendril Crownleaf swung down slowly through the branches, her fangs clenched. When she reached solid ground, she stalked toward Thorn and Nut, never taking her burning eyes off them.

Thorn held his breath, his heart hammering painfully. Was she angry? Relieved? Were her bared teeth for them or for the monkey invasion? Did Tendril even feel normal emotions?

"Strangers," she murmured, pacing a circle around them. "You are strangers no longer."

Thorn's breath escaped in a great rush of relief.

"You arrived here as interlopers," she went on in her strange flat voice, "but you remain as friends. We are bound by the blood spilled in this battle."

Tendril sat back on her haunches and extended a regal paw. Thorn blinked in the silence, shooting a glance at Nut, who looked as relieved as Thorn felt. All the same, unease nibbled at Thorn's belly. The power of Tendril's stare was something he could feel on his hide and fur.

"Crouch," she commanded.

Instantly, they both obeyed.

"From this day, you owe your allegiance to Crookedtree," intoned Tendril. "You fight and work and live for us. You leave us only if you die for us."

Thorn could only nod. Together he and Nut rose to their paws.

At least we're safe. For now. We can work out later how we get out of here.

"What are your ranks?" Tendril looked from Thorn to Nut and back, lifting her brow. "You will be given appropriate roles."

"We're both Highleaves," Nut lied quickly.

Thorn gave him a startled look. *Skies above, Nut's trying to be nice. I'm not going to argue.*

Now that the fight was over, Thorn was much more aware of his torn ear; it throbbed and stung badly. He touched it again with a paw and winced. Tendril eyed him, her head tilted.

"You're wounded," she said brusquely. "Go to the Goodleaf. Behind that canopy."

Thorn padded in the direction she'd indicated and pulled aside thick fronds of creeper. Sure enough, the small glade within was full of injured baboons, some lying on the ground, some slumped against trees, many of them barely conscious. Among them a single Goodleaf baboon worked in silence; she stepped over a baboon with an oddly angled, bloody leg and pressed a pawful of crushed jackalberry leaves and honey to his wound. *I'm not as bad as he is. I can wait.*

Thorn studied the Goodleaf as she worked. Something about her niggled at him. She was about Tendril's age, he guessed; her fur was unusually pale, streaky and golden. Where the sunlight filtered through the canopy and fell on her, it almost glowed. Leaning over the badly wounded baboon, the Goodleaf touched his forehead gently. Something about her seemed familiar; so familiar, Thorn felt instantly at ease and already comforted.

As if she felt Thorn's stare, she turned suddenly and beckoned to him with a forepaw.

"Where should I sit?" he asked her. "I don't want to get in the way. My ear's not that bad."

Without a word, the Goodleaf took hold of his paw and drew him farther into the glade. As she nodded in encouragement, he gazed into her golden eyes, mesmerized. Without being told, he sat down meekly.

"Have . . . have we met before?" he stammered.

The Goodleaf shook her head. She was already crushing

leaves and honey between her paws, mashing them into a poultice, and she reached up to press it to his torn ear. He closed his eyes. It felt so soothing, the pain was already ebbing.

Gratefully, Thorn began to sit up. "Thank you, Goodleaf. I'm all right. I won't take up more of your time. . . ."

Her forepaw pressed on his shoulder, making him subside obediently. She smiled, her kind face close to his, and pushed the leaf poultice into his paw. She gestured to her ear, then his; then she pointed at the dressing and gave him a nod of encouragement.

"I understand." Thorn raised the poultice to his ear and held it there as she'd indicated. And then he realized.

It's not that she won't speak to me. She can't.

Now he saw the sadness in her huge amber eyes: it was like a physical force, almost tangible. He sensed it was an old, dark sorrow, one that was always with her. Thorn relaxed back on his haunches, gazing at the mute baboon with pity.

What happened to her?

CHAPTER 10

Rain fell in a relentless gray torrent, heavy enough to obscure not only the horizon but even the acacias dotted across the savannah. Fearless trudged on, rainwater dripping from his ears and tail; he had almost given up shaking it from his eyes. Beside him, Valor was soaked too: her golden coat had darkened to a muddy brown.

"How far is this waterfall?" she asked him. "I think I'm turning into a hippo."

He gave a tired chuckle. "Not much farther. I promise, Valor."

Valor opened her jaws, catching the streaming rain on her tongue. She seemed to hesitate, then asked, "Fearless, are you sure you want to do this?"

"What, claim my pride?" Fearless glanced at her in surprise. "Of course. Why wouldn't I?"

"Plenty of reasons." Valor's next step splashed into a pool of reddish mud; she paused to raise her forepaw and shook it with distaste. "You're not old enough to be a pride leader, for a start. You haven't even got your mane yet!"

"I've got more experience than a lot of grown lions," he insisted proudly. "Who else knows as much as I do about—baboons, for instance? Or elephants, or hyenas?"

Valor gave him a skeptical look as they padded on. "It's not just that you won't be grown for another whole year," she went on. "They're Dauntlesspride lions, and they won't want to be led by an outsider. You think they're just going to roll over, show their bellies, and accept you?"

Fearless scowled. "I'll make them accept me."

"Uh-huh. And even if that happens, what use is a pride of cubs against Titan? That won't keep us safe. We'd be better off finding a friendly pride with a proper full-grown leader."

"What pride is going to want us?" Fearless huffed in exasperation. "It's all right for you, but remember what Mother said? Normal prides don't want too many growing males. And anyway, it's not the point. I want to lead my *own* pride."

Valor lashed her jaws with her tongue again. "I know one adult lion who'd take us in," she growled.

"I told you, I'm not going back to Loyal!"

"We may not have a choice." Valor nudged him gently with her muzzle. "I know you've fallen out with him, Swiftbrother. And I don't like oath-breakers any more than you do. But Fearless, he *cares* about you. That's obvious. I'm sure we could patch things up. . . ."

"Absolutely not!" Fearless wished she would stop going on about this; he'd made up his mind. "This is the best thing to do. I need my own pride so I can take on Titan."

"You can't do that," sighed Valor. "Not yet!"

"But when the time comes to face him, I'll have my pride and I *will* be ready!" Fearless gave his drenched fur a violent shake. "I know I can do it. The Great Father knows I can do it!"

Valor's shoulders sagged in resignation. "All right, Fearless. I can see you won't change your mind."

"No, I won't." He shot her a sidelong glance. "If you really hate the idea . . . you could just hang back out of sight. You don't have to help or anything."

"Of course I'll help you," she snapped. "I'll do what I can, you know that. I always will."

Fearless gave her a quick lick of gratitude. "Thanks, Valor."

"I still think it's a terrible idea," she added, rolling her eyes. "But it's not as if it's your first. . . ."

Even the roar of the waterfall sounded muted in the torrential rain. The river narrowed between slabs of rock before tumbling over the edge in a foaming rush; it plummeted down a rock face that was at least three times as high as the tallest tree at its foot. The pool, far below the spray-misted edge, was churned by the falls and pitted by rain; clinging to the cracks in the flat rock around it were a few limp and scraggy trees.

Fearless and Valor crouched on a high outcrop of sandstone, peering down at the small gang of lions who sprawled on the rocks beside the pool. The exiled Dauntlesspride youngsters looked thoroughly bedraggled and miserable.

"A fine-looking pride," murmured Valor.

"I'll soon knock them into shape," Fearless growled defiantly. Still, even he could see that was going to take some work.

They had clearly not set any kind of lookout; no lion was stationed beyond the pool, alert for either enemies or prey. One scrawny female lay on a small crescent of gritty sand, dabbling her forepaw in the water. Another lay on her back on the slabs, paws curled, staring listlessly at the sky as she let the rain soak her. Two young males were squabbling over an old gazelle carcass; it looked like leftover rot-flesh, blackened and stringy, and Fearless doubted they'd killed it themselves. Though their hides were no more sodden than his and Valor's, the Dauntlesspride lions looked a whole lot worse: scratched and skinny, their ribs protruding.

He recognized only one of them: a cub of about his own age, a little smaller but long-legged, with a sharp, clever face. It was Keen, Dauntless's own son, who had tried his best to fight off Titanpride. Fearless had helped the cub escape, and Titan would have killed him for that disloyalty—if little Ruthless hadn't saved him by lying to his father. Fearless swallowed hard, shuddering at the memory of how close he'd come to death.

Keen's dark gold fur was soaked to a dull bronze; his shoulders sagged and his tail drooped as he crouched beneath a dripping thorn tree, watching the quarrel over the rot-meat. With a deep inhalation that made his ribs stick out more than ever, he padded over to the two cubs and butted the bigger one.

"There's no need to fight!" Fearless heard him snap. "We have to divide it up fairly!"

"Why?" retorted the other lion, a thick-necked cub with a blunt face. "I'm the biggest, I get most. That's how it works!" With a glare of defiance, he wrenched the bulk of the carcass away from his rival; it ripped easily, leaving the other lion half a blackened leg bone.

Keen gave a grunt of anger. "Who do you think you are?" He lunged for the bigger cub, snapping his jaws; the cub dodged and bit him back. In moments they were tussling on the flat stones, clawing and tearing at each other.

"Skies above," murmured Valor to Fearless. "What a hopeless mob."

"I've seen enough," growled Fearless. Rising, he bounded down the steep shelf of rock, landing on a jutting boulder just above the fighting lions. He opened his jaws and gave a commanding roar.

They broke apart, yelping. The other cubs, too, were scrambling to their paws. The lioness at the pool twisted so quickly, she almost tumbled into the water; the one who'd been lying on her back panicked and lashed her paws, struggling to right herself. The others were stiff with shock.

That would teach them to keep lookout, thought Fearless with satisfaction, as Valor sprang gracefully down to stand at his side on the boulder.

The big, aggressive cub was the first to recover. "Who are *you*?" he snarled.

Keen, though, pushed past him, eyes brightening. "Fearless? Fearless Gallantpride, it's you!" He took a bounding pace forward, then stopped and stared up nervously, his whiskers quivering. "It's, uh . . ." he stammered. "You look good!"

Fearless wanted to respond with something similar, but it was hard. Keen, like the rest of them, really did look wretched.

Keen seemed lost for anything more to say. Swishing his tail, he turned to the others. "This is Fearless Gallantpride," he told them with a note of awe. "He's the lion who saved me when Titanpride took over."

"Oh." The lioness by the pool came forward, flicking drips from her paw. "*That* Fearless. Wow." She sat on her haunches and stared up at him. "I'm Rough." She nodded at the young female who'd been stuck on her back like a beetle, and who still looked mortified at her loss of dignity. "That's my sister, Tough."

Fearless exchanged a glance with Valor, but just as quickly looked away, for fear her stifled laughter would be catching. The two lionesses looked anything but rough and tough. They were both rangy, with thin faces and slender legs, and water pooled beneath their dripping pale-gold pelts.

"This is Hardy," said Keen, nudging the smaller, dark-tawny male who he had been fighting. He was stocky and short-legged, with a tenacious set to his jaw. As an elegant, delicate-featured female crept from her shelter beneath a rocky outcrop, he added, "And that's Gracious."

"And I'm Snarl," broke in the biggest, pugnacious cub. He glowered at Fearless with an air of defiant aggression.

Fearless gazed around them all, blinking. His tail began to tap the boulder, so he stilled it with an effort. It seemed important to look calm and dignified and in control.

"This is my sister, Valor," he told them. "She was in Titanpride with me, but we've struck out on our own."

Keen glanced nervously at his friends, then back up at Fearless. "So . . . what brings you here?"

Fearless drew himself up, tilting his head high. "I've come to make a fine and strong pride of all of you," he declared. "From now on, you will be Fearlesspride!"

For a heartbeat, they simply stared at him, dumbfounded.

Then, as one, they burst into roars of laughter. "What?" yelped Snarl.

"That's ridiculous!" Hardy threw his head back, grunting with amusement. "What makes you think we'll let you do that?"

"Because we won't," added Snarl, his blunt muzzle curling. "Who do you think you are—Titan?"

"You're not even one of us," Tough pointed out scornfully.

Keen wasn't laughing quite as hard as the others, but he gave Fearless an apologetic look. "I'm sorry, Fearless, but I'm the son of Dauntless, after all. We are Keenpride now."

"No we're not," snapped Snarl. "Who made you the leader? We're Snarlpride."

"Just hang on." Hardy butted between them, glowering. "We're Hardypride, I thought I told you!"

Rough gave a grunt of derision. "You males! You're all useless and you never stop fighting. It would work a lot better if Tough and I were leaders together."

"You can't be," growled Snarl, glaring at them both. "You're lionesses. Lionesses are only good for hunting and having cubs."

Tough gave a high-pitched yelp of anger. "Say that again, you big idiot!" Without even waiting for Snarl to repeat his insult, she pounced on him, closely followed by her sister.

Snarl fell over, roaring in anger, snapping back at the two furious lionesses. "Hardy! Get them off me!"

"Oh, sun and stars!" exclaimed Valor, springing down from the boulder to butt them all apart. She bared her teeth and growled, studying them all with contempt. "No one is in charge here—that's obvious. Look at you! Eating rot-flesh like some pack of hyenas! And *fighting* over it! You call yourselves a pride?"

They backed off from one another, looking shame-faced. Even Snarl hunched his shoulders and averted his eyes, grumbling.

"Have you set up hunting parties?" demanded Valor. "Have you posted lookouts? You didn't see us coming, so I'm guessing not. Have you planned where you'll hide if Titan comes looking for you? Because he will!"

At that, the young lions' eyes widened and their jaws

went slack. They stared at Valor as if the thought had never occurred to them. Not one of them spoke up to reply, because the answer to all her questions was so obviously *No*. Fearless sprang down to stand at his sister's flank. He felt a ripple of pride; she looked so fierce and authoritative.

"Valor's right: you need a proper leader." He looked into each lion's eyes, feeling severe and stern—and quite grown-up in comparison. "I can be that leader."

"Pfft!" Snarl broke the silence. "We know what to do—we just haven't gotten around to doing it."

"That's right," piped up Hardy. "We can do all that without you."

"Sorry, Fearless." Keen shook his head. "We don't need your help."

"We'll pick our own leader," declared Rough.

"Or leaders," put in Tough, with a conspiratorial look at her sister.

Fearless lashed his tail, dumbfounded. He hadn't expected an outright rejection. Snarl was already turning and stalking away, and one by one the others went after him. They would have looked quite impressive if they hadn't all been dripping wet.

"And don't follow us!" called Snarl over his shoulder.

Together Fearless and Valor watched the Dauntlesspride lions pad away through the misty spray of the waterfall and over the rocks. They jumped down from the sandstone slabs and vanished around a jutting outcrop toward the lower grassland.

For long moments, Fearless and Valor were silent. Valor licked her jaws.

"This is for the best," she assured Fearless at last, shaking her head. "Honestly, what a rabble. Our own father couldn't whip that lot into shape."

Mention of Gallant gave Fearless a pang of sudden, aching longing.

His father had been so strong, but so kind. Gallant had known exactly how to inspire loyalty in any lion. He'd led with wisdom and confidence, and he'd never had to bully a lion to command them. Valor was wrong, he decided. Their father could have turned even this scrawny, hopeless gang of lions into a powerful pride of loyal hunters.

And it would honor his memory if I could do it too.

"I'm not giving up!" he growled suddenly. "I know how to make that mob take me seriously."

"Fearless, wait—"

But he ignored Valor, breaking into a loping run after the Dauntlesspride lions. He heard his sister's exasperated growl, and then her running paws on the sandstone behind him.

The young lions hadn't gone far. When Fearless rounded the rocky outcrop, he could see them through the murk, not far ahead, slouching aimlessly across a narrow stretch of rain-drenched savannah. Splashing up gouts of mud, he raced after them and overtook them easily. He slid to a halt, facing the cubs, paws slipping in the squelching dirt.

They froze, blinking in surprise, as Fearless glared into their eyes. He opened his jaws and gave a great roar of challenge.

"By the laws of our ancestors—I, Fearless, come to claim this pride!"

There was no sound but the dull thunder of the rain. A thrill rippled across his skin, raising his fur on end. Then, distantly, a lonely eagle cried, like an echo of his challenge.

I feel as if Bravelands itself is listening to me!

The words he had roared seemed to hang quivering in the air. The first time he'd heard them was on the terrible day when Titan challenged and killed his own father.

And now I've spoken them myself, for the first time.

Hardy gave a sudden coughing snarl, and the spell was broken. "We could just ignore him," he said.

"No." Keen shook his head, still staring at Fearless. "Hardy, the words have been spoken, according to the laws. We have to accept the challenge."

"Anyway," broke in Tough, her narrow muzzle wrinkling, "we can beat him!"

"Of course we can," agreed Rough.

"That's settled, then," said Snarl. "Who's going to fight him?"

"Us!" chorused Rough and Tough together.

"You can't," scolded Gracious. "There's two of you!"

Fearless was quite surprised to hear her voice—since she'd hardly spoken—but secretly grateful too.

The two sisters subsided, grumbling complaints under their breath.

"Me, then." Hardy clawed the ground fiercely with his stocky paws. "I'll see him off."

"You're far too small," scoffed Snarl.

"It really should be me," pointed out Keen, though he sounded less than enthusiastic. "I'm Dauntless's son."

"And you never shut up about it," said Snarl with a roll of his eyes. "Look, it's obvious. I'm the biggest, and I'm good at fighting. I'll take him on."

"Fine," sulked Hardy.

"It's not *fair*," growled Rough. "Lionesses can fight as well as any lion. But since you won't let Tough and me fight him, I suppose we'll agree."

Gracious simply sighed through her nostrils, looking resigned.

Keen nodded. "All right, we're agreed. It does make sense for Snarl to do it, I guess." Quickly he added, "But that doesn't mean we're Snarlpride!"

"We'll see about that," growled Snarl, but he bounded forward to face Fearless, giving an arrogant toss of his head. "By the laws of our ancestors, I, Snarl, fight to keep this pride!"

Fearless exchanged a glance with Valor. She twitched her whiskers and puffed out a snort of amusement.

"Well. That didn't take long," she murmured. "Good luck, Fearless."

Fearless drew himself up and stalked toward Snarl, eyeing him. Though he had no intention of underestimating this burly cub, Snarl didn't look to be in much better condition than the rest of his pride. Still, Fearless knew he would have to be careful.

Snarl was first to spring. Fearless was expecting it; he

dodged the attack and crouched, letting Snarl crash over him. When the cub's exposed belly was right above him he lunged up, flinging him off-balance. Snarl fell heavily onto his side and rolled in the mud, then sprang back to his feet.

"Well done, Fearless!" Valor roared.

Snarl's muzzle curled in frustration, and he struck again. This time his claws raked Fearless's side, but the scratch was shallow, and after the first stinging pain Fearless barely felt it. The teeming rain would clean away the blood.

He reared back onto his hind paws, striking and swiping at Snarl; as his claws lashed out he felt them sink into Snarl's broad shoulder. The cub gave a yelp of shock and scuttled back, panting and slithering in the rain-soaked earth.

"Yield, Snarl!" he roared.

"Never!" Once more the big cub charged; once more, Fearless struck him away and ducked his retaliatory blow.

It wasn't going to be hard after all, Fearless realized. Snarl was already out of breath, and his ribs heaved with the effort of his furious attacks. He thundered in again, but Fearless was too quick, swerving aside and landing another strike, this time on the side of the cub's skull. Snarl reeled, staggering.

"Come on, brother," called Valor, her voice easily drowning out the uncertain yelps and growls of Dauntlesspride. "End this!"

She's right. He must not let this drag on; he didn't want the underfed cub to collapse and die of exhaustion. Nimbly Fearless veered and pounced, raining blows on Snarl's flank and shoulder, pummeling him to the wet ground. The big cub looked dazed, lying there in the pouring rain, and Fearless leaped to straddle him. Reaching down, he fastened his jaws around Snarl's throat.

"Yield," he growled again, through a mouthful of stringy muscle and fur.

Snarl could hardly speak. His breath rasped in a harsh whistle and his whole body was limp. "I yield," he whispered. "I yield."

Fearless released his grip and took a pace back. After a moment, Snarl raised himself up on his forepaws, panting. He staggered to his feet, his head hanging. But his eyes still blazed, and the expression on his face was one of defiant fury. His friends watched him, looking disappointed and rather shocked.

"Congratulations." Valor padded up to Fearless and licked his ear. In a murmur she added, "I think. To be honest, I'm still not sure about this."

"I am." Fearless felt filled with new energy and pride. He threw back his head and gave a roar of triumph, striking the sodden earth with a paw. As the rain teemed down, his new pride watched his celebration, sullen and silent.

My new pride . . . My new pride!

He was a leader of lions at last. Fearlesspride had begun!

CHAPTER 11

Sky was exhausted, and not only from the relentless heat. It was so hard to plod on across the broiling savannah, and to nurse the glow of hope inside her, when false trail after false trail seemed to take her farther than ever from the truth. Sometimes she thought the only thing keeping her going was keeping cheerful about it all for the sake of Rock and Silverhorn.

Each rumor had brought such high hopes, and such crashing disappointment. There had been Great Mother Tufthorn, a giraffe who had turned out to be a singularly vain and silly creature. There was the antelope who believed a tree had spoken to him, until remembering—after a few questions from Sky—that it had happened in a dream. A leopard who had somehow dragged half a small buffalo up a tree had been convinced that his feat made him Great Father, without question. A malevolent hippo had even tried to play a prank on her.

"Come into the water, little elephant," he had crooned, turning toward a bask of grinning crocodiles on a sandbank. "One of these crocodiles has proof that she's Great Mother!"

Rock had told the hippo exactly what he thought of him, and Silverhorn had nudged Sky back from the river's edge, assuring her it was a cruel trick. *I wanted it to be true so much that I might have fallen for it, too.*

"We're all tired, Sky." Rock butted her gently. "There's a big fever tree over there; let's rest for a while."

"Oh, I'd love that," she agreed. She followed close to Rock's flank as he strode toward the shade of the spreading branches. Silverhorn trudged at her side.

"Thank you both for staying with me," said Sky. "I know we've had a lot of bad information, and we've walked so far to follow up all the rumors. But we have to keep trying."

Rock touched her trunk with his. "Sky, don't forget what the old vulture told you. He said the Great Parent would have to be ready to accept the Great Spirit. So maybe it's not that we can't find the right creature—they might not be ready yet."

"Maybe the next Great Parent hasn't even been *born* yet," murmured Silverhorn. "So it's not your fault if you can't find them."

They meant to be reassuring, Sky knew, but she couldn't dwell on these possibilities—they meant Bravelands was stuck with Stinger forever. "In that case we could be walking in circles for seasons and seasons," she said. "No, the Great Parent is out there—or I wouldn't have been sent to find them."

But it was hard to stay hopeful. When the three friends

shambled beneath the fever tree, she halted, sagged, and closed her eyes in exhaustion.

"Who is that?" Silverhorn's voice made her start, and Sky blinked and followed the rhino's gaze.

A small brown figure was loping across the plain toward them. It was a baboon, Sky realized, squinting, but a very small and skinny one, his eyes huge in his little face. He had an anxious, diffident look, but he ran straight toward them and halted just beyond the tree's shadow, licking his jaws.

"Hello," said Rock, peering at him in surprise. "Who are you?"

The little baboon smoothed his fur with careful paws. "I . . . I'm Mud Driftleaf. Mud Lowleaf was my name before. I've been sent by Great Father."

"Driftleaf?" Sky flapped her ears forward with curiosity. "Like the baboon we saw with the buffalo?"

"Yes, that would be right." He cleared his throat. "I was supposed to be assigned to the elephant herd, to, ah . . . look after them, keep them in touch with Great Father." He gave a helpless shrug. "But I can't find them."

Good, thought Sky with satisfaction. Of course Mud Driftleaf couldn't find her family: they'd gone far away, to the Plain Of Our Ancestors, and no animal knew the way there but the elephants themselves. Still, he looked so nervous and scared, she lowered her head to the little baboon in sympathy.

"That's a pity. What are you going to do?"

"Well, that's the thing. Stinger—I mean, Great Father—he

heard you were traveling all over Bravelands, so he suggested I come and be your Driftleaf instead!" He smiled at her a little too brightly, as if he half expected rejection on the spot.

Rock looked at Sky. "I don't think we need a Driftleaf, thanks all the same."

"No." Silverhorn swung her horn and peeled back her long upper lip to blow at Mud Driftleaf. He flinched back, gulping.

"But I . . . I'm supposed to." His eyes were so wide and anxious, Sky could see the whites. "It's my job."

"Rock. Silverhorn." Sky reached to touch them, then remembered not to and curled back her trunk. "It's not Mud's fault. Don't take it out on him." She turned back to the little baboon, whose paws were shaking. "We don't want a Driftleaf spying on us, Mud, I'm sorry. But you can tell Stinger you're watching us, because we're certainly not going to be seeing him. Is that a deal?"

Mud hesitated for a moment, then gave a violent nod. "Yes. Yes, so long as Stinger doesn't find out. I'm sure he'd be quite angry with me. But to be honest, I couldn't see you agreeing." He twisted his muzzle, looking downcast.

"Run along then," said Rock with strained patience.

"I will, but—listen. Stinger asked me to pass on a message when I found you. He's called a Great Gathering for High Sun today, at the watering hole. Will you go?"

Sky tilted her head and frowned down at Mud. "Why does Stinger want a Great Gathering now?"

"For you," blurted Mud. "He really wants you to come, Sky

Strider. So that he can unite you once again with the Great Spirit."

I am already one with the Spirit, thought Sky. But it was pointless trying to explain that to Mud. "Let me talk to my friends," she said.

Rock and Silverhorn ambled after her as she withdrew a little way, to the far side of the fever tree. "What do you two think?" she murmured.

Rock bent his head close to hers, his dark green eyes very serious. "I think it's a bad idea, Sky. A really bad idea."

"What Rock said." Silverhorn nodded vigorously. "You can't trust Stinger Crownleaf. Remember what we told Thud and his herd?"

Sky stirred the red dust with her toes. "I'd usually agree," she said quietly, "but this could be a rare chance. I can spread the word about my search—so many animals attend a Great Gathering. We wouldn't have to walk miles to find all the different herds. The Great Parent might even *be* there."

Pensively, Rock stretched up his trunk, snapped off a leafy branch, and began to chew on it. "You have a point," he said at last.

"I don't like it." Silverhorn sighed. "But I think so too. And what would Stinger dare to do, with every creature of Bravelands watching?"

The four odd companions made their way across the broad, exposed plains, the elephants and rhino trudging steadily, the baboon scampering at their side to keep up. Somehow the heat didn't seem so oppressive this time to Sky. She had a destination to reach—and quite possibly a destiny, too.

The sun climbed to its zenith in the blazing blue of the sky. Mud kept giving it anxious glances, but their progress was quick and purposeful. *We'll be there soon*, thought Sky.

But as the familiar dark line of the trees came into view, Silverhorn stopped and raised her head, flaring her lip to snuff at the air.

"I smell lions," she rumbled.

"More than one?" Mud rose onto his hind legs, alarmed, and peered around.

Sky glanced about quickly. There wasn't much shelter, except for a tumble of rocks beyond a dry riverbed. She bent her head to Mud. "Go and hide over there," she said. "Wait for us."

She watched him bound at speed across the parched riverbed; no sooner had he scrambled behind the tumble of rocks than Silverhorn gave a grunt of warning. From the other direction, the lions came running: a huge pride, stretched out in hunting formation. Just ahead of them, herded by lions on both sides, raced a smaller, lighter figure: a cheetah, its legs a blur of speed as it sprinted to escape the hunters.

Sky knew immediately why it was running so hard, and why the lions were in pursuit. The black mane of the huge leader made him instantly recognizable: *Titan!*

Now that the big cats were in earshot, Sky could hear the orders he roared to his pride as he bounded alongside the main formation.

"Now's your chance! Move, you lazy idiots! Prove your Steadfastpride days are over—prove you are true Titanpride lions!"

The cheetah was racing full tilt for Sky and her friends now, not even trying to avoid them; clearly her only priority was to escape Titanpride. She was close enough for Sky to see her black-streaked face: eyes wide and terrified, pink tongue lolling.

"What by the Great Spirit are they doing?" trumpeted Rock.

"It's like your little Moon all over again," cried Silverhorn in fury. "They're going to kill that cheetah!"

"I don't see how one cheetah would feed a pride," said Sky grimly. "I bet they're not planning to eat her. Like that buffalo they wasted."

"It's killing for killing's sake," growled Rock, his dark eyes flashing. "They're breaking the Code."

A deep anger filled Sky. "We're not going to let them."

"Good," declared Rock. "But we don't have much time! She looks slow. She must have been running for too long already."

He lowered his head, his creamy tusks gleaming, and plunged forward. Sky and Silverhorn charged after him, tusks and horn lowered in furious threat. As they ploughed forward the cheetah had to bank and swerve; this must have used her last reserves, because when Sky risked a glance back, she saw the cheetah flop to the ground behind them, her flanks heaving.

The three companions stopped to form a line, right

between the lions and their prey. Rock drew himself up, his gray skin as dark as a storm cloud, his massive ears flapping in threat. To Sky he looked fearsome and magnificent, and she did her best to look equally intimidating.

Next to her, Silverhorn was grunting and pawing the ground, her black eyes flashing. The lions skidded to a halt, facing them. Behind them Sky could hear the cheetah's high-pitched, rasping pants.

Titan himself bounded through the perplexed lions and gave an enraged roar.

"What do you think you're doing? Do you dare to come between Titan and his prey?"

Sky let her gaze roam swiftly over the scattered lions. Their meticulous hunting pattern had disintegrated into chaos. Some sat back on their haunches, looking bewildered; others were still on all fours, pacing back and forth, growling in protest. There was no sign of Fearless Gallantpride.

"Move, I tell you!" snarled Titan.

"No." Sky fixed her eyes on his, staring him down. "You won't break the Code again—not when we can stop you."

"*No* creature gives me orders!" His roar rose almost to a scream. "Resolute, Honor—to the left! And you three lazy idiots—go the other way!" A trio of younger male cubs instantly scrambled to obey.

Sky shifted to block them—but Rock simply gave a blaring trumpet of rage and charged the main pride. There was a heavy thunder of huge feet, and before the shocked lions could dodge or flee, he lowered his head and caught a big male on his tusks. With a jerk of his neck, he tossed the big cat to the side; it hit the earth with a sickening thud and lay limp.

Rock spun with astonishing nimbleness, glaring around at the panicked lions. Almost beneath his feet, a young maneless cub cowered, its eyes fixed in terror on the massive elephant.

This time Rock swung his trunk, knocking the small lion sideways; it bounced and rolled, yelping in terror, and Rock followed. He raised one great foot over the terrified creature.

"No!" Sky cried.

Rock raised his head and looked at her, his eyes blazing. "It's what they all deserve! These Codeless savages killed your cousin, when he was no more than a baby." His foot quivered and he glowered down at the helpless cub. "Now I'll smash one of their young."

The cub pressed himself tight to the ground, as if that might save him from Rock's crushing foot. "Father," he whimpered. "Help me!"

His pleading eyes were locked on Titan.

"You're Titan's cub?" bellowed Rock. "So much the better. This will teach your father never to break the Code again!"

Titan roared in insane fury, clawing the ground. "How dare you. I know who you are—the elephants who attacked Stinger Crownleaf. You're no better than we are, so *do not lecture me about the Code*! You elephants don't give a dry bone for it!"

"That's not true!" cried Sky.

"Stinger himself told me how you tried to break it," snarled Titan.

"Stinger?" Sky frowned. "You've been speaking to Stinger?" But a whimper from the cub drew her to where he quivered beneath Rock's gigantic, hovering foot. She trotted over. "Don't be scared," she told him softly. "Rock! *Let this cub go.*"

Rock stared at her for long, agonizing moments, but Sky did not drop her gaze. At last Rock shifted his foot and planted it with an angry thump on the hard earth.

The young lion crawled clear on his belly, a low whimper in his throat. He scuttled between two of the larger lions and crouched submissively.

A strange, hoarse bark of a roar came from Titan, and Sky realized he was laughing.

"So," he sneered. "Elephants have no principles, and no guts either." Twisting, he glared beyond the elephants and the rhino, straight at the cheetah. She squatted with her head hanging low, her flanks still heaving. "You may have stopped me killing that cat-vermin, but Titanpride will find different prey soon enough. One day, Striderbrat, all my rivals will be dead. I'll rule Bravelands as I always should have—and on that day, you'll be sorry."

Without so much as a glance at his cringing cub, Titan stalked off back across the plain. His pride fell in behind him, silent. Sky watched the cub clamber to his paws and follow, his head and tail drooping. The youngster looked thoroughly dejected, and no wonder: Rock had come within a breath of killing him, but his father had not given him a single comforting word.

"You shouldn't have done that," Sky said to Rock. "How can we ask anyone to believe in our search if we break the Code ourselves?"

Rock shifted his great feet, lowering his tusks. "I know," he said softly. "I don't think I really would have done it."

"I'm glad. But don't you remember what happened to Rain?"

"I'm sorry, Sky. It won't happen again."

The lions were a distant, shimmering blur of tawny yellow by the time Mud Driftleaf crept back from the rocks to Sky's side. His terrified eyes were rimmed with white; he couldn't take them off the retreating lions. Leaving her companions, Sky walked back to the cheetah.

"Are you all right?" she asked, blowing softly through her trunk.

"I am now," said the cheetah, dipping her head. "Thank you. I'd be dead if it wasn't for you . . . all of you." She stared at Sky and the three companions beyond her.

"I'm just glad we were here," Sky told her. "Titan had no right!"

"No, he didn't. He and his pride left a fat zebra carcass to come after me." The cheetah rubbed her ear with a paw, then shook her head slowly. "I'm sorry . . . it's just . . . I've never seen a herd like yours. I've seen elephants and rhinos and baboons, but I've never seen them all living together." She licked her jaws. "Are you . . . a herd?"

Sky's ears fluttered in surprise. She glanced back at Rock, Silverhorn, and the scrawny Mud Driftleaf. "I . . . suppose we are. Except for the baboon; he's only here for the moment. But yes; we're a *herd*." Her heart lightened as she gazed at Rock. "I hadn't thought about it, but I like that. We're like a family!"

"And you look as if you'll have a family soon, too," observed Silverhorn, chewing on a mouthful of leaves as she walked over to the cheetah.

The slender cat glanced at her belly. Sky could see now that it was round and protruding, and her eyes widened.

"Oh! You're going to have cubs!"

"Yes." The cheetah purred. "So you saved them as well as me. I'm Rush, by the way."

Rock ambled over to join them. "No wonder you were having trouble outrunning Titanpride," he said with a note of amusement. "I knew cheetahs were usually faster than that."

Rush gave him a wry look. "They caught me off guard. I didn't expect to be hunted. But the good news is that I feel the cubs stirring; they haven't been harmed."

"I'm glad." Sky gazed at Rush's belly, fascinated. "Rush . . . I'd hate to think of Titanpride coming after you again." She hesitated, blinking nervously. "Would you like . . . to join our herd?"

"Me? In a herd?" Rush frowned. "We female cheetahs don't live with others."

"We female elephants don't live with bull elephants and rhinos," said Sky with a smile. "But we're safer together. We can help protect your cubs when they're born."

Rush brightened and got to her paws. "You would? Then I'd be glad to join you. Thank you!"

Delighted, Sky nuzzled the slender cat at last with her trunk. *The warm sense of squirming life inside her . . . the joy of running free across the plains . . . the terror of Titanpride, subsiding now that she was safe . . .* "Welcome to our herd, Rush," she murmured.

Rush submitted to the greetings and touches of Rock and Silverhorn, who looked a little bemused but happy. "I am grateful I met you," the cheetah bleated softly. "Bravelands is a dangerous place to be alone right now."

"Yes, Rush," agreed Sky, "it is." She lifted her head, feeling a renewed, powerful urge to return to her mission. "But I'm hoping to change that soon. . . ."

CHAPTER 12

The watering hole was almost entirely obscured by the great mass of animals that had gathered at Stinger's summons. A troop of vervets perched in one cluster of trees, glaring at a troop of colobus monkeys that must have traveled from a distant woodland; Sky hadn't seen them before. The colobus ignored the rival monkeys; they were too busy grooming one another's black-and-white fur and messily scoffing dates. A graceful gerenuk with sweeping horns reared up on its hind legs, pawing at a bush with its delicate front hooves and nibbling at the leaves. A vast herd of gazelles mingled with impalas; zebras and wildebeests milled on the shore, churning it to mud; three giraffes looked down their noses at the chaos below. A couple of leopards crouched at the water's edge; farther out, the usual crocodiles drifted hopefully, their slitted eyes monitoring the mass of potential meat on the shoreline.

Sky took a breath as she walked toward the Gathering; all she could see was a hopelessly huge and confused crowd of potential Great Parents.

"I need to get to the front," she told Rock, anxiety making her heart beat hard. "I need to tell them about my search."

She was glad to have Rock's reassuring bulk on one side and the sturdy Silverhorn on the other. Mud bounded a short way ahead, looking a little purposeless; he seemed in no hurry to get back to the other baboons. After all, thought Sky, he'd failed to find the main elephant herd and bully them into shape—though the thought of the scrawny Mud doing any such thing was almost ridiculous. Rush, meanwhile, was hanging back, looking unsure. Her bushy-tipped tail was balanced elegantly behind her, though the tip of it gave an occasional nervous twitch.

"Are you scared?" whispered Silverhorn.

"A bit," admitted Sky. "But I've got to do this."

No sooner had she said it than a wildebeest turned from his gossiping group, and his eyes widened. He snorted. "What are *they* doing here?"

One by one, animals lifted their heads and stared. A group of buffalo stamped their hooves and grunted aggressively; impala and gazelle heads shot up, ears swiveling.

Sky took a deep breath and walked on into the fringes of the crowd. Cries of surprise and resentful mutters rose around her.

"Elephants! Didn't we banish them?"

"They've got some nerve."

"Have they forgotten they're not welcome?"

The aggression only got worse as they pressed on through the throng. It was hard work trying to avoid touching any of the animals, since Sky didn't want to see their memories of hunts and howls and frantic gallops from predators; the atmosphere was bad enough without that. Snuffle and his family of warthogs harrumphed and snorted, turning their stiff little tails on the friends. A giraffe dipped its head close to them, its thick lashes blinking rapidly.

"Tree and grass! What kind of herd is *this*?"

A young hippo hauled itself dripping from the water and trudged in for a closer look. "I've never seen anything like it."

A jackal screeched a high-pitched laugh, and its comrades joined in. "An elephant-rhino-cheetah pack! Now I've seen everything!"

"This isn't funny," added a snooty-looking kudu. "It's quite against the natural order."

The laughter quickly turned to hostile rumbles. A gazelle nodded. "It's wrong. Somebody tell Great Father!"

"Great Father already knows," declared a silky, resonant voice.

Sky took a breath and halted. *The False Parent.* While she'd trudged on, flinching away from the other animals and staring at the ground, her little group had made it through to the front of the Gathering. And there stood Stinger Crownleaf, high on a smooth sandstone boulder, his eyes glittering with cunning.

"Mud Driftleaf," he went on, extending a paw toward the

nervous little baboon. "Thank you for bringing our esteemed guests."

"You expected them, Great Father?" cried a surprised zebra.

"Indeed, and let us make them welcome. Make room for our friends, my children." He bestowed a regal, friendly smile on Sky. "Come and stand with me, child."

She bristled with loathing, but she had no choice but to obey. Every nerve in her body alert for a trick, she stood beside the boulder, Stinger to her side and the hordes in front.

"I have heard of your adventures in Bravelands, Sky Strider," declared Stinger. He stood so high on the boulder, he could touch her cheek with a paw. "And such stunning news—you are searching for a Great Parent!"

Sky could feel the eyes of every animal on her hide, aggressive and resentful. Desperately she sought out Rock and Silverhorn; the big bull elephant nodded at her encouragingly. "Yes . . ." she croaked. "You see . . ."

"A Great Parent to replace me!" Stinger went on, talking over her. "I confess, Sky, I don't understand this quest. If the Great Spirit has chosen me—*which it did*—why would it insult me so? Or perhaps . . ." He furrowed his brow, as if trying to understand. "Perhaps this quest does not come from that sacred Spirit at all? In which case . . . surely the insult is to the Great Spirit itself."

The crowd erupted in howls, brays, and hoots of anger. Stinger let them holler for long moments, then shushed them gently with an outstretched paw.

"Really, Sky Strider, who are you to claim you know better than the Great Spirit?"

Sky's whole body felt hot with anger; hotter than she'd felt on the long meandering trek across the plains. Above them, a great bank of dark cloud had slid across the sky, but far from cooling the land, the heat was more intense than ever.

She raised her trunk, and was glad it trembled only a little.

"I have a message to deliver," she cried. "And the Great Spirit's message is true—Stinger Crownleaf is not the Great Father!" She cleared her throat. "The Great Spirit is in me."

"*You?* The Great Mother?" a wildebeest bellowed as the animals roared their scorn. *"Nonsense!"*

"No! I'm not. I never said that!" Sky raised her voice, desperate to make them listen. "I'm carrying the Great Spirit—searching on its behalf. It wants me to find the true Great Parent. And if anyone knows who that might be, please come and find me. I'll be waiting here by the lake and—"

Once more the crowds roared and brayed with derision and fury. The racket was so loud this time, Sky couldn't make out any of their words—and she was glad.

Stinger calmed his audience again. He gave a gentle, rippling laugh. "Oh, Sky Strider, what nonsense is this? Where is your proof? You are young, so we must make allowances, but the Great Spirit is not to be mocked!"

And at that moment, abruptly, the dark clouds burst. Torrential rain lashed from the sky, soaking every creature.

Sky gasped, tilting her head upward. Rain ran into her ears and mouth, and she lifted her trunk. Then she snapped her head back to gaze at the gathered creatures.

"Look at this weather—here is your proof! It's never been like this before, you all know it. If Stinger were truly the Great Father, balance would have returned!"

"Nonsense!" bellowed Stinger again, over the crash of the rain. Raising his voice gave it an edge of desperation that hadn't been there before. "The Great Spirit has been angered, it is true—but we all know why! Great Mother was *murdered*. Stronghide the rhino thrust himself forward, claimed the role of Great Parent—but he was a liar, a usurper. And now this elephant claims that I am not the Great Father. Of *course* the Great Spirit is furious!" He stretched out both paws. "My children, we must work harder than ever to appease the Spirit. Follow your Great Father's guidance, and all will be well." Jarringly, he gave a sudden laugh. "I thought elephants were said to be wise. Yet this one does not understand something *so simple!*"

Horrified, Sky stared at the crowd as every animal joined in his laughter. Only Rock, Silverhorn, and Rush gazed at her with sympathy, although Mud Driftleaf wasn't laughing either. He looked uneasy.

I know why Stinger brought me here, she realized, her gut heavy. The baboon hadn't just wanted to humiliate her—he'd *needed* to, to solidify his position. He wanted to make sure that no animal of Bravelands ever took her seriously again.

And he might have succeeded.

Sky's legs shook. She wanted to run now, run far away and never think of the Great Spirit again. *No. No, Stinger can't win!*

Desperately she pointed with her trunk to the nearby trees. They were empty of birds.

"Look!" she cried. "All of you! Remember when Great Mother used to call our Gatherings? The trees and rocks would be covered with vultures, bringing news and messages and bones. And not just vultures—all the birds of Bravelands. Even Stronghide had his oxpeckers, but where are the birds for Stinger? If he is Great Father, why don't they follow him?"

Stinger chuckled again; she could tell from his smug expression that he knew he was winning. "Oh, Sky. I am not an elephant—didn't you notice? I am not a rhino either—I'm a baboon!" He grinned at his crowd as they laughed. "Things change and evolve, and we in turn adapt; my own troop knows that. The birds do not follow me. So what?" He shrugged. "The rest of Bravelands does."

The laughter of the animals was turning into jeers. Sky felt hot and cold all at once; rain drenched her hide and she realized how pathetic she must look: a sodden, young elephant, spouting crazy claims.

"Poor little elephant," crooned Stinger, twisting the claw of condescension as if to finish her off. "I think perhaps her matriarch's death, so soon after her grandmother's, may have sent her a little mad. Please understand, my children. It's not her fault."

"Get out of here, Sky Strider!" a zebra brayed from the crowd.

A buffalo bellowed, "Yes—clear off!"

"You elephants!" That was a little round hyrax, wrinkling

her whiskery snout. "Just can't let go of your power, can you?"

"Take your weird herd and go," shrieked a jackal. "We don't want you here, insulting our Great Father."

They were pushing forward, crowding toward Sky; Rock and Silverhorn hurried to flank and protect her. Rock glared and trumpeted at the mocking creatures, but they didn't stop.

In the melee, Stinger leaned close to Sky from his high boulder. She shuddered as she felt his breath close to her ear, heard his malevolent whisper.

"Yes, Sky Strider, go. I'll make sure you're a pariah in Bravelands. You'll be welcome nowhere; every beast, every reptile, every *insect* will laugh at you. Go!"

"Come on," Rock murmured. "Let's get out of here."

"No, wait! We have to make them understand—" But the tone of the animals' shouts and roars was growing uglier. They were crowding around her now, faces cold with contempt. One of the buffalo was stomping the ground, readying for a charge. Sky sensed something break within her, like a branch snapping from a tree.

It's hopeless.

She felt Rock's strong flank against hers and—ignoring the flash of memory she saw, a pair of dark elephant eyes fanned by long lashes—she let him nudge her out of the chaos and shepherd her away from the lakeside.

They stumbled away through the lashing rain. Silverhorn and Rush trotted after the two elephants, casting glares over their shoulders at the almost hysterical herds. The mob was cheering Stinger to the skies now. However far she went from the watering hole, Sky decided, she would never get rid of the echo of jeering howls in her ears.

"You did your best, Sky," Silverhorn comforted her. "You couldn't have done more."

"The rhino's right," chirped Rush. "I don't know you well, but you're too good to take any notice of those fools back there."

Sky glanced over her shoulder. Mud was loping after them at a distance, looking downright miserable. *At least our Driftleaf didn't seem to enjoy that either.*

"Thanks, Silverhorn," she mumbled. "And you're kind, Rush. But it's all hopeless now. If Stinger makes me a laughingstock, why would anyone listen to me? He's turned my search for the Great Parent into a joke."

"Don't worry about what they think," Rock told her. "They'll find out what Stinger really is—eventually."

"But Rock, that's not what matters, is it? I don't really care what they think about me." Sky focused on placing one foot after the other in the muddy earth. Her body felt so heavy; she wanted nothing more than to lie down in the dirt and sleep. Yet at the same time, she felt as if she would never sleep again. Everything hurt, especially her heart.

"It's over. I've no chance of finding the true Great Parent. Stinger Crownleaf has won."

CHAPTER 13

In the dense, damp undergrowth of Leopard Forest, every crack and creak seemed ominously magnified. Hunting with the Crookedtree Highleaves, Thorn couldn't repress his unease; the shadows moved oddly, and he did not know where to watch for dips and fallen branches and treacherous rocks. He'd known every cranny and hollow of Tall Trees. Focused as he was on where to place each paw, he couldn't be so alert for sounds and movement, so each snap of a twig made him start. Ahead of him Nut looked equally ill at ease, his head twitching and his ears flickering nervously.

Nut jumped and stifled another yelp. "Did you hear that? Was that a leopard?"

"I doubt it." Their leader, a rangy female called Burr, flared her nostrils. "I've never seen a leopard around here."

"Really?" Thorn raised his brow. "I thought this place was called Leopard Forest?"

Burr smirked at him. "And who do you think called it that? We did. Crookedtree Troop chose the name, seasons ago. Keeps other baboon troops nice and far away."

"Its real name is Shadow Forest," added one of the other hunters, Root. "Because it's so dark. Scares you, does it?" Chuckling, he loped away after Burr.

Nut's shoulders slumped; he looked cross at being fooled by the forest and mocked by the hunters. He yanked a handful of berries from a nearby tree and crammed them into his mouth, but instantly spat them out.

"Yuck," he whispered to Thorn, wiping yellow juice from his muzzle. "Even the fruit tastes bad here. It's nothing like Tall Trees. I don't think I can stand this place much longer. Or these creepy baboons."

Thorn glanced in both directions to make sure the others had moved on. "I'm itching to leave too," he whispered back. "But we've got to stay long enough for Stinger to give up. I want him to think we've died of starvation on the plains."

"I miss Tall Trees," sulked Nut.

Thorn sighed patiently. "So do I, but I'd settle for the new camp at the hyena den. Even hunting like this makes me miss home." He felt a pang of longing to see Berry running at his side; he wished Mud could be here, too. His small friend had always relied on Thorn to wait for him when he fell behind; Thorn hadn't minded helping him up the steepest slopes, or covering for him when he didn't catch much. Mud had repaid him simply by being the best company. Nut just wasn't the same. . . .

"Come on, Nut. We'd better catch up." Thorn scrambled over a mossy dead branch that lay in his way. His fur felt sticky and damp; even the thin spears of sunlight that pierced the canopy were ferociously hot. As he avoided a small patch of blazing sun, keeping to the shade, movement caught his eye.

It wasn't a trick of the light this time, or a fallen twig. Something bright green and quick was darting along a low branch; Thorn leaped for the snake and snatched it by its tail, then caught its neck. "This will keep Burr happy!"

"It's a mamba," said Nut. "Don't let it bite you!"

"No way." It was trying to strike, glaring at him and hissing what must surely be curses in Sandtongue. Thorn let go of its tail, grabbed it near its neck, and yanked both his paws apart, breaking its spine.

"What's that you've found?" Burr was clambering back through the bush, clutching an armful of figs. "Oh, snake. Tasty."

The other hunters appeared behind her, bringing berries and roots and a limp, spiny-tailed lizard. "Surely we've got enough," said Root, holding up the lizard and staring at it. "I had to go beyond the trees to get this, and I hate doing that."

"We've got enough," Burr confirmed. "Especially with that snake. Good catch, Thorn Highleaf. It's nearly as long as you are."

Thorn was pleased at the compliment, and relieved too.

They needed to make themselves indispensable to this troop. He bounded after Burr, clutching his snake with pride.

They hadn't gone as far from the camp as Thorn had thought, and the hunters were soon home. As Burr and the others displayed their haul to Tendril, Thorn drew Nut aside.

"I'm going to tear off a bit of this snake and give it to the Goodleaf," he muttered. "You take the rest, will you?"

"All right, but don't leave me alone with these crazy baboons for too long." Nut shifted his pawful of figs as Thorn chewed off a chunk of mamba-tail, then took the rest of the carcass from him. Clutching his gift, Thorn loped off toward the veil of creepers that hid the Goodleaf's glade.

She was padding around the clearing, tending to the baboons who hadn't yet recovered from the monkey attack. Thorn's heart lightened. The Goodleaf had never shot him a suspicious look or turned her back to avoid him. Of all the baboons of Leopard Forest, she was the one he felt most at ease with.

His ear would always have an ugly rip, but the edges had healed well and it didn't hurt anymore. The mute Goodleaf clearly knew her job, and he was grateful to her. Padding over, he touched her arm and placed the chunk of snake-meat in her paw.

"Thank you for helping me," he said, smiling.

Her huge eyes softened as she looked at the gift, and she smiled back and nodded her thanks.

Thorn didn't know what to say now, and besides, the Goodleaf was turning away to resume her work. Thorn frowned, searching his memory. *Why does she seem so familiar?* He was sure he had met her before. If only he could talk to her properly and ask her . . . If nothing else, he'd like to know her name.

But she was busy, and her priority was the wounded baboons. With a frustrated sigh, Thorn pushed back through the trailing vines and padded toward the main camp.

Nut was with Burr, helping to sort the food into separate piles for Highleaves, Middleleaves, and Lowleaves. As Thorn approached, he could hear Burr giving Nut a low-voiced scolding.

"And don't nibble on the lizard, either."

"I wasn't *pilfering*," Nut grumbled. "A baboon's got to eat, especially when he's been hunting."

"We've all been hunting," she told him. "Bad enough that Thorn took a piece of the snake. Yes, I *know* it was for the Goodleaf, and we'll let it go this time, but you two have got to learn the Crookedtree way."

Thorn bounded over, anxious to make amends. He didn't want Burr to turn against him now, after his triumph in catching the mamba. "Can I help?"

Burr gave him a grumpy look. "Yes, by not raiding the food before the whole troop can eat. Here, divide these berries between the three piles."

Meekly, Thorn sat down and set to his task. Burr had fallen silent, concentrating on dividing up the snake carcass. Thorn licked his jaws nervously.

"Burr, can I ask you something?"

"Go ahead." She pulled a bit of the translucent meat in two. "Do you know why the Goodleaf doesn't speak?"

"Hmph." Burr shrugged. "Pear? She's been like that for a while. Since her mate stole her daughter and ran away."

"What?" Thorn and Nut said it simultaneously. They exchanged a shocked glance.

"Why would a father steal a baby from its mother?" Thorn asked, horrified. *Poor Goodleaf!* "Did they have a bad fight?"

"Not exactly," growled Burr. "He was thrown out of the troop for murdering the Crownleaf."

Thorn's jaw went slack. Inside his chest, his heart thudded and raced. He stared at Nut, and saw that he too was staring open-mouthed at Burr; his paws had frozen on his bunch of berries.

Thorn cleared his throat. "What happened?" he asked hoarsely.

Burr scowled at the snake and ripped another piece off, rather violently. "Seed—that was his name—Seed got Marula Crownleaf from behind, the coward. Hit her in the back of the skull with a rock. I mean, every baboon in the troop knew he wanted to be Crownleaf himself, but we had no idea that was how he was planning to do it."

"He was going to kill his way to the Crown Stone," whispered Thorn.

"That was his plan, I suppose. But he was found out. Before we could bring him before the troop, he fled, and he took his baby daughter with him. Tiny, she was. Poor Pear was devastated. Hasn't spoken since. As you've seen."

Thorn couldn't speak himself for a moment; he felt too sick. His heart was thrashing and his head spun. The story sounded so horribly familiar.

He coughed to clear his throat. "When did this happen, Burr?"

"Dunno. Maybe seven years ago?"

Thorn and Nut exchanged a glance of awful realization. "Seven years ago," whispered Thorn. "Nut. That's when Berry and Stinger arrived at Brightforest Troop."

Nut nodded slowly. "Father and daughter. They must be the same baboons."

"And Pear Goodleaf must be Berry's mother." Thorn swallowed hard and closed his eyes. "No wonder I thought she looked familiar."

The sickening ache inside him turned into a sudden burst of angry energy. Thorn leaped to his feet, gritting his jaws.

"Nut, we have to tell Tendril about this. Burr, I'm sorry, but we need to go right now!"

"Well, if it's the same baboon you're talking about . . ." Burr said pensively.

"It has to be," agreed Nut. "But Thorn, I don't know how telling Tendril helps."

"Because she already knows Stinger!"

"So?" Nut shrugged and picked at his bunch of berries. Thorn swatted them from his paws. "Hey! What was that for?"

"Listen," said Thorn fiercely. "This changes everything. I couldn't tell Brightforest Troop the truth, could I? No one would've believed me. But Tendril will!"

Nut looked blank. "Why do you think that?"

Thorn resisted the urge to shake him. "Because she knows what Stinger's capable of! She knows he's already killed their Crownleaf. When she hears what he's up to now, she'll have to help us get rid of him for good."

Burr shook her head with a dry laugh.

"You're crazy," Nut told him. "Even if Tendril believes you, she won't even let us *leave*, let alone help us."

"Well, I've got to try." Thorn turned and bounded for the Council Glade. He heard Burr's mocking *"Good luck with that!"* drift after him, but to his surprise, Nut was following at his heels. When he glanced around, Nut looked surly and reluctant—but at least he was there.

Tendril was reclining on her mound of black feathers, idly chewing at fruits handed to her by her adoring coterie. The young females spun around as Thorn rushed into the glade, their expressions shocked and angry.

"What's the meaning of this?" snapped the biggest of them. "How dare you interrupt Tendril Crownleaf?"

"I'm sorry," panted Thorn, as Tendril herself blinked at him with stony indifference. "I really am, but there's something you need to know, Tendril. Something I've just found out. It's about Seed."

A few of Tendril's retinue gasped; the biggest gave a growl and narrowed her eyes. The Crownleaf herself craned forward, her blank gaze sharpening. "Seed?"

"The baboon who—"

"I know who you mean," she snapped. "Tell me what you know."

Thorn took a deep breath. "There's quite a lot to tell. . . ."

"Then get on with it."

He did. He told them how Stinger—Seed—had arrived with his baby daughter in Brightforest Troop, seven years ago. He explained how Stinger had been Thorn's own mentor and friend: how he had risen to become a Highleaf and a trusted council member who was one of Bark Crownleaf's most loyal advisers.

All the while, Tendril's eyes remained locked on him, her impenetrable expression unchanging. Thorn paused for breath. "But he murdered Bark Crownleaf. By smashing her skull from behind. *With a rock.*"

Tendril's face tightened.

Thorn clenched his fists. "And after he'd killed Bark—and who knows how many others—he planned the murder of Great Mother. He tricked Stronghide the rhino into doing that, and becoming Great Father—and then he got rid of him. And now he is the Great Father of Bravelands."

As he finished his story, his heart was pounding. There was silence in the glade. Slowly Tendril rose to her feet.

"Seed," she murmured. "Seed is the Great Father? Rumors reached us that a baboon had risen to be Great Father, but I wasn't sure they were true."

"It is true," said Thorn. "All of it."

"And I can believe it." Tendril gazed around at her retinue, who wore expressions of horror and revulsion. "I am sorry indeed to hear what he has done; we have our own experience of Seed's villainy, as you now know."

Thorn's heart soared with hope.

"But," Tendril went on, "the creature is no longer Crookedtree's problem. Because of what he did, we vowed to close our troop to strangers, and to remain hidden from all other baboons forever. What you tell us is terrible, Thorn Highleaf, a shocking story. But it changes nothing."

For a moment, he could not believe it. His limbs felt numb. "You can't mean that. Don't you want revenge?"

Tendril gave a languid shrug. "What use is revenge to me?"

"Then stop him doing this to anyone else!" Thorn's fists clenched.

"And why would I care what he does, if he does it beyond the bounds of Shadow Forest?"

Thorn could barely contain his frustration and fury. "Your troop will want to help me!"

"No," she said calmly, "they will not."

Cold anger gushed through Thorn's veins, and his control snapped. "Why don't we ask them?" Baring his teeth, he barked, "Nut! Gather the rest of Crookedtree Troop. Now!"

Nut's eyes popped, but he was too taken aback to argue. He bolted from the glade.

Tendril reared up on her hind paws. "How dare you! I am Crownleaf of this troop!"

"Stinger came from your precious troop," snarled Thorn. "And now he's destroying Bravelands. He's your responsibility too. It's up to every creature to stop him!"

"Highleaves!" shrieked Tendril, finally losing her cool indifference. "Where are they? My retinue, fetch the Highleaves!
Seize this troublemaker!"

But baboons were already spilling into the clearing, chat-
tering and hooting: Highleaves and Middleleaves, Lowleaves
and Deeproots. At the head of them was Nut, his anxious eyes
on Thorn. *Don't ruin this*, he seemed to be saying with his piercing stare. *Don't mess this up for both of us!*

A crash of branches came from the left; Thorn spun to see
the burlier Highleaves bounding through the trees. He had to
be quick—and persuasive.

"Crookedtree Troop!" he yelled over the hubbub. "Listen to
me! I know where the Codebreaker Seed is!"

The racket died. All around, baboons stared at him,
blinking.

Thorn's chest heaved. "It's true. He's called Stinger these
days, not Seed, but he is the same vicious, cunning baboon
he always was. The difference is, he's now calling himself the
Great Father of Bravelands. But he's a fraud and a pretender!
He's fooled and twisted every creature to get where he is. I
wanted to take him down—I wanted to see him punished for
the dreadful things he's done—but he was Crownleaf of my
old troop, and they believed his word over mine. *That's* why
Nut and I were banished." Thorn licked his jaws, gazing
around at the baboons; he certainly had their attention. "They
wouldn't believe me, but they'll have to believe Crookedtree
Troop. He's lied and manipulated and murdered, and he has

to be stopped. Are you with me? *Will you help?*"

For a long moment, there was silence but for the dripping leaves. Even the Highleaf patrol had come to a halt at the edge of the glade, fascinated and uncertain.

"This is an outrage!" Tendril's scream split the glade. "*No baboon can leave Shadow Forest. Seize him!*"

Her Highleaf fighters snapped out of their indecision. They charged at Thorn, hollering and whooping with fury. Nimbly, he twisted and sprang for a branch.

The Highleaves rushed him again, their faces twisted with frustrated rage. Thorn leaped up into the closest tree, scrambling through the branches. Below him the Highleaves spread into position, surrounding him, glaring up with cold menace.

Panting, Thorn stared around the glade. *It didn't work; they're too much under Tendril's paw.*

He'd hoped he and Nut could stay here until they found a safe way to leave, and a safer place to go to, but that certainly wasn't an option anymore. *Poor Nut. He didn't want me to ruin this.* With a glance at his unlikely comrade, he realized Nut's face was tormented and frightened. But surely he, too, realized it was over. . . .

"I'm leaving!" Thorn snarled at the stunned troop. "Will any of you join me?"

In the glade there was a terrible quietness. Every baboon looked from Thorn to the Highleaves to Tendril.

Then a baboon walked forward from the back, the surprised troop making way for her. She turned to face them. A sweet, slightly hoarse voice spoke, resounding eerily through the trees.

"Seed stole my daughter," said Pear Goodleaf. "The baboon you now call *Stinger* took my baby from me. I will go with you, Thorn Highleaf."

For a moment Thorn forgot the Highleaf fighters, and his perilous position. He was not the only baboon gaping at Pear Goodleaf; every Crookedtree troop member had turned to watch her in disbelief.

Seven years! Thorn realized. *She's just spoken for the first time in seven years.*

Her unexpected words had sparked something in other baboons. Three young males loped forward to join her. "We will too!" cried one of them.

"And me," declared one of Tendril's retinue. She stepped away from her sisters as Tendril's jaw widened in disbelief.

"I'll challenge a baboon who steals babies," growled a mother. She bounded forward, her own tiny baby clinging to her belly.

Thorn's heart swelled with delight and hope and pride. *They're turning!*

"No!" Tendril screamed again, pummeling the mound of feathers. "Leaving—is—*forbidden!*"

Nodding, the Highleaves began to scramble up the tree after Thorn, but Nut growled and sprang at them. Baring his fangs, he bit at their haunches, grabbed and dragged at their tails. Taken by surprise, they twisted and clawed ineffectively at him; Thorn took his chance to spring over their heads and down from his perch. The Highleaves, cursing wildly, turned and chased Nut instead.

"Capture them!" Tendril's voice was growing ever more high-pitched. "And those stupid renegades who want to leave. Take them all!"

The renegades exchanged apprehensive looks; then, with whoops and growls of defiance, they charged the Highleaves. In moments the glade became a turmoil of slashing claws, clattering jaws, and sprayed blood. Baboons snarled and snapped at each other, grabbing opponents and wrestling them to the ground, or yanking at their tails to drag them back to be beaten. It was hard for the bewildered Thorn to tell who was on his side.

"Pear!" Nut barked suddenly. "Thorn, the Goodleaf!"

Thorn spun his head; the golden-furred baboon was at the edge of the glade, backing warily away from a big Highleaf fighter. Thorn raced toward her, followed by Nut, and together they wrenched the Highleaf away from her and flung him to the ground. Nut straddled him, pummeling his chest and yelping with fury, as Thorn grabbed Pear's arm.

"We've got to get out of here," he told her. Jumping onto a low fig branch, he hollered over the noise of the fight, "If you want to come, follow me now!"

At once some of the baboons began to tear themselves from their individual battles, ducking and lashing as they crawled and scampered out of reach. Thorn was soon joined by about a dozen of the rebels, along with Nut and Pear. Root the hunter was there, and the young mother and her baby, as well as some of Tendril's retinue and three young males.

"This way!" cried Thorn. He spun and raced into the forest, sprinting as fast as he could from the Crookedtree camp. He could hear the pounding paws of his followers, and their desperate pants.

And he could hear Tendril's increasingly shrill commands to her Highleaves. *"Get back! Come here and help. Leave them! Let them go!"*

Was it a trick? But despite his gasping breath and the pounding of his blood in his ears, he guessed there were eleven or twelve baboons behind him at most. *Only the Crookedtree dissenters.* The Highleaves were not coming after them.

She must need them to keep control of her remaining baboons. Thorn glanced with sudden understanding at the former members of Tendril's retinue; perhaps her devoted troop wasn't quite as loyal as she pretended. *And she's probably terrified the Highleaf fighters will abandon her, too*, he realized. *If they had any sense, they would. She's mad.*

But all that followed them through the trees was her terrible screeching voice. Tendril Crownleaf sounded demented with fury.

"You can never come back! *None of you!* Rebels! Renegades! You're banished! *You'll pay for this, Thorn Fallenleaf!*"

Thorn ignored her wild threats. He ran on, leaping over fallen logs, crashing through tangled undergrowth, birds scattering in alarm from the treetops above him.

He couldn't worry about Tendril and her crazy troop; he didn't even want to think about them anymore. Hope was building to a thrumming pitch inside him. He had allies now, friends, a small troop of his own—and they knew the truth.

Now I have a chance to take Stinger down!

CHAPTER 14

"*How long do you think this* will take?" asked Silverhorn nervously. She swung her horn at the line of hostile wildebeests that almost surrounded them. The herd had edged closer all morning, snorting and stamping; gradually they had formed into an intimidating semicircle, and were growing more aggressive by the moment. Yet Sky and her friends could not retreat—not right now.

"Honestly, Silverhorn, I don't know," admitted Sky. She lowered her head in warning as one wildebeest risked a pace forward. "I watched Moon being born, but I've no *idea* how long it takes cheetah babies to come out. Rock?"

"Well, don't ask *me*," he grunted, stamping a threatening foot at the herd.

Behind them, the bushes rustled again. There was a faint, mewling chirrup of distress, and the sound of heavy panting.

Rush's cubs had not picked the best moment to be born, thought Sky. The wildebeests had been tracking their steps all day, and they did not look as though they were here to offer congratulations on the impending birth.

"Why are you still in Bravelands?" brayed their leader, a stubborn-faced bull with a scarred nose. "You and your unnatural herd aren't wanted here!"

"Why are you following us, then?" retorted Silverhorn. "You seem to want our company, since you haven't left us alone since the Great Gathering."

"That elephant"—he jerked his horns at Sky—"insulted Great Father. She insulted the Great Spirit itself! She needs to leave!"

With a grunt of anger, Rock charged forward and swung his tusks. The wildebeest neighed in alarm and dodged, but the tip of one long tusk gouged his flank. With a bellow of pain he fled, and his herd stampeded after him.

"Look who's leaving now!" shouted Rock. He strode back to Sky. "Idiots."

"They may be idiots, but there are a lot who agree with them," sighed Sky. "It looks like Stinger's plan to turn Bravelands against me is working."

A faint mewling came from under the bush, and both elephants turned, angling their ears toward it. "Oh, stars!" exclaimed Sky. "They're here! Come on, Rock, let's look!"

"You go right ahead," he rumbled nervously, taking a step back.

Sky trotted over to the bush and gently eased the branches

aside with her tusks. Rush lay there on her side, her fur damp; she looked exhausted but happy. Two tiny, fluff-headed cubs nestled at her belly.

"Oh, Rush! They're *beautiful!*"

Rush lashed her tail proudly. "I'm going to name them Nimble and Lively. Look how alert they are already!"

The little creatures squirmed and pushed at each other, suckling hungrily; Rush craned her head to lick them. Sky watched the small family, struck by a sudden pang of grief. *This is how my own mother once looked after me. And I used to love taking care of Moon.*

Rock must have gotten over his queasiness about the birth, because he stepped suddenly to Sky's side and reached to tap her with his trunk. Sky didn't have time to flinch away; abruptly she was in his memories.

He was thundering across the plains, so fast and hard, and his mind was foggy with grief and anger. He lifted his trunk and gave an earth-shuddering trumpet—

Quickly Sky yanked herself free of his mind. It wasn't fair to invade his privacy—yet she couldn't help feeling a rising curiosity. What had happened to Rock? What had driven him to run like that?

"Sky, look." He pointed his trunk across the savannah. "There."

A broad, stolid figure was trotting toward them; it was coming from the direction of the river, and Sky realized it was a hippo. She took an apprehensive breath and turned her rump on Rush and her cubs, protecting them; Rock and Silverhorn shifted to stand on either side of her.

"Hippos can be brutal," rumbled Silverhorn. "What does he want?"

"Good question," said Rock. "Why has he left the river?"

"He's probably come to tell me to get out of Bravelands," murmured Sky.

"He can take that back to his muddy pool and choke on it," growled Rock.

The hippo was much closer now, still trotting stubbornly toward them despite their hostile stance. He came to a halt right in front of them and looked from one to the other. Then, to Sky's surprise, he gave a clumsy bow of his head.

He opened his colossal jaws; his teeth were blunt but terrifyingly huge. "Greetings, Sky Strider!"

Sky was at a loss for words. "Greetings, uh . . ."

"Wallow, of the Fever Swamp Pod. I heard you speak at the Great Gathering."

Sky creased her eyes. "I think I remember you." He was the young hippo who had splashed out of the watering hole to exclaim at the oddness of her herd; she recognized a split in his front tooth.

"You could be the Great Hippo of the Thunderclouds," said Silverhorn acerbically, "but that's nothing to us. What do you want?"

He shot a wary glance at the rhino. "It was madness at that Gathering. There was something in the air; maybe it was the storm driving every creature wild. But I listened to what Sky Strider said. She told us to come to her, and here I am."

Surprised, Sky took an impulsive step forward. "Do you know anything about the Great Parent?"

"No. I don't know who it is or where to look." He shook his heavy head. "But I don't for a moment think it's Stinger. Power has gone to his oh-so-clever head. He's declared crazy, random boundaries all over Bravelands. He says it's to spread the grass-eaters evenly among the flesh-eaters, but now my pod isn't allowed to go to the Fever Swamp. We're the *Fever Swamp Pod*! It's where we graze!"

Sky took a breath, exchanging looks with Rock and Silverhorn.

"It's an outrage!" the hippo went on. "I want to help you find the true Great Parent—because we can*not* go on with this one."

Sky didn't want their hopes to be built up only to be dashed again—but she couldn't help the wave of relief and happiness that flooded through her. "Then you're welcome, Wallow! Will you join our herd?"

He lowered his head respectfully. "I'm yours to command, Sky Strider—as are all of Fever Swamp Pod, if you will have us."

"We would be glad to," said Sky. With another bow of his head, Wallow trotted away to fetch them. Rock nudged Sky and nodded to the west. A small crowd of gazelles was approaching, their tails in constant back-and-forth motion. Not far ahead of them, tinier animals were running fast across the plain, and as they drew closer Sky recognized a mob of meerkats. The two groups arrived almost simultaneously, the meerkats popping up and down to get her attention, the gazelles shying back at the sight of Rush but holding their ground.

"Stinger sent our clan a stupid Driftleaf, and he hurt one of our pups!" squeaked a meerkat.

"Yes! Yes! Stupid Driftleaf!" chorused his mob. "Bad Stinger!"

"We were stuck inside the wrong boundary," complained a gazelle, butting in, "and our leader was killed."

Sky had no time to answer. More animals were drifting across the savannah; she saw Snuffle and his family trotting toward her, tails high and stiff.

"Snuffle! I'm surprised to see you!" she managed to exclaim through the hubbub.

"You turned your back on us at the Gathering," said Rock, more bluntly.

"Well, well," harrumphed the warthog, scraping at the ground with his small hoof. "It was a difficult situation there; a very awkward business. Something in the air, you know. We've had time to think since then. And we're not at all happy about this Stinger and his self-important notions."

Something in the air. Wallow the hippo had said the same, Sky remembered. There *had* been a horrible fever at that Gathering—but now there seemed to be something else in the air, she thought with rising excitement: something clearer and fresher. *Stinger might have bitten off more than he can gnaw. . . .*

"We all want to help you find the true Great Parent," declared a bushbuck as she strode to join the gazelles.

"True Great Parent!" squeaked the meerkats as one.

"Th-thank you, all of you," Sky stuttered. "Are none of you the Great Parent, then?"

All the animals shared quizzical glances, then shook their heads. "No, we're not," whinnied a zebra from behind her. Sky hadn't seen his herd arrive; she turned and raised her trunk in startled greeting.

"But we're all smart enough to *know* when we're not the Great Parent," bleated the gazelle, and her herd whickered their agreement.

"And humble enough," put in Wallow. "That Stinger is so *arrogant.*"

Sky felt dazed with happiness. The animals who had come to her were only a few of the many herds of Bravelands, she knew that—but at long last, the river might be flowing the other way.

"I'm glad to see you all," she cried, raising her voice. "We know the truth—that's what's important. The more of us there are, the safer we are from attacks—by Stinger, and by the likes of Titanpride."

The gazelles and zebras nodded vigorously.

"You're all welcome, and . . ." Sky stopped. A small figure was pushing through the herds to the front. Mud the baboon hopped to a halt in front of her, looking nervous.

She ground her jaws together, suddenly apprehensive. *He's Stinger's spy. He's so sweet, I'd almost forgotten.*

"Mud Driftleaf," she rumbled gently. "I'm sorry—I know Stinger has given you orders to watch us, but I can't have you here, spying on us. I know this makes things hard for you, but I haven't a choice."

Mud blinked at her, his eyes huge and miserable. Then, to her shock, he flopped down to squat on the ground, rubbing his furry head with his paws.

"I should never have trusted him," he howled. "Stinger Crownleaf. I'm so stupid!"

"Mud?" She nudged him with her trunk. *Hunting for scorpions with his best friend Thorn, competing to send rocks rolling and tumbling.* Sky pulled away from the bittersweet memory and cocked her head. "Mud, are you all right?"

His arms dropped limply to his sides and he gazed up at her. "I've turned it over and over in my head. All the things you said at the Great Gathering. You said Stinger's not the Great Father."

"That's right," said Sky firmly. "He's not."

"No, he's not," wailed Mud. "He's not, he can't be. He's so cruel. He's mean to the whole troop. He makes bad rules for the herds, so bad that animals *die* of them. It's like he's a different Stinger." He sniffed and rubbed his muzzle. "Or maybe the real one."

"Oh, Mud." Sky knew he wasn't faking his distress; she'd seen his memory of happier days, felt his aching longing and regret. "You're not the only one Stinger has fooled. He's good at it. *Very* good. Look how he manipulated the rhinos."

"What?" Mud snuffled and blinked.

Sky glanced at Silverhorn, then back at the little baboon. "Mud, Stinger's the one who convinced Stronghide's crash to murder Great Mother—and then Stinger killed Stronghide, too."

"So he could become Great Father himself." Mud's wide eyes were appalled. He opened his jaws and howled. "How could I have believed Stinger's lies? Now Thorn's dead and I can never say sorry!"

"Mud, Mud!" Anxiously, Sky stroked his head, not caring about the flashes of memory that assailed her. "Thorn Middleleaf isn't dead!"

He choked on his latest howl and blinked. "But Stinger said—"

"Stinger lied," put in Rock grimly. "As usual."

"I stopped Fearless killing Thorn," Sky assured the little baboon. "He got away."

Mud leaped to his feet. "He's alive? Thorn's alive!" He looked joyfully around at the herds as if he expected Thorn to come running to meet him. "Where is he?"

"I don't know," Sky told him. "But I know he's all right."

"Oh, Sky, this is the best news." Mud hugged her leg. "I'm going to help you. I'll look everywhere for the Great Parent, I promise. And no way will I spy on you for *Stinger*!" He spat out the name. "What I'll do instead is keep an eye on Stinger for you! I'll tell you everything he gets up to."

"Oh, Mud. Thank you!" Sky enveloped him with her trunk. *Riding with Thorn on Fearless's back, happily planning a strategy for the Three Feats . . .* "Welcome to the Great Spirit's true herd, Mud Lowleaf!"

* * *

That night was so different from the previous nights Sky and her friends had spent on the plains. All around her were the snuffles and grunts of creatures settling to sleep, and the stir and occasional hoofstep of an alert sentry. A zebra foal gave a squeaking whinny in a dream, and its mother hushed it. The pipe and rasp of frogs and crickets grew in volume as the land vanished into darkness.

Farther away there were less friendly voices; jackals and hyenas screeched and barked, mocking Sky's quest from a distance. They had formed a well-practiced call-and-response since the Gathering at the watering hole.

"Mad Sky Strider, running around a tree!"

"She dashes in circles like a crazy big bee!"

Tonight, Sky took no notice; even the taunting packs couldn't spoil her newfound hope. But it was more important than ever, now that so many creatures had gathered to join her, to keep watch. So Sky remained on her feet, idly brushing the grass with her trunk, alert for any attack.

Rock too had refused to sleep, promising to keep her company until it was his turn to stand guard. "Today went better than we expected," he murmured.

"Much better," she agreed. She pointed her trunk toward the clusters of sleeping animals. "Look how many more sets of eyes and ears we have! This will make finding the Great Parent so much easier."

"Well . . ." Rock hesitated. "Perhaps the Great Parent has already been found."

"What do you mean?"

His green eyes glittered in the dark. "Sky, you're carrying the Great Spirit! The Great Parent has always been an elephant—at least for as long as anyone remembers. You have visions, you read other bones, the animals follow you . . . I think you might have misunderstood what the vulture told you. Isn't that possible?"

"No." Sky shook her head again, more firmly. "No, Rock, you're wrong. I know it."

All the same, she shifted a little closer to him, without letting their hides make contact. It was touching that the big bull elephant thought so highly of her, and she felt a renewed surge of affection for her loyal, powerful ally.

Despite his insistence that he would stay awake, Rock's eyelids were drooping, and in a short while Sky realized he was asleep. *Good*, she thought fondly. *He may be strong, but he needs rest like any of us.*

She must stay alert, though. Blinking hard, she peered into the darkness. Her night vision was good, but it was hard to distinguish dozing friend from approaching foe. Shadows moved in the darkness; oddly, they seemed to be dropping from the sky. Sky stiffened.

Yes: the shadows were definitely drifting from sky to ground. One by one they came, then more and faster, until the last of them landed; a great cluster of winged shapes.

Am I dreaming? Did I fall asleep after all?

If the shadows had really had wings, they were folded now. They made a black mass of hunched shapes against the paler gray grassland, and they did not stir. Were they watching her? She could not see their eyes, but she could feel them. Sky shook herself; she had to investigate. With trepidation, she moved toward the shadows.

Birds, she realized. *Vultures!* The biggest and oldest of them turned toward her, and now she saw its eyes: they were eerie glowing orbs in the night.

"Windrider," she whispered in awed recognition.

It was the venerable old vulture who had led her to the mountain—and to the even more ancient bird who had given her the gift of reading the living.

Windrider did not answer her, did not even nod; the great bird spread her vast wings and took off into the star-filled sky. Her flock immediately followed, circling Sky in a cloud of black wings. They soared a little way, then swooped in a circle again.

She wants me to follow her again. What did the vultures want to show her this time?

A bolt of excitement went through her. *The Great Parent—it has to be!*

Her heart racing, Sky trotted back to Rock and Silverhorn and nudged them awake.

"I need to go. Rock, will you come with me?"

"What? Yes. Yes, of course, Sky." Rock shook himself into wakefulness.

Silverhorn grunted. "I'll come too."

"No—stay and keep watch. Please!"

"Of course I will," said the rhino as she and Rock exchanged quizzical glances.

Sky's blood buzzed with eagerness. "Then let's go!"

The two elephants strode through the night, eyes constantly searching the darkness for the flock. Yet again Sky's heart warmed with gratitude toward Rock; he had not questioned her instincts, but simply nodded in agreement when she explained why they must follow the vultures. The great birds soared on ahead, doubling back now and again as if making sure they were still following.

The stars were gradually blotted out by a vast bank of cloud, and scattered drops of rain swiftly became a drenching torrent; but the elephants ploughed on, ducking their heads into the downpour. It seemed a very long way, Sky thought for the umpteenth time; and just then she saw that a faint glow was lightening the eastern horizon beyond the cloud bank.

The streak of dawn light seemed intensified by the rain clouds that covered the rest of the sky. A pale ray of sunlight pierced the gloom, illuminating a narrow valley that spread out before them. Sky came to an abrupt halt.

The vultures wheeled above the valley, then swooped on into it. With an apprehensive gulp, Sky shambled after them.

Already the heat of the day was building, but Sky's steps felt unusually light. *The Great Parent could be here in this valley. . . .*

The valley opened out suddenly before them, a broad, sloping dip in the land striped with early-morning shadows. Grass grew long and yellow, and vines crawled over patches of tumbled boulders. Sky could see no animals: no grazing impalas or even scuttling lizards.

Then she gasped in horror.

There were indeed no living animals here at all, just a jumbled mound of discarded bones, many with flesh still clinging to them. The size of the pile was grimly breathtaking; it towered above even Rock's huge head. Around it soared the vultures, their flight path growing ever tighter and lower, until at last they settled on the earth around it, stretching, then folding their wings.

Windrider was still airborne. In her talons, Sky saw, was a single leg bone, but the bird did not drop it onto the grisly mound. Instead she lurched down to stand before Sky and laid the bone at her feet. Then she flapped once more into the air and drifted in a slow circle above their heads.

The other birds hunched in a grim semicircle, watching in silence over the pile of remains.

The sight of the mass of bones was unspeakable; the smell of death worse. Scraps of fur and skin clung to broken skeletons. An entire small rib cage, perhaps once a monkey's, perched at the summit. Halfway down, a slender leg bone jutted out, a shiny hoof still attached; beneath it lay the horned half-skull of an oryx. Dead grasses were tangled through a cluster of tiny meerkat skeletons. The grinning, loose-toothed skull of a zebra was tilted at a crazy angle toward Sky; the empty sockets stared straight into her eyes, and she felt almost as if it were mocking her.

She stumbled a pace backward, her trunk trembling.

"What is this?" Rock's voice was hoarse and stunned.

Sky had no idea, but she couldn't even reply. Murky cloud slid across the sun once more, and the bright glow of its light was dimmed. All around and above her—even inside her—she could sense the shifting, restless spirits of the dead creatures, and their whispers crept into her head like rustling spiders.

She had to know. She already suspected, but she had to be sure what had happened to them.

Very hesitantly, she extended her trunk and touched the last bone, the one Windrider had laid at her feet—and she was a buffalo once again.

He was trudging home toward his waiting herd, the heat intense on his broad back. This path was not his normal one, but Stinger Crownleaf had recommended it. It seemed good. There was shade from the high rocks on either side. Skeletal trees dotted the steep slopes that rose around him. No grass to nibble, but soon he would be home with his herd: he was their protector and guardian. Their Great Father.

He knew it now, because that sweet young elephant had been wrong: the Great Spirit was within him. Stinger Crownleaf had told him so, his voice full of wonder. He himself had been only a temporary leader, Stinger had whispered humbly. He would stand aside, Stinger said, once he had told his herd the good news. And then he would take his rightful, Spirit-given place as Great Father of all Bravelands.

Something rolled and rattled above him; loose stones tumbled down the slopes to lie at his hooves. Slow and curious, he raised his heavy head.

The boulders crashed toward him with astonishing speed, bouncing, flying, unavoidable. One slammed into his flank, knocking him sideways. He stumbled, fell to his knees. A shadow loomed above him. Another great rock, and then another. As they hurtled toward him, he lowered his colossal horns, instinctively, hopelessly.

The last thing he heard, before the boulders crushed him, was the triumphant shriek of a baboon.

Sky jerked away from the bone. She stumbled backward, heart thrashing, breath coming in terrified gasps. Oh, *Thud.* Poor, stupid, good-hearted Thud, who had only wanted the best for his herd. . . . Her heart wrenched.

Staggering to the mound of bones, Sky touched another. *Drowning, drowning in mud she hadn't known was there.* Sky jerked away and lunged for another. *The branches! They're breaking! How could the baboons do—* Another bone. *Jackals! No! The babies . . .* And another . . . and another . . .

With a keening wail, Sky backed away. Desperately she cast her head up, searching for Windrider. "All of them. Was it him? *Was it?*"

Who knew if Windrider understood her plea? But she must have recognized the meaning behind it, because the vulture fixed Sky with a long, lamenting gaze, her wingtips twitching.

And then Windrider nodded.

"Sky! Sky, tell me!" Rock's trunk reached for her. "What *is* it?"

"Stinger killed these animals," she rasped, staring in horror at the bones. "Rock, he killed them *all.*"

Rock laid his trunk across her neck and drew her closer; this time she let him and did not protest. The flashes of his past were suddenly a radiant comfort compared to the terrible last moments of Thud, and the gazelle, and the poor little meerkats. . . .

Rock stared at the vultures. "Why did the birds bring you here?" he demanded angrily. "What good does it do you to see this wretched place?"

He drew back his trunk and cantered toward the circling birds, rearing onto his hind legs to swipe at them with his tusks. They careened away, screeching and swirling above them.

Then Sky understood.

"I know why they brought me here."

"What?" Rock dropped back to the ground.

"They've shown me what to do." She looked up at him. "How many more will Stinger kill if I just carry on my search? Too many, Rock."

"So what will you do?"

She gazed at him steadily. "I may not be Great Mother, but I have strength of my own, and now I have allies. I can still fight for Bravelands."

"Are you saying—Sky, do you mean . . ."

She nodded, once, determined and certain. "I have to stop Stinger. I have to stop him *now*."

CHAPTER 15

The heat was almost unbearable; his fur was prickly with it. Running, chasing, hunting: it seemed like the worst prospect that had ever faced Fearless. It was the last thing he wanted to do.

But hunt he must. Somebody had to.

Behind him, through the long grass, plodded the former Dauntlesspride lions, their eyes blank with boredom. However enthusiastic they'd been at the start, the long stalk and the careful ambush-planning seemed to have drained them of energy. *Maybe it's the heat*, Fearless thought with a roll of his eyes. *Or maybe they really are just useless.*

"When do we get to pounce?" came Hardy's plaintive voice.

"Be quiet!" growled Valor.

She and Fearless had been trying for days to knock the principles of hunting into the young lions' heads; Fearless knew his sister was running very short of patience. Tentatively raising his head above the grass, he eyed the gazelles on the plain. Some stood alert, ears swiveling and eyes huge, but most continued to graze peaceably. They still didn't know the lions were there. Fearlesspride had a chance to make their first good kill.

"Look, Fearless," murmured Valor. "There's an old one at the back—or maybe it's sick. We could take that one easily."

"Right." Halting, crouching low, Fearless waited for the others to slink next to him. "Remember what we taught you," he told them. "Gazelles are fast, and they'll pronk when you first come after them."

"They'll do what?" said Snarl, curling his muzzle.

"So you *didn't* listen," muttered Valor.

"They'll spring high in the air," explained Fearless patiently. "Then they'll land and run. It's supposed to throw you off, but just keep your focus and watch where it twists and comes down."

"We need to spread out along the target's likely route," added Valor. "Then when one lion starts to run out of breath, another can take over. If we can drive it farther from the herd, so much the better."

"Grab it by the throat when you can, and don't let go." Fearless tensed his muscles and prepared to rise. "Suffocate it; then it can't struggle so much. The quicker and cleaner the better. That's in accordance with the Code."

Valor nodded approvingly. "Now, Rough, Tough—you slink around to the right. Snarl, Keen, and Hardy to the left. Gracious and Fearless and I will drive the target toward you."

"And whatever you do, wait for Valor's signal!" Fearless warned them.

Stealthily the lions crept into position. Fearless watched the two ambush groups head toward their stations. The lagging gazelle was trudging after its herd, falling farther behind, and Fearless felt a wave of pure optimism. *This'll be great experience for my pride. And we'll eat tonight!*

The two ambush groups were no more than broken tawny shadows in the grass now. Fearless picked up his pace, trotting lightly after the oblivious gazelle. It had veered a little to the left, tantalizingly close to its stalkers.

Then a lion broke cover.

Snarl! Fearless gave a growl of fury. The young lion bounded straight at the startled gazelle, which duly pronked, shooting into the air on four stiff legs. Fearless could only watch with frustration as it came down. Snarl had completely misjudged its bounce, and as he swerved, slithered, and scrambled after it, its hind feet caught him in his gaping mouth. Something small and bloody flew into the grass.

Fearless, Valor, and the others were racing after Snarl by now, but the gazelle had found a new lease on panicked life. It was bolting for its herd, and the whole lot were fleeing in fear. Valor made a last mighty effort to spring after their target—Fearless had a sudden flash of memory of their mother, Swift—but the gazelle zigzagged, cut back to the herd, and was lost among them. The entire herd was far away in moments.

One by one, the disappointed lions trudged to Fearless. Snarl slouched back too, his jaw dripping blood; one of his fangs had been broken. Fearless did not feel even remotely sorry for the impetuous young lion. He sat back on his haunches, trying and failing to contain his anger.

"What was that?" he roared. "It was a *mess*!"

"You didn't listen to a word I said," growled Valor, stalking back to the group.

"Valor's the best hunter there is!" Fearless went on, getting to all fours again. "You're fools for not listening to her."

Snarl glowered at both of them. "Why should we take orders from outsiders? You're not our boss. And you need your sister to help you hunt!"

Keen gave a grunt of objection. "Fearless is our leader now, whether you like it or not, Snarl. We should follow his instructions."

"We were better off without him." Sullenly, Snarl rubbed his wounded mouth against his foreleg, streaking it with blood. "If Dauntless hadn't been weak enough to lose the pride to Titan, we wouldn't be in this state."

Keen sprang forward, growling in fury. "Don't you insult my father!"

"I'll insult him all I like!" And in moments the two cubs were rolling in the grass, biting and scratching and snarling.

"Stop it! Right now!" Fearless plunged in, swiping them apart and baring his fangs. "Fighting among ourselves will get us nowhere. We'll try another hunt when we get a chance. In the meantime, stay on the lookout. And behave yourselves!"

It was all very well giving them orders, but the young lions just couldn't seem to keep their focus long enough. By the time Fearlesspride had walked on for what felt like moons, the cubs were once again bored and restless, sniping at one another and pouncing at beetles.

Fearless had to admit that he knew how they felt; he was as hungry and fed up as they were. *But I'm still going to act like a pride leader!* "Come on, Gracious, keep up," he urged her. "We've got to be ready for a hunt again at any moment. Rough, Tough—leave those lizards alone, we'll find something better soon."

Rough suddenly straightened, her eyes brightening as she looked beyond her leader. "The gazelles have settled!"

Fearless glanced over his shoulder. The young lioness was right; the pride had walked far enough to catch up with the herd, who had obviously decided the danger was over and were grazing once more.

"Right, everyone: same as before. Get into position—and this time, Snarl, do *not* move till Valor gives the signal!"

Snarl, his mouth still bleeding, muttered something inaudible.

Fearless eyed his pride as they moved into position; then he lay down, forelegs extended, and studied the gazelles. They were drifting nearer to the cubs, cropping at the grass. The lions' last prey-target was nowhere to be seen, but a pair of elderly-looking does were wandering ever closer to their trap.

Valor, nor far from Fearless, began to creep through the grass. Fearless followed her example, belly to the ground.

"Now!" cried Valor. She sprinted for the does.

As he raced after her, Fearless was pleased to see his pride was keeping its formation this time. There were Snarl, Keen, and Hardy, running hard on the left flank; Rough and Tough were a blur of tawny fur, closing in from the right. Gracious was working hard to keep up with him and Valor, her face tight with determination.

The gazelles were fleeing, but Fearless knew his pride was making good ground. Ahead of him, Valor was speeding toward her prey, paws pounding like thunder across the arid grassland. Keen, coming in from the side, was a claw's breadth from one of the fleeing rumps, and Valor suddenly roared, "Keen! *Now!*"

Keen coiled his muscles, sprang—and missed.

Snarl, racing across at an angle, crashed into him, and the two of them tumbled and rolled.

"Keep going!" yelled Fearless, aghast.

Gracious, though, took no notice; she skidded to a stop beside the two fallen lions. "Are you all right?" she asked anxiously, nudging them both.

Fearless gave an anguished growl of frustration and looked over to where Rough and Tough were still bolting furiously after the gazelles. But they'd misjudged the creatures' direction and were dropping back. And when Fearless caught sight of Hardy, the youngster was trailing behind at an exhausted lope, his energy reserves already spent.

"Oh, sun and stars!" Fearless swore, and tried to sprint after the gazelles with Valor. But they had no ambush to drive them into now, and both were tired and slowing. Fearless trotted to a halt, flanks heaving, and Valor too finally drew up ahead of him, cursing. As the old does glanced back, Fearless could have sworn they were laughing at him.

"These lions are no good at *all*," growled Valor. "At this rate we'll all starve before Titan can kill us."

"It's Snarl who's the problem," Fearless told her, scowling. "At least the others are trying their best. He tried to run straight over Keen, the idiot. Oh, what *now*?"

A little way back the pride was snarling and snapping at one another, voices raised in accusation and furious denial. Tails lashed, ears were pinned back, and fangs were bared.

"You messed it up!" Snarl was yelling at Keen, as Fearless and Valor trotted back to them.

"You can't talk," retorted Keen sharply. "You messed up the first hunt because you *couldn't wait!*"

"At least I can catch a gazelle when it's right in front of my mouth!"

"Quiet!" roared Fearless, bounding into their midst. "Shut up, all of you!"

"It's him!" Snarl yelled, jerking his head at Keen. "He thinks he can get away with being useless because he's Dauntless's son. Every wrong thing he does—it's all *Oh, but my father was Dauntless and I'm special.* Well, he cost us that gazelle and he should pay!" He lunged once again for Keen's shoulder.

Fearless reared back and swept a paw at him, knocking Snarl off-balance before his unbroken fang could sink into Keen's flesh.

"Enough!" Fearless snarled. "No lion is useless! You're all learning, I understand that—we are, too. I won't punish anyone for honest mistakes, but I *will* hurt someone if they damage the pride! Got that?"

Snarl glowered at him, breathing hard. Then he turned on his heel and stalked off, tail lashing.

"Go and look out for prey again," Fearless told the rest of them in disgust. "You'll keep searching until we succeed."

Looking thoroughly shame-faced, the young lions turned and padded away. Fearless sat down on his haunches and glared after them. Valor stood beside him, shaking her head.

"This is harder than I expected," he mumbled to her. "I thought they'd all have good instincts, at least."

Valor grunted comfortingly. "I did warn you. But every pride leader finds it hard at the beginning, Fearless. Even Father struggled when he first took over his pride, you know—Mother told me stories." She licked Fearless's ear. "What's important is that you not show them how worried you are. If you're confident, they will be too."

"That makes sense." Fearless gave a heavy sigh. "I still think Snarl's a problem, though. He's going to keep pushing, isn't he? Challenging me over everything?"

"I think that's a certainty," growled Valor.

"I can't put up with it, Valor. Fearlesspride will fall apart before it's begun."

"What can you do, though? You can yell at him all you want; he doesn't care." Valor wrinkled her muzzle. "Throw him out of the pride?"

"I can't do that. I need all the lions I can get." Fearless sighed. "And he *is* a good fighter."

"Anyway," growled Valor, "he'd probably take half the

others with them. They're none of them very sensible."

"I wish I had Stinger's authority," said Fearless wistfully. "He can get his troop to do whatever he wants, because they love him."

"Baboons again," snorted Valor. "Ask him to lead your pride, if he's so wonderful."

"I can't do that." Fearless stood up, brightening. "But you've given me an idea, Valor. I know what I *can* do!"

"Oh no." Valor lowered her face onto her paws, groaning.

"I'm going to go to him." Fearless stretched his muscles, filled with new resolve. "I'm going to seek advice from the Great Father!"

CHAPTER 16

Tree frogs piped in the darkness, and cicadas whirred, but they sounded more subdued than usual, as if the heat were pressing too heavily on even the smallest creatures. Nightfall hadn't brought much relief from the oppressive weather. Thorn and Nut crept though the humid darkness of the tree belt, placing their paws with caution to avoid dry twigs.

They'd left their new Crookedtree Troop allies hiding in a dense patch of woodland farther back, and Thorn was glad. Numbers weren't always strength, not in every situation. Right now, what mattered was staying undetected. If the Strongbranches spotted them, they were both dead.

As they slunk across the open grassland toward the hyena den, Thorn's heart beat rapidly and his breath felt shallow. This place had been home for long enough to feel familiar, and with every nervous breath he caught the scents of baboons he knew.

But he was returning as an enemy. And Nut too was an exile; Thorn vividly remembered how the troop had driven the terrified baboon out of Tall Trees, their savage whoops and hollers filling the forest as they harried him from his home forever. No wonder Nut looked as uneasy as Thorn.

If I can just find Berry and talk to her alone, my plan might work. . . .

The den and its surroundings were eerily quiet. Thorn's apprehension only grew as the two baboons trod cautiously along the foot of the escarpment toward the tunnel mouth. No pawstep crunched, no sentry called out. There was a lingering foulness in the air from the hyenas that had died here, but even the baboon scents seemed stale.

Where are the sentries? The Strongbranches?

Thorn placed his paw on the rock at the entrance, and with a deep breath edged into the darkness.

"Nut," he said aloud.

"Thorn, shush!" hissed Nut in alarm. He scampered across the bare gritty earth and flattened himself against the rock.

"It's all right," Thorn said clearly. "There's nobody here."

"What?" Nut's eyes glowed pale in the darkness.

"They're gone." Thorn spread his paws in a helpless gesture.

It was obvious now. There were no fresh scents, no growls or hoots or even rustles from the depths of the den. The hyena smell was the strongest of all, and Thorn had no intention of probing deeper and finding out how much of the rotting carrion Brightforest Troop had left behind. He'd eaten that stinking rot-flesh for days, and he had no intention of touching dead hyena again, as long as he lived.

"So where do you think they—"

Something scraped against stone, deep in the tunnels.

Thorn and Nut froze, their eyes locked. Was that padding footfalls?

"Just rats," whispered Nut.

Of course it was. Thorn flared his nostrils, lifting his snout. That dead hyena smell was pungent, all rot and grease and coarse fur and . . . Was that scent actually *dead*?

A soft yip echoed from far below. And was answered.

"They're back!" croaked Thorn. As one, he and Nut turned and fled from the den.

They ran across the arid grassland, paws skidding and stumbling in the dust. The darkness was almost complete, but Thorn didn't dare hesitate, not even when he tripped on a rock and turned a complete somersault; he just leaped back to his paws and bolted on.

They came to a halt deep in the tree belt, craning their ears and trying to pant silently. The cicadas and tree frogs were still piping merrily, and a distant jackal screeched out on the plains, but no pawsteps came racing from the direction of the den.

Thorn sagged against the tree. "That was something I am *never* going to do again."

"Close one," Nut agreed, breathing hard. "Where do you think Brightforest Troop went?"

"I can't imagine." Thorn shrugged. "But there's only one place to ask. . . ."

In silence they loped back across the dark savannah toward the watering hole; it remained shrunken by heat despite the rainfalls, but what was left of it gleamed in the night like a pool of starlight. After the eerie darkness of the hyena den, it was a welcome sight. *Brightforest Troop must be somewhere near here*, thought Thorn. *If they're here, Stinger will be too.*

And if Stinger was here, Berry wouldn't be far away. . . .

An impala sentry stood by its dozing herd, head high and alert. Thorn bounded up to it.

"Excuse me," he said, clearing his throat politely. "Do you know where Stinger is?"

"Great Father?" The impala looked surprised, and shook his head a little too quickly. "I don't know. Ask the zebras."

The zebra herd was right next to the impalas; their sentry turned and snorted as Thorn approached, his huge eyes glowing.

Thorn dipped his head quickly. "Do you know where I can find Stinger?"

The zebra shook his mane and gave a nervous snort. "No idea."

This is ridiculous, thought Thorn. Stinger had to be nearby. He tugged lightly on the tail of a bushbuck. "'Scuse me. Any idea where Stinger is?"

The bushbuck's eyes widened a little, and he stamped a hoof. "Don't ask me."

"*Somebody* must know where to find him," pointed out Thorn.

"Well, not me." The bushbuck took a rapid step away from him.

"Don't ask me either," hissed a tiny dik-dik before Thorn could even open his mouth. "Try the warthogs, they know everyone's business." It turned and trotted into the tree line, twitching its tail in alarm.

"They all seem a bit reluctant to talk," Thorn remarked to Nut in a low voice.

"I would be too," murmured Nut. "Getting on the wrong side of Stinger is never a good plan. I should know."

With a sigh, Thorn beckoned him to follow and then loped along the water's edge until he spotted a group of warthogs. It wasn't Snuffle's sounder, he realized as he drew closer; he didn't know this group. *Warthogs like a bit of flattery*, he remembered. Mud had laughed about it once, saying that they loved to think they knew secrets and gossip that were a mystery to every other animal. He slowed respectfully and nodded to the sentry, a snooty-looking creature with badly yellowed tusks.

"Greetings, and may your sounder find sweet roots!"

It snorted disdainfully. "It's the middle of the night! We're not *eating*."

Thorn swallowed a sigh of frustration. "None of these animals seems to have a clue where Great Father is," he told the sentry, gesturing at the sleeping herds. "I'm sure *you'll* be different, though."

"Hmph!" The warthog tilted his head back and peered at Thorn over his snout. "I don't know that it's any of your business."

"Maybe not," said Thorn, putting on his most charming smile. "But I bet it's yours. Warthogs know *everything*."

"True," rumbled the warthog. "Well, if you don't spread it around *too* much . . . see that jutting bit of land at the far side of the bay?" He gestured with his flat tusks. "He's over there. Baboon Island, he calls it."

Thorn and Nut exchanged a grin. "Thanks." Thorn bowed and scampered away along the shoreline, Nut at his heels.

They slowed as they approached the border where the peninsula met the land. Glancing left and right, they crept more carefully forward, senses keen for Strongbranches.

"There's a good mahogany tree," whispered Nut, pointing. "The one with elephant damage. Maybe we should wait up there for a while?"

Despite the long gashes on its trunk, it did have an abundance of dark green leaves. Thorn nodded and bounded for it, and the two baboons scrambled up to conceal themselves among the dense, drooping foliage. Just in time, Thorn realized: dawn was paling the horizon, and a thin gray light seeped across the watering hole.

Together they peered out at Stinger's well-defended retreat. At the entrance, several big Strongbranch guards scratched themselves and bared their teeth at any animal that came near. Beyond them, in the camp itself, Thorn could make out baboons moving busily around, clearing bedding and sorting food. There wasn't any of the usual chatter that accompanied the morning chores; the baboons loped from place to place without a word or a glance to their comrades. Their gazes were downcast, their shoulders slumped, and they set about their various tasks without apparent enthusiasm. Thorn frowned.

Nut shifted a clump of leaves aside and pointed. "Stinger," he mouthed.

There he was, the Crownleaf and False Great Father, sitting on top of a gigantic sandstone boulder. Before this new and much bigger Crown Stone, their heads respectfully lowered, a line of baboons waited in meek silence. There were no councilors at his side, of course; back at the hyena den, Stinger had done away with the Council with a casual wave of his paw.

Now that he's Great Father, he thinks he can do as he pleases. Stinger was acting on every whim that entered his head—which might explain why his troop looked so cowed.

The undergrowth below their tree rustled. Both Thorn and Nut shrank back as a larger, tawny shape approached Baboon Island. *Fearless!*

Thorn hadn't seen the lion since Fearless's gaping jaws had loomed above him, closing in for the kill. His pulse beat hard in his throat as he watched his old friend pad confidently toward the guards. The Strongbranches drew back to let Fearless enter the camp.

"What does Big Talk want with Stinger at this hour?" whispered Nut.

Thorn couldn't repress a dark stab of resentment. "Getting his latest orders?"

The lion had paused just inside the camp entrance, dipping his head to speak to one of the baboons within. She had gold-streaked fur and a delicate face—though right now, it wore a frown of irritation. And she was tailless.

Berry! Thorn's heart leaped inside him. With her were more Strongbranches, who waited with clearly strained patience as she talked to Fearless. When she parted from the young lion and padded past the guards on the border, the Strongbranches walked with her.

Accompanied by her escort, she headed away from Baboon Island, passing quite close to Thorn and Nut's mahogany tree. Thorn could not take his eyes off the beautiful young baboon. He ached to jump down from the branches and run to her— but that would be suicide. He glanced in frustration at the big Strongbranch guards, then back at Berry. She still looked annoyed, but to Thorn it seemed her huge brown eyes were worried, too.

"This might be my only chance to talk to her," Thorn whispered to Nut. "We have to follow!"

"All right. It's better than waiting here."

Nut followed Thorn down the tree, both of them trying not to snap thin branches or rustle leaves. Keeping at a safe distance, they shadowed Berry and her escort along the shore, then through the scrubby tree line and deeper into the forest. Thorn picked up speed as they entered a patch of thick undergrowth. He couldn't bear to lose sight of her.

Berry's familiar voice drifted back to him through the trunks and scrub of the woodland. "This is ridiculous," she snapped at the Strongbranches. "I'm perfectly capable of hunting by myself."

"Your father's orders," one of them replied. "It's for your own protection."

"You can't go anywhere by yourself." That was Grass's sneering voice, and Thorn's fur bristled. "There are rebels and traitors everywhere, as you well know."

Thorn stopped and crouched behind a croton bush, clenching his fists in frustration. "How am I going to get past those guards?" he muttered. "They're never going to leave her alone."

"Don't worry." Nut grinned. "Those idiots didn't scare me when I was in the troop, and they don't scare me now."

"Nut, wait! Things are different—"

But Nut had darted away already, bounding to within a few paces of the Strongbranches. "Hey, you!" he whooped cheekily. "Remember me? I'm back!"

The Strongbranches turned as one, their jaws slack with disbelief. That didn't last long; as their faces hardened in recognition, fangs were instantly bared and they snarled in rage.

"Murderer!" screamed one guard. "Traitor!"

"Kill him!" screeched another.

Nut was already running, leaping and darting through the trees, and the Strongbranches followed in hot pursuit. Hanging on to a branch, Thorn watched them go, his heart in his mouth. *You crazy baboon.* Nut had no idea of the danger the Strongbranches posed these days.

But now Thorn was free to run to Berry, and he couldn't waste the chance Nut had given him. Dizzy with hope, he pushed through the bushes and ran forward on silent paws—

And stopped. His heart sank: one of the Strongbranches had stayed at Berry's side.

Grass! It would be. Thorn curled his muzzle.

Grass was slinking close to Berry. "Don't worry, Berry Highleaf. I'll stay right here and protect you from that traitor." His long arm slid around her shoulder; Thorn had a powerful urge to run over and bite it off.

But there was no need. Disgust tightening her nostrils, Berry shoved the Strongbranch away. "Get your paws off me, Grass."

"You know I'm your father's most loyal soldier," he reminded her in a wounded tone. "I don't see why we can't be friends." Once again, he snuck his arm around her.

Thorn could bear it no longer. He launched himself from the bushes, snatching up a rock. Drawing his arm back, he flung it at Grass's skull.

His aim didn't fail him. The rock smacked straight into the big baboon's head, just above his ear. Grass swayed and keeled over, landing face-first with a dull *thwack* in the mud.

Berry stood frozen with shock, staring at Grass's prone body. Her head jerked up as Thorn bounded toward her, and she recoiled, opening her jaws to scream.

Thorn threw himself at her, clamping his paws around her muzzle. Her eyes were bright with terror as she stared into his.

"Berry! Berry! Please don't scream."

She wriggled, tearing at his paws. He was glad he couldn't hear the names she was trying to call him. Muffled snarls came from beneath his grip.

"Berry, I *swear* I'm not a killer! You know me! Please don't be scared. You can call me what you want, send me away—turn me over to your father—" He gasped, grabbing her with one arm while trying to keep the other paw over her mouth. "But please, listen just a moment! There's someone I need you to meet. Will you do that? Just this one thing?"

Berry's struggles subsided. Her eyes narrowed. Then she gave a sharp nod.

Hesitantly, slowly, Thorn withdrew his paw from her muzzle. She rubbed her mouth and glared at him.

"Thank you," he whispered.

"If you are planning to kill me, Thorn Middleleaf," she growled, "you'd better be ready for the fight of your life."

"I swear by the Great Spirit, Berry—I would *never* hurt you." He panted, meeting her furious gaze, desperate to make her believe him. "Come with me. This way. Please?"

He stretched out his paw. Ignoring it, she spun and stalked in the direction he'd indicated. Thorn scampered to overtake her, his heart hammering, and gave her a humble look as he led the way through thick scrub.

The woodland where the Crookedtree baboons were waiting was not far away; Thorn was glad of that, because he didn't know how long Berry would stay. At any moment he expected her to throw a curse at him, twist, and sprint back to Baboon Island. But each time he glanced over his shoulder she was still there, shooting him a glare of edgy suspicion.

He scrambled onto a shelf of gray rock and turned back to her with a pleading expression. "Here," he told her softly.

Still eyeing him, Berry climbed onto the rock beside him. Then she turned to follow his gesture.

A baboon padded toward them, her fur glowing golden in the streaks of sunshine that pierced the canopy. Her eyes were wide and soft on Thorn, filled with anxious hope. When she turned her gaze to Berry, she gave a gasp and put her paw to her mouth.

Berry stiffened. She half rose onto her hind paws. In a small, scared voice she said:

"Mother?"

Pear Goodleaf seemed to have fallen mute again. Her eyes were moist, and she simply nodded, hard and swift.

"Mother." Berry leaped from the rock and flew into Pear's arms. The two baboons clutched each other as if neither would ever let go, swaying and rocking.

"I knew it was you," Berry was sobbing. "I knew, but I was so scared it wasn't, that I was dreaming. I'd still know you anywhere."

"My daughter, my daughter," was all Pear could say, over and over again.

"Father told me you'd died!" cried Berry.

The Goodleaf drew back a little, her eyes shining. "Oh, Berry, my beautiful daughter." She hugged her close once more. "I would never have left you, not even if the Great Spirit had tried to drag me away.

"And I never, ever will."

CHAPTER 17

"He just complains, all the time," Fearless told Stinger. "Nothing I do is ever right, and Snarl simply won't accept that I'm leader of this pride now. He questions every single order. It's undermining me in the eyes of all Fearlesspride!"

"Hmm." Stinger scratched his chin fur, contemplating the problem. "This is a difficult one, Fearless. Get control of a strong cub like that, and he could be a very useful ally."

There was something in Stinger's voice that made Fearless glance up at him with curiosity. But he must have imagined it; Stinger was shaking his head as if still lost in thought.

"It sounds," the baboon went on, "as if Snarl saw himself as the leader of this pride. Would that be right?"

Fearless gave a gloomy nod.

"Hmm, I thought as much. Well, he has lost that purpose, Fearless of Fearlesspride. You must give him a new one."

"But what, Great Father?" Fearless scowled. "You've never seen such a hopeless hunter."

Stinger hopped down from his Crown Stone and ruffled the lion's neck fur. "Remember when I made you Protector of Brightforest Troop? You could do exactly the same with Snarl. Send him out on patrol! Make him feel important! It sounds as if that's what matters to him."

"Oh. Of course!" Fearless bent to touch the baboon's head with his muzzle. "You are so wise, Great Father. Thank you for this. It's a wonderful idea."

"Don't mention it, my Cub of the Stars," said Stinger fondly. "I'm glad to help in any way I can. I can tell you're already becoming a very fine pride leader."

Fearless's heart swelled. As he padded away from his audience with Stinger, he felt happier about the future of Fearlesspride than he had since it had begun. *I'm so lucky that I can turn to the Great Father himself for advice.* As he passed the line of queueing baboons, he nodded respectfully to them; they had stood aside hastily when Stinger commanded it, letting Fearless go straight to Great Father without waiting.

He always enjoyed his visits to Baboon Island; he had so many friends here. There was Mud now, entering the camp as he left.

"Hello, Mud!" Fearless called.

But Mud only raised a limp paw in response. He looked quite distracted and anxious; perhaps he was on an important mission for Stinger.

The trek back to his pride was a long one, but Fearless was

too full of energy and optimism to mind. Valor had found them a cave in a stony kopje, sheltered from the wind and almost concealed from view by a sharp, vertical blade of rock. Since there wasn't any wind at the moment, the hideout in fact felt quite hot and stuffy, but he knew Fearlesspride would appreciate it when the weather changed.

Which it surely would soon, he was certain. Fearless gave an impatient glance at the blazing blue sky and the dark cloud that loomed at the horizon.

Padding around the vertical rock, he crouched to crawl into the cave. His pride was sprawled lazily on the sandy floor, snoozing or licking their paws or, in Rough and Tough's case, indulging in a little mutual grooming. At the sight of Fearless, they sprang to their paws.

All except Snarl. He blinked slowly at his leader, his muzzle curling, then rolled over so that his back was to Fearless.

Bristling, Valor gave a bellow of annoyance. "Snarl! Show your leader respect!"

"Hmph," came a muffled grunt.

Fearless stalked over to him and swiped the back of his head with a paw. "Get up," he growled. "There's work to be done."

"Like what?" Snarl twisted and propped himself up on his forepaws with bad grace. "Another useless hunt with the worst pride leader in Bravelands?"

"No," snapped Fearless. He was striving to recall Stinger's wise words about making Snarl feel important, and he forced patience into his voice. *What would Stinger say . . . ?* "I've been thinking, Snarl. You're so big and strong, and it seems silly to waste you on a hunt when other lions can do it." He managed to look at the cub with bright approval; Snarl's ears had pricked forward. "I've got a special job for you. You could go out and patrol the boundary around the den, where I've scent-marked it. Make sure Titanpride doesn't come anywhere near us. Or hyenas, for that matter."

One of Snarl's ears flicked back, and he gave a truculent growl. Under his breath Fearless heard him mutter, "Because you're scared to do it yourself, I suppose."

Fearless dug his claws into the sandy earth, his hold on his temper cracking. "My job is being the leader. Try to remember that, *Snarl Fearlesspride*. You're big and strong—so get out there and patrol."

When Snarl's rump had vanished around the rock gateway and into the sunlight, Fearless turned to the others. They were watching him with trepidation, and he made an effort to look a little less ferocious.

Keep looking authoritative, though.

He drew himself up. "Right. Follow me, Fearlesspride. We're going hunting."

"Zebras!" Rough's ears pricked forward in excitement. "I love zebra."

"Me too," said Tough.

"Every lion loves zebra," Fearless reminded them with amusement. "So let's get some. This time, try to remember everything you've learned. Gracious, you go with Hardy and

Keen. Ambush formation, like before. Valor and I will drive them."

The pride spread out as planned, and Fearless and Valor began to creep through the long grass toward the zebra herd. A lone big colt had strayed recklessly far from his companions; Valor shot Fearless a glance, and he nodded.

The other two groups were in place ahead, little more than their bright eyes visible in the yellow grass. Fearless caught their obedient gazes and nodded at the careless zebra.

The pride looked ready—or as ready as they were ever likely to be. Fearless rose, keeping his head low, and began to trot silently toward his target. A little way from his flank, Valor did the same.

Closer . . . Just a little closer . . . Wait until the time is right. . . .
Now!

Fearless opened his jaws to call the signal, but he didn't get the chance. A golden-maned, fully grown lion burst out of cover, speeding toward the very zebra Fearless had chosen.

Fearless recognized him in an instant: the scarred face, the crooked tail. *Loyal!* He gave a strangled snarl of frustration as his former friend sprang for the fleeing colt, dragged it down by its haunches, and sank his jaws into its throat.

One striped leg flailed in distress; the zebra's head rose, trying to scream a distress call that could not get past the lion's jaws. In moments, it was all over.

"Wow," said Valor at Fearless's side. "You've got to admire his skills."

Fearless did, but he wasn't about to admit it. "That oath-breaker just stole our prey!"

"To be fair, it must have been his prey to begin with. I guess he'd been waiting there for a while." Catching a glimpse of Fearless's face, Valor added quickly: "He's still a rotten oath-breaker, though."

The lions of Fearlesspride were slouching back, their faces morose and disappointed.

"So that means no food again tonight," grunted Hardy.

"No zebra," moaned Tough.

"It means no such thing," growled Fearless. Drawing himself up, he bounded to the place where Loyal still crouched over his victim.

"Fearless!" The big lion raised his blood-drenched face to grin at him. "It's so good to see you. Are you all right? I've been worried!"

Fearless stiffened, taken aback by the older lion's blunt friendliness. "I'm fine," he said coldly. "I have my own pride now. Fearlesspride."

"Oh!" Loyal turned his head to peer at them. "That's great news. Well done! Listen, Fearless, I'm glad I ran into you." The big lion's scarred face had become serious. "There's something you need to know."

"Oh?" said Fearless. Despite himself, his curiosity was pricked.

"It's Titan," said Loyal. "He's been having secret meetings with that absurd baboon, Stinger."

Fearless's hackles sprang up. "Stinger's the *Great Father*," he growled. "And anyway, you're wrong."

"I wish I was. But I've seen them together."

Fearless snorted, tossing his head. "I don't believe you. Why do you hate Stinger so much? He's never done anything to you."

"It's what he might do to *you* that concerns me." Loyal's orange eyes flashed. "Any ally of Titan's is bad news, so I suggest you keep your distance from this so-called Great Father."

"Stinger is *not* Titan's ally!"

Loyal opened his jaws as if to say more, then hesitated. He tilted his head, his scarred face softening once more.

"It's hard when friends let you down," he said at last. "I understand, Fearless. And I know you were close to that baboon when—heh!—when you were one yourself."

Fearless was too annoyed to reply. Loyal thought he was making a friendly jibe, did he? Well, he *had* once been a member of Brightforest Troop, and he was proud of it. Fearless settled for curling his muzzle in a disdainful, silent snarl.

Loyal watched him for a moment, then shrugged. "Anyway, there's more bad news, I'm afraid," he went on. "Had you heard? Titanpride took over Forthrightpride, just yesterday. They were one of the prides from the southern plains. That's several days' walk from here."

"I . . . didn't know about it." Fearless licked his jaws. That was a long reach Titan was developing.

"Well, you know now. Titan's growing ever more powerful, Fearless. Be very careful."

"I know how dangerous Titan is," snapped Fearless. "I watched him kill my own father, remember?" But as he turned to stalk away, Loyal spoke again.

"Hey, Fearless."

He glanced over his shoulder, still angry.

Loyal nudged the zebra's lolling head toward him. "You should take this. You and that pride of yours look hungry. I think you need it more than I do."

"I'm not taking your leftovers!" barked Fearless.

"They're not leftovers if I haven't even started it." Loyal gave him a grin. "And I'm not going to eat it now. I *refuse* to eat it. So if you don't take it, you'll be making me a Codebreaker as well as an oath-breaker. Do you really want that on your conscience?"

Fearless found himself opening and closing his jaws again, like the idiot Loyal used to call him. At last he realized there was no face-saving way out of this. Except one.

"Fine," he growled. "We'll take your zebra. It was ours anyway before you butted in."

Loyal rose and gave him an affectionate lick before he could flinch away. "Look after yourself, Fearless."

And before Fearless could come up with a suitably barbed reply, Loyal had walked away.

The young lions of Fearlesspride were bounding toward him across the grass, panting with excitement. "Wow, Fearless!" exclaimed Keen. "You made that thief give up the zebra!"

"That was pretty amazing," agreed Rough.

"Yes, amazing," echoed Tough.

"I'm impressed," Hardy told him, looking suddenly a lot more awed by his leader.

"I could never do that," said Gracious shyly.

"Oh, you'd be amazed what you can do," drawled Valor, with a dry and knowing glance at Fearless. "Can we stop admiring Fearless now and start eating?"

As they fell on the warm meat, gnawing and tearing and licking their bloodied jaws, Fearless felt a warm rush of gratitude toward his sister. Valor hadn't let on to the pride the real story: that he hadn't intimidated Loyal in the slightest.

And I'm not going to tell them the truth. This was his pride's first good meal since Dauntlesspride had fallen, and Fearless wasn't about to spoil their sense of triumph. Besides, it had worked out for the best, he had to admit: Loyal had made him look very good in front of his new pride. And maybe, he told himself grudgingly, that had been no accident.

With an inward shrug, he set to gnawing at the zebra's haunch. At this moment, he couldn't be angry with anyone.

"Fearlesspride, don't eat everything," he told them cheerfully. "Save a chunk for Snarl."

He was deep in a dream about hunting. *That careless zebra was running in front of him, far too slowly. Fearless could see Loyal racing in from the side, but the big lion was even slower than his terrified prey. Fearless was outpacing his rival easily, and there was a look of awe and admiration in Loyal's eyes. Springing, almost flying—no, actually flying—Fearless slammed into the fat, delicious zebra. All alone he brought it to the earth, and his fangs sank into its rich, juicy haunch.*

"Fearless!" Keen was pulling him back from the zebra, patting and pawing at him. Fearless growled in anger —

"Fearless, wake up!"

He woke with a start. Keen's face was peering into his, wide-eyed and anxious.

"What?" he growled irritably.

"I'm sorry, Fearless, but Snarl hasn't come back yet. He's been gone all night. I'm worried."

Fearless lifted his head and blinked at the den entrance. Pale sunlight poured in at the narrow crack. His heart clenched and he sprang to his feet.

"Wake up," he ordered, nudging and butting the other lions. A sense of dread filled him: Snarl was far too lazy and disobedient to patrol the border all night without a break. "Rough, wake up! Hardy!"

The bleary pride crawled out of the den and blinked in the morning brightness.

"Where do you think he's gone?" asked Gracious, shivering with trepidation.

"I don't know." Fearless trotted down the kopje and paused to stare toward the boundary he'd marked so carefully. Yes, there was the lone acacia he'd marked, and the dry riverbed running down from the gully to the east of the kopje. *It's pretty obvious we'd make our den in the kopje. If Titanpride attacked, wouldn't they search for us there first?* But there had been no sign or sound of them.

Yet now, there was no sign of Snarl either.

"Gracious, Hardy: you check the southern border. Rough

and Tough, you go with Valor and look in the little ravine. Keen and I will go this way." Fearless set off at a trot toward the north, Keen jogging behind him.

The ground was quite open here; only an occasional acacia dotted the landscape. Within the northern boundary there were a few heaps of tumbled stone, but although Fearless and Keen sniffed carefully at them and pawed loose boulders aside, Snarl was not among them.

"Is there somewhere he might have gone?" Fearless asked Keen, frowning. "Any friends he might have decided to join?"

"No, I can't think of any." Keen shook his head in bewilderment. "I'm sure he—"

His words dried up, his jaws still open, as Valor's grunting roar echoed across the flat grassland.

"The gully," snarled Fearless. "Quick!"

Doubling back, paws pounding, Fearless and Keen raced across the low slopes and flat stretches of grassland, heading for the sharp slash in the land that Fearless had noted as the most treacherous spot in their territory. Valor, Rough, and Tough stood gaping in hopeless horror down its steep slope.

Vultures were circling; Fearless knew with a sick plummet of his stomach what he would find at the foot of the precipice. When he reached its lip, he stared down, wordless. Keen gave an appalled, grunting cry.

A big flock of vultures was already hunched over a pathetic lion carcass, tearing off strips of bloody flesh. From time to time one hopped back, stretched its black wings, then flapped to the feast once more. The short grass around the young lion's body was streaked and stained with blood.

Fearless licked his jaws, hardly able to move his limbs. Guilt and horror shuddered through his bones. Around him, Fearlesspride stood as helpless as he was, growling and shivering; Gracious whimpered in distress.

But slowly, one by one, the young lions turned to stare at Fearless. He froze, shocked at what he saw in their eyes.

It was fear, and awe, and respect.

CHAPTER 18

"Every time I close my eyes," said Rock, "I see all those bones. I don't think I'll ever forget them."

They were back with the herd. As well as Rock, Silverhorn, Rush, and the cubs, a vast crowd of different animal herds milled around Sky, grazing and stamping and chatting.

"I hope I don't," she said. "They deserve to be remembered."

Rock's green eyes were watching her closely. "Life in Bravelands will go back to normal once Stinger is dead."

"You think I should kill him?" she said sharply. "No, Rock. That's not what the Great Spirit wants."

Rock looked confused. "I thought we were going to fight Stinger. What's the sense of fighting him if not to kill him?"

Sky pressed the tip of her trunk against her head. The cloying air seemed to be sucking every drop of energy from her, and she was struggling not to be overwhelmed by the spirits that clung to the bones in the valley. Discovering their deaths at Stinger's command had changed the course of her quest, but flashes of their dying memories were stopping her from planning their next move.

A giraffe ran for her life across the baking plains, harried by a pack of slavering hyenas. As the hunters clawed at her legs, sending her crashing to the earth, their screams of triumph echoed: "Tell Stinger we have her! She'll never question him again."

A wildebeest stood at bay in a narrow gully, surrounded by baboons whose eyes glittered with malevolence. They flung rocks; Sky felt the sharp pain as each one struck her head and chest and forelegs. "Not sure Stinger's the Great Father, eh? We'll show you what faith is!"

She swayed, sick with horror, as each vision rushed through her.

"Sky?" came Rock's sympathetic rumble. "Are you all right?"

She nodded, trembling as the images faded. She wasn't a wildebeest—she was a young elephant, standing on a familiar stretch of savannah. And she had a new mission.

"I'm sorry, Rock, but killing Stinger would break the Code. Anyway, we've tried to kill him already, haven't we?"

"And Rain died," he said softly.

"While Stinger lived." Sky looked up at him. "No, it won't work. Our best chance is to drive him from Bravelands forever."

Rock was silent, his eyes downcast in thought. At last, he blew through his trunk in resignation. "Then that's what we'll do."

Before Sky could reply, she reeled on her feet; the memories had surfaced again.

Blood soaked from her wounds as baboons tore at her: now she was a vervet monkey, and they were ripping her to pieces. "We've never liked you monkeys. A baboon is Great Father, get used to it!"

Cries of alarm from her huge, motley herd of allies brought Sky back to the savannah. Some were spinning and stampeding a little way; others were grunting in challenge, lowering heavy heads or sharp horns. Through the growing hubbub she heard one clear word: *"Lion!"*

Sky gasped. "Titan?"

"Let's go look." Rock snorted an aggressive blare, lowered his head, and began to push through the herds to where the commotion was most intense. Sky followed him, cold with trepidation.

A little way ahead of them, creatures were growling and tossing their heads, backing away from a single, tawny shape. Indifferent, the lion stalked on through them, toward Sky and Rock, his black-streaked mane rippling and his crooked tail twitching. His scarred face looked determined.

At Rock's side, Sky puffed out a sigh of relief. "Rock, it's all right. I recognize him."

A shivering gazelle turned to gaze at her, still tensed to spring. "Isn't he from Titanpride?"

"No, he's a friend of a friend," Sky called back to her as she walked on. "That's Loyal Prideless. He helped Fearless rescue the lion cub I told you about, the one the cheetahs abducted." For a moment she hesitated, one foot hovering above the ground. "I wonder if he's helping Stinger, too?"

"Only one way to find out," Rock pointed out.

With the big bull elephant striding protectively at her side, Sky walked toward the lion. She came to a halt, coughed nervously, then raised her trunk.

"What do you want here, Loyal Prideless?"

He sat back on his haunches, then dipped his head. "Sky Strider, I believe you and I both want the same thing. My friend Fearless is under Stinger Crownleaf's spell, and that can only hurt him in the end. I want to make him see the truth."

Sky stared at him, taken aback. "But why have you come to me?"

"I've tried to tell him the truth," said Loyal, his crooked tail twitching, "but the cub's got river mud stuck in both ears when it comes to that baboon. He might listen to you, though."

"Me?" Sky flinched. "But why?"

"Because you're carrying this spirit-creature—or so you say."

"Careful," rumbled Rock, lowering his tusks. "I'd show more respect if I were you."

Loyal returned the big elephant's glare, but his tone softened. "I don't believe in the Great Spirit," he said. "No lion does—except for Fearless. If you can convince him that you're carrying the Great Spirit, he might be persuaded that you have its power and support." Loyal's eyes narrowed. "And Stinger trusts Fearless. Fearless can get close to him. And then—well. No more false Great Father."

Sky looked from Loyal to Rock, and then at Silverhorn,

who had trudged supportively to her flank. *Here it is again*, she thought. *They all want to kill Stinger and throw the Code to the wind.* Torn and doubtful, she gazed around at the herds. Wallow and his pod of hippos were gathered at the front, a family of meerkats beside them. Wildebeests, gazelles, and kudu mingled together, a group of giraffes watching closely from behind them. Every animal stood still and attentive, waiting for her response to the lion.

"But Loyal, Fearless won't believe me," she said at last. "I tried to tell him the truth about Stinger already—I talked to him at the Great Gathering, but it made no difference. He's completely convinced that Stinger's the true Great Father."

Loyal gave a dismissive grunt. "That's only because Stinger's been manipulating him since he was a tiny cub. Fearless doesn't know any better, and Stinger's turned him into his own personal tooth-and-claw. He doesn't deserve to be used like that—used against his own Bravelands!" He stalked a little closer to Sky and gazed intently into her eyes. "Great Mother helped Fearless, when he needed to rescue Titan's cub from the cheetahs," he reminded her. "Will you now do what she would have done? Will you help Fearless?"

For long, aching heartbeats, Sky stared at him. How could she persuade Loyal Prideless he was wrong? Helplessly she glanced at Rock. She was sure he didn't have any more faith in the lion than she did, but he was saying nothing, simply watching her with those deep, dark green eyes of his.

A memory came to her: Great Mother's ancient face, wrinkled and wise. Warmth flooded Sky's bones, as if a fire of adoration and respect had kindled inside her. Her grandmother had always been so gentle, so strong: so filled with protective love for Bravelands and every creature that lived there. Besides, maybe the Great Spirit wanted her to bring Fearless onto their side—maybe he had some part to play in Stinger's downfall.

She raised her tusks and trunk so that the herd could hear her; her voice was strong and calm and level.

"Yes, Loyal Prideless," she said. "I *will* help you."

CHAPTER 19

The big eland bull had no idea it was in danger. *And that's exactly as it should be,* thought Fearless with satisfaction.

It ambled across the flat grassland, unconcerned, its humped shoulders and thick body looking impossibly heavy on those slender legs. Fearless licked his drooling jaws as it lowered its horned head to graze. *So big. So broad. No doubt so deliciously tender . . .*

He slunk through the long yellow grass, Keen and Gracious behind him. He knew the two cubs were there—he could smell them—but they made no sound. Somewhere off to his right stalked Valor, Rough, Tough, and Hardy, but they too gave no sign of their presence. Rough and Tough had spent a long, patient time seeking out a likely eland from the herd; they were turning into excellent scouts. And Valor finally seemed to be whipping the whole pride into an efficient hunting team.

Fearless didn't even have to raise his head above the grass; he could hear the clicking of the creature's split hooves, a good distance from the muted chorus made by the rest of its herd. The bull was close.

"Now," he snarled.

Keen and Gracious sprang forward with him; Keen's long legs ate up the distance, while the lioness bounded in elegant strides. Off to his right Fearless saw the blur of gold that meant Valor and her team were running too, keeping pace, heading the eland away from its herd.

It was galloping now, its spiral-ridged horns raised as it barked out an alarm. The herd was running too, but that didn't matter; the bull was effectively cut off. *It's even bigger than I thought*, Fearless realized as he closed on its flank. His head was barely level with the top of its legs.

He leaped for its haunches, felt his claws sink into its flesh. It faltered, but didn't fall. Fearless clung on and jerked himself higher onto its back. He was aware of Keen flashing past him as the eland stumbled; the young lion launched himself at the great dewlap of flesh beneath the bull's neck and hung grimly on. The weight was too much and the world tipped. They slid together across the grass.

The eland was kicking, thrashing, but it was on the ground, and in moments the rest of the pride had piled on. Valor joined Keen at the bull's throat, crushing it at its narrowest point. The huge antelope subsided, thrashed once more, and gave a long groan. Under Fearless's heaving flanks, he felt it go still.

Slowly, he released his jaws from its back. "That was perfect!" he exclaimed.

"We did it!" roared Rough with glee.

"Well done. Well done!" A fierce pride surged through Fearless. *We're a team at last!*

Though, if they were a team, why were the others suddenly backing off? He glanced at them in surprise, his claws still hooked into the eland's spine.

Ah, the successful hunt must have earned him some respect as the pride leader at last. Still buzzing with triumph, Fearless sank his fangs into the eland's neck. *They're letting me taste the first blood.*

But as he flicked his eyes sideways, he realized the others still weren't joining him. Rough and Tough were reversing awkwardly away from the kill. Keen and Hardy crouched on the flattened grass, watching him with wary eyes. Gracious sat respectfully, her eyes downcast.

Valor blinked as she looked around. Fearless jumped down from the eland's hunched back, frowning. Now that he thought about it, they looked more nervous than respectful.

"Come on," he urged them. "We all brought this down, let's eat it together."

Hesitantly, they slunk forward, exchanging wary glances. As they began to tear at the eland's flesh, Fearless started to work at the belly. Blood spilled out across his muzzle, and he licked his jaws; he could hear the others talking in low voices through mouthfuls of warm meat.

The intense heat had brought out more flies than ever, and

Fearless flicked his ears irritably, whipping his tail. It was a while before he bothered to listen to the talk going on around him. Near him, Keen and Hardy were tearing at the flank, and as the others lapsed into a temporary but intent silence, he heard Hardy's whisper.

"I'm telling you, Keen, I wouldn't cross him. Look what happened to Sn—"

Realizing there was sudden quiet, the two male cubs looked up guiltily.

Fearless's jaws went still; he couldn't believe what he'd heard. "What? What did you say?"

Keen and Hardy blinked and swallowed. "Nothing, Fearless!" they yelped in unison, and returned to their intent ripping and gnawing.

Valor, at his side, nudged him. "Leave them be," she growled. "It's no bad thing."

Fearless was still staring at the cubs. "They think I had something to do with what happened to Snarl," he muttered.

"Fearless, just eat," said Valor.

But Fearless had lost his appetite. "I feel awful about what happened. I shouldn't have sent him off on his own."

"He did something stupid, and it got him killed." Valor shrugged. "Who knows what? Pounced at a bird and fell? He was far too overconfident, you know that. It's a shame, but it wasn't your fault. And if it's made them respect you more, you should make the most of it."

"I don't want that kind of respect," protested Fearless. "I don't want them to think I'll kill anyone who challenges me!"

"Why not?" Valor rasped flesh from a rib bone. "*I* may know you wouldn't do that, but they don't. They're taking you seriously at last. This hunt was the result."

"No." Fearless stared at the other lions. "They've already had to run away from Titan. If I act like that brute, I'm no better than he is."

"Don't even think—" Valor stopped as Rough sprang to her feet.

"Elephant!" the lioness yowled, as Tough jumped up to stand at her side. "Coming from the west!"

"What does it want?" Fearless asked, getting to his paws in surprise.

All the lions were standing up now, staring across the parched grassland, tail-tips flicking nervously. The young elephant wasn't full-grown, but no wonder his pride was intimidated: she loomed larger with every step, her vast ears flapping wide, her steady, swaying gait implacable. Fearless recognized her: it was Sky Strider. The last time he'd seen her, she'd smashed her head into his shoulder to fling him off Thorn. *What does she want with me now?* His hackles rose defensively.

"We should run now, right?" came Keen's doubtful voice behind him.

"No. Wait here." Swallowing his nerves, Fearless set out at a trot toward the elephant.

As he drew closer through the trembling heat haze, he saw that she wasn't alone. In the long grass ahead of her paced a lion, leading her toward Fearless, his familiar scarred face full of determination.

"Loyal!" grunted Fearless, bounding forward. "Why are you here? Fearlesspride is fine without your help." He halted some distance in front of the older lion, scowling.

Loyal's black-and-gold head turned to the elephant as he muttered something. Sky paused, waiting, and he trotted forward alone to meet Fearless.

Fearless curled his muzzle. "I thought I told you to stop interfering! Why have you brought her here?"

"I'm not going to stop *interfering*," Loyal told him grimly, "until you understand the truth about Stinger Crownleaf."

"Oh, not again." Fearless gave a rumbling growl of irritation.

"I've told you: I've seen Stinger with Titan, but you won't believe me."

"Because it isn't *true*." Fearless slashed at the grass with his claws.

"So you keep telling me. That's why I've brought Sky." Loyal flicked his crooked tail toward the elephants. "She's the one who's carrying the Great Spirit. Not that devious baboon."

Fearless laid his ears back and gave a guffaw of scorn. "You don't even believe in the Great Spirit!"

"But *you do!*" Loyal drew himself up, snarling. "So stop doing everything Stinger tells you, and *listen* for once!"

"It's true, Fearless." As Sky strode toward him, Fearless had to force himself not to take an instinctive step back. Her head alone seemed larger than his entire body, her legs like great logs. Her tusks, though still short, looked like they could easily tear lion-flesh. Worst of all were her eyes: she was staring at him intently, as if she could see his deepest thoughts. He dropped his gaze.

"A vulture took me to the mountains," Sky said, in her rumbling voice. "There another vulture spoke to me. He told me that the Great Spirit was within me, and would be until the new Great Parent emerged."

"He already has," muttered Fearless.

"No," said Sky firmly. "Stinger is not the Great Father. And you've seen the Great Spirit guide me with your own eyes. Remember that day I found you in the forest, with Thorn?"

"I'm not likely to forget it."

"The Great Spirit brought me to you. I knew nothing about what was happening, but it made sure I found you. It wanted me to stop you breaking the Code."

Fearless met her eyes at last. "You think *I* was breaking the Code?" He tossed his head. "Thorn's a murderer. Great Father wanted him gone before he killed anyone else. *You* broke the Code by stopping me!"

"Fearless!" Loyal snapped. "Can't you see that Sky's trying to help you? Shut up and listen to her."

Anger roiled inside Fearless. "*You* listen, Loyal Prideless. You don't know Stinger, and nor does Sky. He's never done anything but help me. From the moment he rescued me from that eagle's nest, he's been there for me."

"Because he's using you!" roared Loyal. "He's always used you! All that cunning monkey wants is an obedient lion to boss around."

"And why should I take your word for that?" yelled Fearless. "You're an oath-breaker! Stinger bosses me around? That's funny, coming from you. You're not my father—you have no right to tell me what to do."

"You young fool!" Loyal's eyes blazed golden with fury. "If you father *was* here, he'd tell you exactly what I'm telling you."

The rage within Fearless boiled up like a gushing spring. Lunging, he lashed his paw across the older lion's muzzle. Loyal reeled back, and Fearless saw his anger turn to stunned hurt.

"Get out of here!" Fearless stalked forward, forcing Loyal to back away. From the corners of his eyes he saw his comrades—*Fearlesspride!*—pace forward to join him. "Go, or my pride will tear you to pieces. *Go!*"

Loyal was breathing hard. He didn't even look at the other cubs; he only gazed into Fearless's eyes as the relentless sun beat down.

"Be careful, Fearless," he said at last.

Fearless watched him turn and pad away. Sky's eyes were full of disappointment. She swung around to follow Loyal, and the pair of them trudged away across the grass toward the west.

In the silence, Fearless stared after them. Then Hardy sprang forward to his side.

"That was *amazing!*"

"It really was." Keen bounced up to join them. "You scared them off!"

"A big lion *and* an elephant!" exclaimed Rough. "Fearless, you're the best!"

"The best!" put in Tough.

"I never saw anything like that." Gracious sat down, gazing at him in awe.

Fearless's jaws were tense, but he flexed and stretched his shoulders in an effort to relax. "It's . . . nothing, I . . . I always protect . . . my pride." He tried to grin triumphantly, but there was an awful, wrenching shame in his gut.

I struck him. I hit Loyal. He mustn't let the pride see him shaking. He took deep gulping breaths.

He'd never return the blow. I knew I could strike him and he wouldn't hurt me back.

And I did it anyway. Guilt writhed inside him like a trapped snake.

But it didn't make sense. Why would Loyal and Sky tell such lies about Stinger?

They're up to something, he realized, with a sinking sensation. His erstwhile friend was planning some mischief with those elephants. The glances they'd shared, their lies about Stinger—it couldn't be good. And whatever it was, shouldn't the Great Father of Bravelands be made aware?

Fearless didn't have a choice. However bad he felt, however guilty and wretched, he had to act right now.

I have to warn Stinger.

* * *

Rain lashed the lake, raising a thin gray mist that hung eerily over the water's pitted surface. Fearless padded along its shore, the gritty sand sodden beneath his paws. A few animals loitered beneath dripping trees: that gerenuk was still here, front hooves propped against a tree as it ripped listlessly at the leaves. Zebras clustered high up on the shore, flicking water from their ears and shaking their stiff manes. A solitary monkey squatted miserably on a branch, her baby cuddled against her as the rain streamed from her fur. A nearby cheetah scowled at the world as if it was furious with everybody.

"You're wasting your time," it grumbled as Fearless walked past. "Nobody gets to see the esteemed Great Father today. *Apparently.*"

Fearless glanced at the cheetah in surprise. "He'll see *me*," he said curtly, and kept walking.

Certainly something unusual seemed to be happening on the peninsula called Baboon Island. Yelps and enraged screeches came from within, and Fearless could see baboons dashing and darting from tree to rock and back again; they looked panicked but purposeless, as if they were desperate to look busy but didn't know how. The Strongbranch guards at the entrance seemed distracted, craning to stare into the encampment rather than watching for approaching visitors. Fearless was almost upon them when Fang finally started and spun around.

"Cub of the Stars!" He shook himself, dislodging showers of water.

"Hello, Fang. I'm here to talk to Great Father. May I?"

It was only politeness; Fearless didn't expect for a moment to be denied entry. But Fang picked uneasily at his yellow teeth.

"You can try," he muttered. "But Stinger's not really in a mood to talk to anyone."

Frowning, Fearless glanced past the baboon's shoulder. "Why? What's happening?"

"You haven't heard?" Fang swallowed hard. "Thorn's come back. He's taken over another troop and stolen Berry."

Fearless gasped, stiffening. "That traitor? How dare he?"

"Beats me." Fang jerked his head. "Go on in. If Stinger wants to see anyone, it'll be you."

"I'll help Great Father," rumbled Fearless grimly, and strode on into the camp.

Inside, the uproar was obvious. Baboons shot past without even greeting him, their eyes wide enough to show the stained whites. Some of them balanced in the low branches, muzzles peeled and heads tipped back as they chittered and shrieked in distress. From the central glade came a voice that rose above all the others, its guttural tone almost demented with fury.

"Where is she? You useless mob of idiots! *Find her!* What? Do I look as if I care that Grass is injured? The fool *lost my daughter*! Worm, get out of my sight and *don't come back* till you've found Berry and ripped Thorn limb from limb. *No! Wait!* Don't you dare kill him! Bring him here bleeding so I can *do it myself*!"

Fearless trotted urgently between the trees, almost

tripping over the baboons who raced in a frenzy in front of his paws. The central clearing was no longer sun-dappled; it was drenched and hammered by rain, and every baboon who stood there, shaking with fear, looked as if they only wanted to be somewhere else. On the Crown Stone in the center stood Stinger Crownleaf, his fur rumpled and soaked, his long-fanged jaws wide in a scream of rage.

"Get scouts out there! And summon every Driftleaf. Someone saw *something!*"

"But . . . Sti—I mean, Great Father—" a baboon stammered. "Most of the Driftleaves are stationed too far away and—"

"*I don't care!* Get them here, Splinter, and get them here by High Sun or you'll find yourself exiled!"

Splinter spun and fled from the clearing, almost crashing into Fearless as he entered. Fearless couldn't blame Stinger for his anger. *His daughter's been stolen!* He had to do something for his mentor, right now.

"Great Father!" He jogged to the Crown Stone. "How can I help? I heard about Berry. I'm so sorry—"

"So you should be!" Stinger whirled to face him, his eyes blazing with a rage that bordered on madness.

Startled, Fearless took an involuntary pace back.

"This is your fault, Cub of the Stars." Spittle from the baboon's jaws spattered Fearless's whiskers. "If you'd killed Thorn when you were supposed to, this would never have happened!"

Fearless couldn't reply; he could only gape at Stinger's twisted face and his bared yellow fangs, and he could feel his paws beginning to tremble. Stinger had never shouted at him, ever.

He swallowed hard. "Stinger, I'm sorry. I'll do what I can to make up for it. How do you know Thorn's involved?"

With a shaking paw, Stinger pointed to the edge of the glade. "*That.*"

Fearless followed his gesture. Beneath a mahogany tree stood a baboon he knew all too well—or rather, the baboon slumped, supported only by the vicious grip of two big Highleaves.

Nut! The exile's broad face was bloody and swollen, he was missing a tooth, and one of his eyes was stuck shut.

"What's he doing here?" breathed Fearless in shock.

"My Strongbranches brought him here," hissed Stinger, "after they lost my daughter to his accomplice, Thorn. Nut told us everything—with a little persuasion."

"I don't understand," Fearless said hoarsely. *Nut? With Thorn?* None of this made sense. They were enemies. Staring at the beaten captive, Fearless felt his stomach lurch. Of course Stinger wanted to know where his daughter was, but had this been necessary? Had it even *helped?* Nut looked barely alive.

Stinger's chest was heaving, and his muzzle was still peeled back from his long snout to expose pink skin. He bounded down from the Crown Stone in a single leap, to stand close to Fearless's nose.

"Make up for it," he snarled. "Atone for your failure, *Cub.* Get my daughter back, and kill Thorn Middleleaf. Chew him to hyena-scraps. Kill every baboon in his benighted troop if you have to; I don't want a single one of them left alive in Bravelands."

Fearless blinked, his jaws parted as he sucked in shaky breaths. "But Stinger . . . I . . . that would break the Code."

Stinger's red eyes were locked on his. He said nothing.

Fearless ducked his shoulders, trying to placate the incensed baboon. "You're Great Father," he pleaded. "If you explain to Thorn's troop that he's done something wrong, if you tell them what happened, they'll—"

Stinger snatched a broken branch from the ground and smashed it across Fearless's jaw.

Fearless stumbled and fell back in a blur of pain and shock. The hot tang of blood seeped into his mouth, and he reeled. The blow was far, far worse than the one he'd given Loyal, yet as he squeezed his burning eyes, trying to focus, there wasn't a trace of remorse on Stinger's face.

"Get out of my sight." Stinger's snarl hurt almost as badly as the blow, making Fearless's belly clench and twist. "I've done so much for you. And it's time to stop taking, taking, taking, Gallantbrat. Time to *give something back*."

Fearless flinched at the sneering nickname. This couldn't be Stinger. The kindly baboon who had raised him from a cub. It just *couldn't*.

Stinger was still glaring at him. "I even got rid of Snarl for you, and look at you, still useless to me."

For a moment Fearless couldn't breathe. He could only stand there shivering, as the bolt of shock tore through him.

He got rid of Snarl?

"That's right. If you fail me yet again, I have another ally to help me. One who's a lot bigger and stronger than you, Cub. And it won't just be Thorn that Titan kills; I'll tell him exactly where to find you and your pathetic pride."

As the words sank in, blinding fury turned his chilled blood to a burning heat. Fearless sprang, slamming his forepaws into Stinger and sending him crashing to the ground beneath him. The baboon gave a grunt of shock, winded, and Fearless saw sudden panic in his eyes; he pressed his attack, pinning Stinger down and lowering his gaping jaws.

Fingers clutched him, tangling in his fur and digging into his skin. He barely felt the scratch of their claws as the baboons dragged him off their Crownleaf. Every baboon in the clearing had come to rescue their leader, and Fearless, his eyes locked on Stinger's as he was hauled back, saw the Crownleaf's momentary panic turn to a sneering triumph.

Fearless snarled and slashed, writhing to escape, but the Strongbranches and their sidekicks held him tight. Stinger scrambled to his feet and paced menacingly toward him.

"I feel sorry for you, Fearless," he growled silkily. "Poor, deprived cub: give him a little affection and he'll do anything. I realized it the moment I plucked you from that eagle's tree. You've been so willing and useful ever since— well, willing, but not quite useful enough. And sadly, those days seem to be over." He flared his red nostrils and exposed his fangs. "Get out."

The claws that clutched him were abruptly released.

Fearless stood trembling for a moment, staring at Stinger's contemptuous face: his curled snout, his hate-filled eyes. He wanted to summon his anger again, but it felt like a dammed river. He turned and stumbled out of the clearing, blundering through the trees. All around him baboons stopped and stared in astonishment, but he did not meet a single friend's eyes. *They're not my friends. They never were. Loyal was right about Stinger. He was right, and I treated him so, so cruelly.*

Fang gaped as Fearless bolted past him and fled along the shoreline.

Thorn too. He tried to tell me, and look at what I almost did! I nearly killed my truest friend. . . .

Still the rain hammered down, drenching his pelt, dripping from his muzzle, making him slide and stumble on the bank. Lightning crashed above him, and thunder roared like a victorious enemy. It felt as if Bravelands, and his whole world, was breaking apart.

And his mouth was filled with the bitterness of his own blood.

CHAPTER 20

"You did your best for Fearless," Sky told Loyal Prideless, brushing her trunk hesitantly across his mane. "You couldn't have done more."

"No," he grunted. "You're wrong, Sky Strider."

He lay with his forepaws outstretched, panting in the heat, and stared blankly across the drying, steaming grassland. Fresh banks of dark cloud swept across Bravelands toward them, promising more rain. The very skies seemed to share the sense of turmoil. Sky glanced anxiously at Rock, who gave a shake of his head, but she tried again.

"You told Fearless everything he needed to know. It's not your fault he wouldn't listen."

"It's kind of you to say so, Sky," said Loyal bleakly, "but there are things you don't understand. I've never done my best for Fearless. I need to change that—and I can start by telling him the truth," he muttered. "There's something he needs to know."

"The truth?" She blinked in confusion. "What do you mean?"

But at that moment, she caught sight of a small brown figure bounding across the savannah toward them. Mud Low-leaf loped to a halt and smoothed his fur, and he and Loyal exchanged a surprised nod.

"Sky, I've got news," he told her, breathless.

She nodded in welcome. "What's happened, Mud? Good or bad news?"

"Both, but the good parts are very good indeed." His big dark eyes were shining. "Stinger's in a furious temper—and I know that's not good for anyone around him—but it's because his daughter Berry has gone missing. And the word is, she's with Thorn!"

"Berry?" Sky flapped her ears forward, about to exclaim in delighted recognition, but she stopped herself just in time. After all, Thorn's memory of the beautiful, golden-furred baboon was one she shouldn't have seen. *Not that I could help it . . .*

"Thorn's been in love with Berry forever," sighed Mud happily. "It seems he's still alive and well, and now he's with her!"

"That is good news," said Sky, with a happy glance at Rock. "But Mud, you're no doubt right about Stinger. I hate to imagine how dangerous he could be when he's angry."

"Actually, I've never seen him like this," Mud admitted. "He's always so controlled, but it's as if he's lost his mind along with his daughter. He's ranting and raving at everyone, making threats, hitting baboons."

"That doesn't sound good," murmured Rock, "but it could mean he's more likely to make mistakes."

"I've been trying to help him with that." Mud grinned. "I gave him false news, Sky, like I promised. I told him you only have a few allies, and they're mostly weak and needy. That they're just here for what help you can give them, not the other way around. He thinks no one is interested in helping you find the Great Parent."

"That's good work, Mud," said Sky, feeling more cheerful by the moment.

"But . . ." Mud's expression darkened. "Stinger has a message for you. He wants you to meet him at the Lightning Tree, one-on-one."

"Alone?" Rock cocked his ears forward in alarm. "I don't like that idea, Sky. We *know* Stinger is dangerous."

Thoughtfully, Sky stirred the dust with her toes. "I know it's risky. But Rock, you were right when you said he's more likely to make mistakes now."

"That's true, but out of control or not, he's still dangerous—"

"I know. I've seen the bones of his victims." Yet again her heart wrenched at the memory of poor Thud, so trusting and stubborn, and so betrayed. "But if things go wrong, no one else will be there to get hurt," Sky told him firmly. "Besides, what baboon would be fool enough to take on an elephant?"

* * *

The Lightning Tree had an even more sinister look than usual, its forked branches stark against the dark gray cloud bank that slid across the sky. Its bark seemed blacker than Sky remembered, and as a cold breeze rose it brought a stink of charred wood to her trunk. One of the recent raging storms must have struck it once again.

At its roots crouched a hunched figure, long-snouted and thickly ruffed, his eyes glinting with a cunning brilliance. Sky halted, staring at Stinger, and as he rose to meet her the clouds burst.

Rain exploded from the black sky, striking the ground hard enough to raise a spray between Sky and the baboon. But there was no mistaking the expression on his face: a combination of rage and sheer contempt.

"Stinger Crownleaf," she greeted him stiffly.

He didn't even respond with her name. "I am indeed. I am Crownleaf of Brightforest Troop, and ruler of Bravelands. I am the Great Parent, and I will no longer tolerate your insolent challenges to my authority."

Sky stared at him. The edges of his eyes were rimmed with red; his yellow fangs gleamed between his peeled-back lips. His whole body was a shape of sheer menace—but so was a leopard's when it crouched, or a buffalo's when it prepared to charge. How could Sky possibly know what truly lay inside that skin, or what the Great Spirit wanted from her?

There was only one way, and it was the Great Spirit that had given it to her. Closing the distance between them with two swift paces, she touched her trunk to Stinger's shoulder.

Need. The urgent, overwhelming need: for strength, for power, for control. His head was almost bursting with it, and the effort to repress it day after day had curdled it into a hot red malice in her blood.

Now, at least in this moment, it had an outlet: the baboon who idled there beneath the crooked tree, her back turned. The stupid creature did not deserve to live; no baboon who was so careless and complacent had a place at all in this troop, let alone a place at its head. Stinger felt the rock in his paw, rough and heavy; he leaped, fast and silent, and smashed it down onto the Crownleaf's skull.

The Crownleaf didn't even make a sound as flesh and bone crumpled. She fell forward with no more than a gurgling gasp, and Stinger hated her weakness. He smashed the rock down, again and again, till blood streamed and dribbled out, soaking into the Crown Stone of feathers.

It felt wonderful—just as it had the last time. It was a great release, as if he'd done something good. He had done something good. He had rid the troop of a weak leader. He'd assuaged the heat inside his head, and—

"Seed? No! What have you done?"

Stinger spun around. A golden-furred baboon stood there, paws over her mouth, her eyes filled with revulsion and horror. How ridiculous! Why should Pear look so aghast? Wasn't she proud of her mate? Didn't she know that this was how power—

Sky reeled as Stinger struck her trunk away from his shoulder. He skipped back, his snout twisting with rage. "How dare you! How dare you touch me?"

Sky breathed hard, trying to regain her balance. A feeling of sickness was rising from her gut to her throat, and she didn't know if it was from the vision itself, or from the cloying sense of evil that still clung to her.

"You arrogant elephant!" Stinger's voice was shrill. "Do you think you can read me the way your grandmother read old bones?"

Yes. But Sky said nothing. A tawny figure was bounding toward her through the driving rain: a colossal, savage lion. His black mane was plastered to his neck in the downpour, but that did nothing to diminish his menacing hugeness. *Titan!*

The lion slowed and trotted to Stinger's side. He said nothing, simply stood there and stared at Sky with narrowed yellow eyes.

Stinger's face twisted into a sneer. "Ah, Sky. I believe you've already met Titan. No need for introductions then."

Sky's head swam. This was the lion who had killed little Moon. She remembered his powerful leap, his fangs sinking into Moon's neck; his satisfied grin as she'd galloped toward him, too late. She'd known Titan and Stinger were meeting and talking together—Loyal had told her so—but were they now true *allies*? It was a gut-churning shock, and for a moment she couldn't speak.

Stinger's evil genius, backed up by the brutal physical might of Titan—and neither of them with a scrap of respect for the Code. Sky's head swam with the terrible possibilities. *No creature in Bravelands will be safe from them.*

"You wouldn't try to hurt me, Sky Strider?" Stinger was grinning, picking at his yellow teeth. "Titan wouldn't like that at all."

"I really wouldn't." Titan gave a slow, colossal yawn that displayed the full length of his fangs.

"Why did you bring me here?"

Stinger relaxed against the Lightning Tree and spread his paws. "Why, to give you one final chance."

She narrowed her eyes. "Chance to do what?"

"To join me, of course!" His eyes glittered.

"You—you're not serious!" Sky blew angrily through her trunk. "Why would I betray the Great Spirit?"

He tilted his head and scratched at his scar. "Does the Great Spirit not seek what I seek? A peaceful, stable Bravelands, working for the benefit of all. Why would the Great Spirit *not* want that?"

"You're twisting the whole purpose of the Spirit!" cried Sky.

"Oh, I don't think so." Stinger shrugged and smiled. "Bravelands will be run as efficiently as my own troop, with every creature in its place, and food shared fairly. Even *if* the Great Spirit doesn't approve—and I doubt very much that's the case—why wouldn't *you*?"

Sky shook her head. She found it hard to control her breathing; her heart was beating thunderously. "You're right about one thing, Stinger Crownleaf."

He leaned forward. "What is that?"

"I *can* read you like an old bone." Grimly Sky stamped a forefoot into the sodden grass, sending mud flying to spatter his fur. "When I touched you, I saw what's inside you, and it's vile. I've seen what you've achieved so far, Stinger, and it's not peace and stability—it's terror and death!"

For a moment there was silence but for the relentless

hammering of the rain. Then Stinger nodded and rose.

"Very well. There will be no more chances, Sky Strider." Resting a paw against Titan's shoulder, he smirked unpleasantly. "I told you once before that you'd be laughed out of Bravelands. The good news is, I've changed my mind. Exile is just not good enough for you, my little elephant. You, and all my enemies, must die."

For a moment, Sky tensed, wondering if Titan was going to kill her right now. But the big lion didn't move. Sky clenched her jaws. "You're wrong, Stinger. You're the one who will be driven from Bravelands forever."

He gave a rippling laugh. "I see. And who's going to do this?"

She turned her rump on him to walk away and cast her reply contemptuously over her shoulder.

"The Great Spirit will see to it, Stinger. The Great Spirit itself."

CHAPTER 21

The night air was sticky with the humid heat, and it felt much worse under the trees. The rain might have stopped at last, but the forest was sodden with it. Mahogany, fig, and marula nut trees grew in tight, tangled clusters in the woods where the former Crookedtree baboons were hiding; if there was any breeze out on the grassland, it certainly didn't penetrate the forest. Thorn pushed wearily through the branches, his limbs aching and his head throbbing with the heat.

He had searched for Nut everywhere he could think of, but there was no sign of him. Gradually, and with great reluctance, he'd had to admit it to himself: the Strongbranches must have cornered and caught his ally.

It was incredible enough that he and Nut were friends at all, but for Nut to do something for him that was so brave, so reckless of his own safety? It hardly seemed fair that a deed so noble should have gone so horribly wrong. Nut had sacrificed himself so that Thorn could reach Berry, and Thorn knew he'd always blame himself if the worst had happened.

He clambered over a mossy rotten log and dropped down on the other side to find his little troop busy with their night-time routines. It was a reassuring sight after his weary and ultimately hopeless search. Some baboons were eating a last few figs; some perched in the branches on sentry duty; others groomed one another or wriggled into comfortable positions in the forks of branches.

Thorn peered anxiously around the glade, and his heart lifted. Berry was crouched with the young mother called Sage, playing with her baby while Sage chewed on spiky melons. When Berry caught sight of Thorn, she returned the infant to its mother and loped to meet him.

"How's your ear?" Frowning, Berry touched Thorn's wound very gently. "The bite hasn't opened up again?"

"It's fine, Berry. Your mother made sure of that." Thorn smiled.

Glancing past his shoulder into the stillness of the night, she sighed. "No sign of Nut? I'm so sorry."

"I'll worry about Nut. How are *you*, Berry?"

She made a rueful face. "I'll be all right. It hardly seemed believable at first. I hardly *could* believe it. But I have to, Thorn. I'm sad, and I'm angry. But the sadness at least will pass."

If it hadn't been for Pear, Thorn knew it would have been much harder to convince Berry of her father's villainy. But with her mother there—the mother Stinger had told her was dead—Berry had had to accept the truth. She'd been upset, of course, and Pear had spent a long time sitting with her, comforting her daughter and murmuring reassurances.

Still, Berry had not been as shocked as Thorn had feared.

"I told you, I was beginning to have doubts," she said now, as they padded together to their new sleeping-place in a huge fig tree. "My father has behaved so strangely in the last few moons. I was so happy when he became Crownleaf, but he didn't act the way I thought he would."

Thorn pulled himself up onto the lowest twisted branch and reached down a paw to help her follow. "I'm sorry, Berry. About everything."

She settled beside him, her eyes downcast. "None of it's your fault. I wish you'd told me, but I understand why you didn't."

"I was trying to protect you. . . ."

Berry plucked at his fur. "After he became Great Parent, my father really began to change—show his true self, I mean—and it wasn't good. You were right to be worried. The way he treated the troop!" She shook her head in disbelief. "And when I got better after—after the monkey attack—and I woke up to find he'd abolished the Council—well. I could hardly believe it."

"Neither could the Council," Thorn said softly. "I was there."

"And the Strongbranches!" Berry's sad eyes suddenly flashed with irritation. "They wouldn't let me near their precious Crownleaf, but they followed me *everywhere*."

"Stinger wanted to make sure you didn't discover the truth," said Thorn.

"It all still feels like a terrible dream." Berry turned to him, her eyes achingly sad. "It's a dreadful thing to know. That my own father could be so devious and vicious! But one good thing has come out of all this, Thorn." She touched his arm with a gentle paw. "We're together again."

"Oh, Berry." He hugged her closer. "I wish I could help."

"You are, by being here. I'm not grieving for my father, you know—I'm grieving for the baboon I thought he was. That baboon never really existed at all."

Thorn's heart ached for her. He tightened his embrace, but she pulled sharply away, her eyes wide.

"Thorn, I smell lions!"

He jerked around, his heart thrashing. She was right; drifting on the night air came a scent of hot, musky fur and blood.

"Berry, take your mother and climb. Everyone!" called Thorn, jumping down from the fig tree. "Get high in the branches. Quick!"

Their nostrils flaring and eyes widening, the troop was quick to obey. Thorn loped around the glade, harrying stragglers and making sure no one had been left asleep in some ground-level cranny. What were the lions doing in this dense forest? When he had counted all the baboons up into the higher branches, he scrambled after them, hopping nimbly between the trees.

With luck any predators won't even realize we're here.

He had just swung up beside Berry and Pear when there

was a clatter of leaves, a squeal, and a light thump. He heard a screech of raw panic from the mahogany beside them. It was Sage's voice, and she was grabbing branches, peering down desperately.

"My baby! Stalk! He—"

"Don't go down!" barked Thorn, staring at the baby who had fallen into the center of the clearing. "I'll get him."

Backing swiftly down the trunk, he bounded to the wailing Stalk and lifted him gently. The little creature whimpered and grabbed Thorn's chest fur, clinging on desperately.

"All right, reckless one, let's get you back to—"

Thorn's voice choked in his throat as the first lion snout emerged from the tree line, followed by several others. Above him, his troop erupted in shrieks and hoots of alarm.

Moonlight turned the lions' eyes to shining orbs, and Thorn gulped. His heart raced in his chest as he slowly backed away; they were advancing in a semicircle, and there were no trees close enough to reach. *No retreat.* He barely dared to count the pairs of eyes. Six lions? No, *seven.* There was not a mane between them, but there were enough near-grown cubs here to rip him and Stalk to scraps. He cast around desperately, seeking an escape route.

Then the biggest lion paced forward, out of the shadows, straight toward Thorn, and he knew at once he was dead. The cub's face was grim, and smeared and streaked with blood; it was also very, very familiar.

Thorn clenched his jaws, breathing hard. "Fearless."

The lion stared at him darkly, in silence.

"You've come to finish what you started." Instinctively Thorn clutched the baby at his chest with a protective paw.

"I have." The growl was low, resounding around the glade.

High in the trees Thorn heard Pear's frightened cry of warning; a moment later, there was a light thump next to him, and he turned, startled. "Berry! No!"

She drew herself up, not taking her defiant eyes off Fearless. "I stand with you, Thorn. I won't let you face these lions alone."

Thorn's chest was tight with gratitude and fear. Berry truly did still love him, then—but he almost wished she didn't, if it meant she'd stayed safe in the treetops. He closed his eyes briefly in agony.

The infant on his chest moved, squirming in terror. Detaching Stalk as gently as he could, Thorn thrust him into Berry's arms. Taken aback, she clutched the little baboon close.

"Go!" urged Thorn. Turning back to the lions, he glared at his old friend. "Fearless! It's me you've come for!"

Fearless's glowing eyes were unreadable, and his voice was a harsh growl. "Yes, Thorn. It's you I've come for."

Beside Thorn, Berry gasped in terror. "No," she whispered.

"Come on!" Thorn demanded, his fur bristling as he leaped in front of Berry and tensed for the lions' charge. "Get it over with! Kill me!"

"Stinger ordered me to kill you!" Fearless's voice was a hoarse bark. "I didn't say I'd obey him."

For a moment there was absolute stillness in the forest. The baboons high above seemed to be holding their breath;

even the cicadas stopped their constant rasping song. Thorn gaped at Fearless as the lion paced closer.

"You work for Stinger," whispered Thorn hoarsely. "He's your master."

"I *did* do Stinger's work." Fearless came to a halt when his muzzle was almost touching Thorn's. Now that he was so close, Thorn could see the tormented shame in the lion's face, could feel the tremor in his hot breath. "Not anymore."

Thorn opened his mouth and closed it. At last he managed to speak. "You mean it?"

Fearless bowed his head. "I said I'd come to finish what I started: that means finally waking up. I started today, Thorn, because I learned the truth. I opened my ears at last. Stinger's used me and tricked me my whole life."

Thorn's heart beat light and fast in his chest, and his limbs were beginning to tremble with something like relief. "Yes," he whispered. "He's done that to everyone, Fearless."

"I've been so stupid, Thorn." Fearless closed his eyes. "Why didn't I see it sooner?"

Impulsively, Thorn reached out a shaking paw to touch the lion's muzzle. "He didn't let you see it. Fearless, I told you before. You're not the only one who fell for him. So did I, for years."

Fearless pushed his furred cheek into Thorn's paw, then raised his somber eyes to Thorn's. "*You told me before,*" he murmured, "when I was doing my best to kill you on Stinger's orders."

"Don't think about it," Thorn urged him. "It's not what's

important right now."

"You almost died because of my gullibility. *I almost killed you*." Fearless wrinkled his muzzle and growled. "Today I found out Stinger has been working with Titan all along: the lion who killed my father and destroyed my family. That was the moment I realized. Only when it affected *me*."

"Oh, Fearless . . ."

"Stinger ordered me to break the Code; how could I not have seen that sooner? I should have trusted you. Don't tell me it doesn't matter. I'm so sorry."

Thorn's eyes felt hot; he couldn't bear it anymore. He threw himself at his old friend, wrapping his arms around Fearless's muscled neck and hugging him tightly. For an instant the lion seemed surprised, and then Thorn felt his hot breath on his head, his rough tongue licking his fur.

"Maybe it did matter," he mumbled into Fearless's fur, "but *not now*. Stinger has fooled every creature he ever met, but if we can learn the truth, so can others."

"Fearless," came Berry's voice, and Thorn glanced back. Still cradling baby Stalk, she padded to Fearless and stroked his shoulder. "I'm Stinger's own daughter. If anyone should have known, if anyone should have seen through him, it was me. But I fell for his trickery too."

"It's not surprising that Stinger ordered you to break the Code," said Thorn fiercely. "He's broken it himself, countless times. But his days of covering up his misdeeds are over." He pressed his paw to Fearless's neck. "All the time, more of Bravelands sees him for what he really is."

Fearless drew back a little to stare at Thorn. "I know he's deceitful and treacherous, but what else? Tell me."

"Where to start?" said Thorn darkly. "He murdered the Crookedtree Crownleaf; that's the first killing we know of. When his plan to take over that troop failed, he escaped to Brightforest. It was Stinger who killed Bark and Grub, years later."

"Great Spirit," breathed Fearless, stunned. "Actually—*killed* them?"

"Them, and more," said Thorn. "He framed Nut for those murders; he tricked Stronghide the rhino into killing Great Mother. And then he made sure Stronghide himself was driven out to die."

Fearless opened and closed his jaws, looking agonized. "Stinger killed Great Mother!"

"He killed Starleaf and framed me for that." Thorn swallowed hard as he felt his fury rise. "He murders anyone who crosses his path, whether they know they have or not. But Fearless, these are only the deaths we know about. Stinger probably started a long time ago—and I don't doubt he's killed many more."

"I should have known you wouldn't hurt Starleaf," snarled Fearless. "I'm sorr—"

"Don't say it again," put in Thorn quickly. "What's important now is that we know the truth and we can stop him."

He was aware of rattling branches and rustling leaves as the Crookedtree baboons gradually emerged and made their way down from the treetops. They'd recovered their nerve, though they still eyed the lions with awe and disbelief. Berry passed Stalk carefully to his mother, then turned back to Thorn and Fearless.

"And we really *can* stop Stinger," she said firmly. "We must."

"Of course we can." Fearless drew himself up, whacking the mossy earth with his claws and sending gouts of earth and grass flying. A few baboons flinched, then giggled with nerves.

Thorn had never felt such relief and gladness. At last, *at last*, his friend had come to his senses and seen the truth. Both Fearless and Berry were at his side once again, and his destroyed life was slowly being put back together. *If only Mud were here too*, he thought wistfully.

In the excitement, he realized he'd overlooked a very important matter—six matters, in fact. "But who are these lions? I take it you got away from Titanpride?"

Fearless growled triumphantly. "I did—and so did my sister, Valor." Thorn turned as an elegant lioness paced forward. "The rest were lions of Dauntlesspride—another pride Titan conquered. Thorn, Berry, meet Gracious, Rough and Tough, Hardy and Keen!"

"Hello." Thorn's voice came out squeakier than he'd hoped as the last five lions stalked closer: a slender and delicate-featured lioness, two rangy, rough-coated twins, a stocky, blunt-faced cub, and a tall, long-legged cub with dark brown eyes.

Fearless gave a grunting roar and struck the ground dramatically. "We are Fearlesspride!"

"I can see that." Thorn grinned. "Congratulations, Cub of the Stars."

"Don't call me that. Please." Fearless gave a shudder. "You know who persuaded me to found my own pride? Stinger. I guess he wanted more lions to command." He glanced left and right, meeting the fiery gazes of his pride. "Well, he's going to get a shock. Fearlesspride will be fighting *against* him!"

His pride huffed and roared their agreement.

"And this is my new troop," said Thorn, gesturing at the curious baboons who were pressing forward now, losing their instinctive fear of the lions as Thorn and Fearless hugged and nuzzled one another. All around there was a babble of excitement, and even whoops of happy laughter. Berry hugged Thorn and then threw her arms around her mother, her eyes shining.

"I feel better than I've felt in moons," Fearless admitted with a grin.

"As do I." Thorn hopped and scrambled onto Fearless's back. *This is how it ought to be.*

"We have a pride and a troop, and they're both fine ones," Thorn declared to the gathered lions and baboons. "And we're going to take this fight to Stinger. But there's one thing we have to do first—one animal who is central to everything. We can't do this without her."

Berry gazed up at him on Fearless's back, looking delighted

to see the odd pairing once again. "Who's that, Thorn? Who do we have to find?"

"The one who carries the Great Spirit," said Thorn. "We're going to find Sky Strider."

CHAPTER 22

Sky had never seen so many animals, not even at the biggest Great Gathering she'd witnessed. The emissaries who had approached her yesterday were returning now with their herds and families, and the earth trembled with their movement. Dust rose into the air, obliterating the horizon and turning the fierce sun into a hazy blur of white.

Through the dust strode zebras and wildebeests, elands and impalas and gazelles. A black line in the distance drew closer and closer until it coalesced into a great mass of buffalo: Thud's former herd, their faces grim and vengeful. Overtaking them, a pack of hyenas loped steadily toward Sky; they scrabbled to a halt before her, and their leader dipped his scruffy head.

"Titanpride massacred our old and our young while we

attended a Great Gathering," he growled, lowering his head. "For this Code-shattering crime, we are with you in your fight. I am Hardclaw of the Sandstone Pack."

Sky bowed her own head. "Thank you. You and your pack are welcome, Hardclaw."

"And my crash has suffered too," came a familiar voice.

Sky peered through the billows of dust and recognized the rhino who walked with Stronghide's old crash behind her. "Silverhorn!" she cried in delight. "I wondered where you'd gone today."

"This is Grimfoot, our new leader." Silverhorn turned respectfully to usher him forward.

The rhino nodded his heavy, square head. "We hate Stinger for what he did to Stronghide. Many of our crash were misled, Sky Strider. We ask your forgiveness for Great Mother's death, and we request the right to join you in your defiance of the False Parent."

Sky brimmed with conflicting emotions, but to her surprise, anger was not one of them. Instead, she felt another rush of determination that Stinger's poison must be wiped from Bravelands forever. "You have both," she told him. "Thank you for joining us, Grimfoot."

As more animals approached, Sky took a breath and a moment to look around. Loyal was still here, and Wallow's pod, and the leopards and cheetahs . . . and so many more. *So much for being laughed out of Bravelands*, she thought. *The Great Spirit is strong indeed. All of Bravelands flocks to its summons.* "But how will we organize them all?" she murmured to Rock.

"Look at them." He gestured with his tusks. "We have animals here who can fight, like the hyenas and those wild dogs. The buffalo and the zebras and the wildebeests are fierce with their hooves and horns and teeth. The meerkats and the hyrax are small, but they can scout and spy, and we have animals who can protect them. Every one of them can have a role, Sky."

She nodded. "We must divide up the responsibilities properly. I just wish we had some climbers, other than those few leopards; Stinger and his troop are bound to retreat into the trees."

Rock studied her. "You know we can't wait, Sky."

"I know. The more we delay, the more animals will suffer—and the more time Stinger will have to prepare."

"What's more, these animals are all ready to fight." Rock gazed proudly out over the herds. "Everyone's longing to take down Stinger—all they've been waiting for is a leader." He turned to her. "And that's what they've found in you, Sky. Their leader."

She swallowed hard. For an instant, the responsibility felt like a stone weighing her down. Then she shook herself, took another deep breath, and stepped out before the hordes.

The dust was settling now, at least a little; anyone who was coming, it seemed, was here already. Beside her, Rock lifted his trunk and gave a trumpeting blare for attention. Murmurings, brays, and growls faded away; there was a last squeak from a bush squirrel, and then silence.

"All of Bravelands owes you a debt," Sky cried, feeling a

small tremor of nervousness. She cleared her throat to steady her voice. "Thank you for coming today, all of you. Look at us! We have so many strengths. I see power, speed, and endurance; I see cleverness and cunning. I see agility and alertness, strong eyes and sharp ears! Stinger Crownleaf the False Parent is a sly and powerful creature, that is true. To move against him—it's a momentous, frightening decision. But he can't stand against Bravelands itself. We *will* defeat him! We will drive him from these lands!"

Roars, bellows, and grunts of approval rose from the crowd, and Sky felt new strength and determination fill her blood.

"The smaller animals will stay at our rear, to watch for sneak attacks, and alert us." She let her gaze drift to the hares and hyrax, rock rats and striped bush squirrels. "You're important to our strategy, but I won't send you in to fight against Stinger's lions and baboons. You will stay behind us, protected by the strongest and fiercest grass-eaters—Stamp, Crash, and the rest of the buffalo."

"We want to attack Stinger!" bellowed Stamp.

"And so do we," piped a rock rat, though he was almost completely drowned out by the buffalo.

"You are our last line of defense!" cried Sky. "And an important one," she added to the rodents and meerkats. "Send scouts outside the herd, make sure Stinger has no nasty surprises planned. You can move through the grass unseen, then report back to us."

"Oh, all right." There was an audible note of relief in the rock rat's squeak.

"And, Stamp! Please, will you protect our smaller forces? It's vital."

The big buffalo hesitated, then nodded proudly. "Yes. We will do this for you, Sky Strider."

Rock shot Sky a glance of pure pride. As the buffalo trudged forward to encircle the small creatures, she turned back to the crowd. "Rush the cheetah will stay behind too—she has more speed than anyone. She can bring any urgent warnings. We have to be on guard against Stinger's treachery."

Animals hollered in agreement.

"The rest of us?" Sky paused, raising her head and trunk. "We march on Stinger!"

Loyal sprang forward, tossing his mane and roaring. The rest of the assembled creatures erupted behind him, howling, bellowing, braying.

"We march on Stinger!"

"We march on Stinger!"

In the tumult, Rock turned to Sky. "Well done, Sky. You've inspired them."

The Great Spirit has inspired them, she thought to herself. She stared out at them all, hoping she had done the right thing. "Some of these brave animals will die, Rock."

"They know that," he told her. "They know it and they still want to follow you. You're a true leader, Sky. Now the sun is going down. It's time."

Taking a deep breath, she swung around and began to pace across the broad sweep of grassland toward the watering hole.

But she hesitated, one foot lifted, as a voice cried out from the east.

"Wait!"

She stared. Across the plain bounded a pride of young lions and a troop of solemn-faced baboons. She recognized their leaders at once.

"Thorn Middleleaf! Fearless Titanpride!"

"Fearlesspride, now," declared the young lion, skidding to a halt before her. "These are my lions, and we've come to fight for you."

"As have we." Thorn loped to his side. "This is my troop, Sky. We will go into battle under the name Justice Troop, to honor those Stinger has murdered. Many baboons are as sick of his tyranny as anyone."

Happiness thrilled through Sky. "You are just what we needed. Now we have lions on our side, and baboons who can pursue Stinger into the highest trees. Thank you!"

She paused once more to turn to the animals behind her.

"We are the Great Herd!" she declared, spreading her ears and raising her trunk. "We're the defenders of the Great Spirit, and we are fighting for every creature who lives in Bravelands. With the Great Spirit's blessing, we will find the true Great Parent! Now—we march!"

Bravelands filled with the voices of the Great Herd; their roars of determination seemed to spread from the most distant lake to the highest mountain, and into the farthest arc of the dusky, darkening sky.

Billows of dust rose once more beneath hundreds of hooves and paws and tramping feet as they set off toward their destination. At Sky's flanks marched Rock and Silverhorn, with tusks and horn lowered. Sky had never been so certain as she was now: they were doing the right thing. *This* was what the Great Spirit wanted.

Through the dust and the shimmering haze, she made out shapes on the horizon. They were growing in size, silhouetted against the gold-and-violet glow of the setting sun. And as they drew even closer, she saw the faces of the foremost animals, their jaws drawn back in gaping snarls of fury.

Lions. Lions led by a huge, fierce, black-maned brute.

Titanpride.

CHAPTER 23

Fearless bared his fangs as he paced on at the head of his pride. The tremor of the Great Herd's movement shivered up from the ground and into his bones, but there was something more in the earth beneath him. With every pawstep he felt the strength of Bravelands itself rising up and filling his blood. Facing him, Titan advanced, his black mane rippling around his powerful shoulders, but for now at least Fearless didn't feel afraid. He locked stares with his father's murderer as they drew ever closer to one another in the hazy dusk.

There was still enough light to pick out the big baboon who stood on a kopje, overlooking his own forces as they advanced. The sunset surrounded Stinger with an eerie, pallid yellow glow. Fearless stared at him. He felt no grief of betrayal, no longing to have his mentor back—only an angry determination.

Fearless nudged Keen at his side, drawing his attention. "That's Stinger. The one who's behind all the trouble."

Keen twitched his whiskers. "He looks so small next to all his allies."

"Small, but lethal. I wish I'd been able to kill him when I had the chance on Baboon Island."

"You didn't know the truth in time," said a voice close to his ear. "You do now."

Fearless started and swung his head. There at his flank was Loyal, padding grimly into battle beside him. A rush of happiness filled Fearless, mingled with deep shame.

"Loyal!" He swallowed. "You tried to tell me earlier. You tried to help me, but I took Stinger's side instead of yours. I'm sorry. I was ashamed of myself the moment I struck you." He risked a direct glance at Loyal's scarred face. "Can you ever forgive me?"

Loyal turned, an expression of surprise overcoming the grimness. "There's nothing to forgive." He narrowed his eyes at the dried blood on Fearless's face. "What happened to your muzzle?"

"Stinger," said Fearless wryly. "Of course."

Loyal's eyes flashed, and his hackles bristled. "He will live to regret that."

Something warm stirred in Fearless's heart, and he was about to reply when a cheetah nearby gave a growl of alert.

Titanpride was so close, Fearless could almost smell their leader's hot, bloody breath. Beside and behind the enemy lions came other allies of Stinger's: black-backed jackals, rhinos, warthogs, wild dogs, and hippos. Some of the grass-eater herds had chosen Stinger's side too: wildebeests and zebras, hartebeests and elands. And of course, there were Stinger's own Strongbranches and other powerful-looking baboons. But none of Stinger's herds were bush squirrels or meerkats or dormice, realized Fearless. The smaller, more vulnerable creatures must know their only hope lay with Sky Strider.

This will be the fight of my life, he thought. *Of all our lives.*

Near him, just beyond the cheetah, a zebra was trembling; he could smell its fear as the two sides closed to within a river's-breadth of each other. Many of the other animals of the Great Herd looked nervous, too, and Fearless didn't blame them. Even without its allies, Titanpride looked terrifyingly powerful and intimidating; they were all bunched muscles, long, savage fangs, and vicious, protracted claws—the veterans of countless fights.

"Fearless!" Sky's trumpeted call came to him from farther along the front rank. "You are a natural fighter. Can you tell the Herd what they must do?"

Fearless balked a little. "Loyal," he murmured, "I'm not sure I know. I've never seen anything like this before."

"Neither has Titan," growled Loyal. "No creature has. But I know you can do this, Fearless. You don't just have the skills of a lion—you're half-baboon, remember?" He shot Fearless a grin.

Fearless returned it, his confidence already building within him. "Hardy. Gracious. Every one of these enemies looks strong, and some of our Herd won't stand a chance. Can you round those ones up and get them back to a safe distance? I'm thinking the smaller antelopes and the civet cats. They can help later, when the first charge is over."

"As good as done, Fearless," growled Hardy, and he and Gracious twisted and sprinted back through the Great Herd.

Fearless turned to his sister. "Valor, Rough and Tough, and Keen. You know how Titanpride operates. They'll try to surround us so that they can pick us off. So each of you must choose a group of good fighters to lead. Split up, and that'll force Titanpride to split up too."

"I'll do the same," growled Loyal as the others nodded. "I'll take the hyenas with me. Despite our differences, we respect each other."

"Good. For myself, I'll go and help Sky and her group." Fearless lashed his tail. "Good luck, all of you! Fight hard. Fight for Bravelands."

It was a gut-wrenchingly anxious moment, but Fearless shook himself. He might only have known the Dauntlesspride lions for a short time, but he had to trust them as much as he trusted Valor and Loyal. For a moment he watched them bounding through the Herd, summoning animals and giving instructions; then he turned and loped to Sky.

Just as he reached her, the Great Herd came to a rumbling, blowing halt. Only a cheetah-dash in front of them, so did Titanpride and the rest of Stinger's forces. Fearless eyed the enemy—their forces were evenly matched, he thought.

"It's time, Sky Strider," he murmured.

She touched him lightly and quickly with her trunk. "It is.

Thank you for this, Fearless. Whatever happens, we'll know we fought for Bravelands and the Great Spirit."

"We're not just going to fight for them," he told her gravely. "We're going to win."

The Great Herd was still. Just for a moment, not a bark nor a bellow disturbed the ominous silence. Fearless took a last look at their ranks, so brave and steadfast, and then at the lions of his own pride, staunch at their positions. From a distance across the front rank, Keen gave him a nod. He returned it, then gritted his jaws and turned back to face the enemy.

"Fearless Gallantbrat!" Titan's snarl resounded across the short stretch of grassland. Behind the massive lion, the sky was a deep violet-blue; the last rays of the sunset were a hot, angry gold that threw his shadow in a dark line across the plain. Titan's muscles rippled and flexed as his cruel claws raked the earth. "You're as stupidly trusting as your father was, Fearless, and it's led you to the same miserable fate. Tonight is the night I will destroy you. Say your good-byes to the sun; you'll never see it again."

Fearless only gazed at him. He had no retort; he didn't want to give one. *My claws and teeth will give it for me, Titan.*

All of Bravelands seemed to hold its breath. The last dazzle of the sun's rim flared once, then sank behind the far hills. As if that had been their signal, the two opposing forces reared, stamped, roared, and bellowed.

Then they charged.

The onrush was swift and sudden, and they collided in a

tumult of striking hooves, snapping teeth, and raking claws. A zebra bucked a Strongbranch from his back and lashed his hind hooves at a lion. Two leopards had fastened themselves with claws and fangs to Resolute, tearing at the big lion as he roared in pain. Keen led a whole detachment of Grimfoot's rhinos in a charge from the side, their horns lowered to slash and tear. Wildebeests stampeded into an opposing herd of their own kind, kicking and clashing horns. Regal, Sly, and three of the young males of Titanpride were twisting and snarling, lashing out wildly as they tried to dislodge Justice Troop baboons from their backs and shoulders.

Fearless tried to hold his position, but in the melee it was impossible. He found himself swept back by the sheer force of the crush, and his claws scrabbled for purchase on the earth. *Where is Titan? Where is my enemy?*

He saw him suddenly. Titan had plowed deep into the first ranks of the Great Herd, his weight and power carrying him forward easily as animals brayed and screeched and tumbled aside. An eland gave a shrill holler of agony as it was dragged down beneath Titan's claws.

Before Fearless could move toward the huge lion, two baboons leaped in front of him. He knew Splinter and Worm—he'd laughed and played and eaten with them—but he had no choice. He could only snap and lash out, dodging their snarling snouts and vicious claws.

As Fearless sank his fangs into Worm's shoulder and flung her away, he caught sight of Sky and Rock, trampling wild dogs and swinging their tusks violently at more lions of Titanpride.

Hippos thundered in, led by Rough and Tough, to clash into battle with jackals and hartebeests and a small herd of zebras. Just beyond them, cheetahs were darting nimbly through the crush of bodies, harrying a cluster of hyenas; the hyenas' size and strength were of little use to them as the cheetahs bit and clawed and then swiftly withdrew, faster than the hyenas could turn. No sooner had one lithe cat retreated than another flew in from the other side, and the hyenas were panting, twisting, sweating with frustration and fear.

Fearless's flared nostrils were thick with the stink of sweat and blood and churned mud. He spun in the confusion and uproar, trying desperately to make out the tide of battle, and the direction it was flowing. *We're holding our own. Just.*

Valor was suddenly at his side, sinking her fangs into the neck of a jackal that had been creeping toward him. She tossed it away in a shower of blood, and the jackal hit the flank of a rhino and thudded limp to the ground. Panting, Valor grinned at Fearless.

"Watch your rump, little brother."

"Thanks, Valor." He spared her a swift lick and realized his jaws were dripping with blood.

"Splitting up the herd was good sense. It's working." She twisted to dash back into battle, then hesitated and turned with a glint of amusement in her golden eyes. "Maybe you're not such a bad pride leader after all."

He watched her fling herself at a lion that had its claws in Silverhorn's shoulder. Then, catching his breath, he spun again and sprinted at another enemy lion.

It was Proud, he realized: one of Titan's new young males. Proud had the advantage of size, but he looked confused by the noise and the press of bodies. Fearless leaped for his back, clinging on and biting hard down into his neck.

"Get off me!" snarled Proud, twisting and bucking, shaking his half-grown mane.

With a last, violent lurch, he finally dislodged Fearless. Flung away, Fearless felt himself spin briefly and helplessly before crashing down into the mud. Winded for a moment, he could only sprawl there, gasping and staring.

Straight into the eyes of Titan.

The huge black-maned lion looked as if he couldn't believe his luck. A slow grin spread across his muzzle as he exposed his long, bloodied fangs.

"This is perfect," he snarled. "I was hoping you'd end up at my claws, and lo and behold, here you are."

Fearless sucked air desperately into his chest, his paws flailing. Twilight was deepening across the plain, and Titan was a looming shadow above him, his eyes beginning to glow. The sounds of the battle around them somehow seemed to recede, leaving Fearless alone with his nemesis.

"And now, little Fearless, I'm going to kill you as I killed your father."

"What—without honor?" rasped Fearless, panting hard. He scrabbled onto his paws, bunching his shoulder muscles. "You weren't lion enough to fight my father on your own."

"You worthless carrion!" Titan's roar was high-pitched with rage. He lunged forward, both forepaws raised to strike.

Desperately Fearless rolled, feeling mud spatter his face as Titan's paws struck the earth. He sprang to his feet again. "You didn't even blind my mother yourself, you got your over-fed mate to do it!"

"Silence!" cried Titan. He pounced again, his jaws snap-ping on empty air as Fearless ducked and scrambled out of reach.

I shouldn't do this. I shouldn't make him angry. But oh, Great Spirit, it feels good. All the rage and frustration and hatred of his cub-hood came pouring out of Fearless. "Coward! Brute! Every animal in Bravelands hates you! *Every lion hates you!*" He dodged another strike of Titan's claws. "That's why you have to bully them. You're no pride leader!"

Titan's eyes were on fire with mad fury. With a shrill roar, he plunged after Fearless once more. Deftly Fearless rolled again and clawed himself out of reach—

And felt a heavy paw thud onto his tail.

There was a stinging, terrible pain; Titan's claws had pierced the flesh and pinned his tail to the earth. Writh-ing, Fearless lashed out and snapped wildly as a rising panic filled him. Titan dodged his blows, but that enormous paw remained clamped down, and no matter how he fought, Fear-less could not escape. Twisting onto his back, he stared up, panting. Titan's great maned head and shoulders blotted out the darkening sky, and his jaws widened above Fearless in leering victory.

A huge lion streaked through the air and slammed into Titan's flank.

Titan staggered sideways, grunting in shock, and Fearless felt his tail released. In an instant he was up and free. Without hesitation he sprang, fastening his teeth in Titan's foreleg.

Titan roared with pain and reared, and suddenly Fearless's savior was back, lunging for Titan with bared fangs and extended claws. Even in the shadows of dusk Fearless knew the lion's black-streaked mane and his crooked tail.

"Loyal!" he panted.

"Get out of here," grunted Loyal through a jawful of Titan's maned shoulder.

The two huge lions rolled and kicked and snarled, locked together in a bloody struggle. Fearless backed away, torn by indecision. The air was split by Thorn's clear, fierce shout, rising above even the racket of the battle, which Fearless could hear loud and clear once more. "Stinger's running! He's getting away!"

Fearless jerked his head around, searching for his friend. He couldn't locate Thorn in the chaos, but he saw Stinger clearly enough. The big baboon was a dark blur of shadow against the broad crescent of the shoreline, and he was sprinting for Baboon Island. Fearless hadn't realized the battle had moved so close to the watering hole. *We've driven them back! We're winning.*

But if Stinger escaped, it would all be for nothing.

He spun back to Loyal and Titan. The two huge lions had broken their clinch and were stalking around each other, fangs bared and dripping dark blood.

"Go, Fearless!" snarled Loyal. "We'll hold Titanpride back."

Titan gave an infuriated, yowling scream as he prowled around Loyal. Fearless's breath came in harsh rasps. He glanced from Loyal to Titan and back again. The two still circled, eyes locked.

"What are you waiting for?" Loyal roared. "Go, Fearless!"

With a roar Loyal sprang. Titan reared to meet him, and once again the two lions collided in mortal combat, blood spattering the earth around them.

Clenching his jaws, tormented, Fearless turned. Stinger was almost at the entrance to Baboon Island.

Fearless loped into a run, racing after him.

CHAPTER 24

There were no stars; nightfall had brought storm clouds once again, spreading across the deep violet sky till it was black and solid with them. As Thorn hurtled through the trees, seizing creepers, leaping from branch to branch, he could just make out Stinger's fleeing shape, not far ahead.

With startling suddenness, the clouds broke. A violent gust tossed the branches, sending Thorn lurching, and a torrent of rain hammered down, soaking his fur instantly. But he sprang for the ground and as his paws touched it, the wind caught him. The powerful gust was like something alive, and it seemed to help him, driving him on through the trees as if he was flying. Rain streamed into his eyes and down his snout, but he didn't even bother to wipe it away as he ran. All that mattered was catching up with Stinger.

Somewhere behind him raced Mud, Berry, and Pear, and

behind them Justice Troop. As he ran on, a snarl rang out behind him, and he glanced back.

It was Fearless, his huge paws slamming the ground, much louder than those of the baboons. Once again the young lion's face was twisted into the glare of a merciless, single-minded predator, but this time, Thorn knew, it wasn't for him. Fearless's glowing eyes were locked on Stinger's racing shadow.

Thorn was sprinting faster than he ever had, but Fearless overtook him easily, crashing through thornbushes and closing in on the fleeing baboon. As the clouds shone silver with hidden lightning, Thorn saw the lion spring—but as his jaws snapped shut, Stinger jumped for a low branch and scrambled up. Fearless fell back, spitting fur and snarling, his paws thudding onto the earth.

Thorn didn't hesitate. He bounded up into the trees after the escaping baboon. He was so close now, his nostrils were filled with Stinger's smell: the dry tang of scorpion mixed with the hot odor of fear. *We've got him now. There's nowhere for him to run.*

Stinger paused just for an instant and glanced back, his eyes cold.

"Fight me, you coward!" yelled Thorn.

Turning again, Stinger only picked up his pace, springing determinedly through the wildly tossing branches.

Thorn clenched his teeth. The other baboons were racing across the ground below him. "Into the trees!" he yelled down. "After him!"

He had time to see his troop bound up in pursuit, and

then something sharp snatched at his chest. He staggered and almost slipped; a baboon's claws were digging into his rib cage. Fly's chipped fangs leered in his face and he was flung back. Sliding, Thorn tumbled to the ground.

More claws grabbed at him, tearing at his fur. Thorn fought to escape their grip, peeling back his muzzle to yell: "The Strongbranches! They're in the trees!"

And there were more of them. Stinger must have expanded his brutal force, taking in all the bullies and thugs of his troop. Berry's hoot came from nearby; she sounded angry and desperate. "They're everywhere!"

Thorn flung Grit Strongbranch away and bolted for the tree where he'd last seen Stinger. And there he was, pausing to glare back as his Strongbranches defended him.

Grit and Fly were right behind Thorn, judging by the crash of foliage, and ahead more baboons sprang out to block his way, but he snarled and lashed at them. Fang grabbed at Thorn and he dodged, raking his claws across the Strongbranch's chest. Berry flew at Splinter and tore at his face, letting Thorn scramble past.

"You're my father!" Thorn heard her scream after Stinger. "How could you do this? You're a monster! A killer! A liar!"

Stinger did not wait to reply. He leaped into the next tree, and Thorn bounded after him, his breath coming in angry rasps. The Crownleaf seemed to be constantly one tree ahead, and even when Thorn finally shook off the Strongbranches, he still lagged behind Stinger. As the rain lashed down and the trees whipped, Stinger's shadow grew more indistinct, until at last Thorn lost sight of him altogether.

He came to a frustrated halt, gripping a branch tightly with his forepaws. "You can't escape, Stinger!" he yelled into the trees ahead.

From the ground below him came a voice, weak and hoarse. "No. He went . . . that way."

Thorn's heart skipped. He peered down through the foliage. "Nut?"

"Quick. If you go . . ."

Thorn was already scrambling down, jumping to the earth with a thump. Nut lay slumped against the roots of a mgunga tree, his fur torn and sticky with blood and rain, his wavering paw pointing into the trees to the left. His face had been beaten to an almost unrecognizable mess.

But he was alive. "Nut!" Thorn held his shoulders gently. "Pear will look at your wounds. Wait for her. Hang on!"

"Never mind that," slurred Nut through his swollen muzzle. "Get after Stinger."

"I will." Thorn paused, then hugged the broken baboon against him. "Thank you. For everything."

Nut was shoving him away, weakly. "Get off . . ."

As Thorn drew back and gazed into his battered face, he could tell Nut was smiling.

There was no more time to lose. Following Nut's gesture, he sprang once again into the trees and leaped from branch to branch. They were slippery and treacherous, but if he kept up his speed he knew he wouldn't fall. The rain had intensified, and lightning turned the driving torrents of water to brilliant silver.

Somewhere close behind him, Thorn heard Fearless roar. *He's catching up.* Then, off to his left, came the resounding battle-trumpet of an elephant. *Sky!*

The knowledge that his friends were at his back gave Thorn extra energy and speed. Gritting his teeth, he sprinted on. A hind paw slithered beneath him, but he regained his balance. Through the trees he could make out the dull, rain-pocked sheen of the lake, illuminated every few moments by another dazzling burst of lightning. Thunder crashed and rolled constantly, one rumble fading into the next violent explosion.

The trees were thinning as the land ran out. There, right ahead, was the tip of the peninsula, jutting out over the rain-lashed water. Baboon Island. Narrow and long, it tapered to a sharp point. And in the very last tree, a spindly lone mahogany, was the hunched figure of Stinger. His chest was heaving with heavy breaths, and he threw panicked glances left and right.

There's nowhere left to run, False Parent.

Thorn stalked forward along a sodden bough. If his paws didn't slip, he could reach Stinger's perch from here.

Below him, two shapes walked out onto the flat scrubby ground and stood staring at Stinger: a lion and a young elephant. *They're with me. We can finish this together.*

Fearless's snarl was audible, even through the rumble of the thunder. "Let's kill him."

I'm with you, my friend.

But it was Sky who must give the final confirmation, Sky who knew the Great Spirit's mind. Thorn turned to look down at her, just below his tree, and she tilted her head to gaze up at him. Her eyes glowed with an intense light in the darkness, and he held her gaze for a long moment.

Then, out of nowhere, a violent jolt shot through him, rocking him on his paws so that he staggered. White light blinded him and he grabbed for a pawhold, reeling with shock; as his vision cleared, he saw Sky stagger.

Lightning!

Gasping for breath, he clutched a branch. He was still alive, he realized with amazement, and so was Sky, though she looked dazed with pain. But their luck might not hold out in a second strike; it was time to do what they must. Turning, Thorn sprang for Stinger's mahogany.

Stinger had retreated to the farthest branch, jutting out over the watering hole. As Thorn edged along it toward him, he caught sight of the black water swirling below. The ridged backs of crocodiles surfaced, then sank.

He stopped. Stinger was gazing at him, a smile playing on his face.

"Hello, Thorn."

Thorn stayed silent, his breathing harsh.

"I always knew you were a clever baboon," said Stinger, stroking his own chest fur idly. "I could have predicted you'd be the one to find out the truth."

"No," growled Thorn. "It's not just me. Every creature in

Bravelands sees you for what you are, Stinger. Even your allies do—they just don't care. You saw the Great Herd who came to fight you today. You know you're finished."

Stinger gave a light shrug. "I suppose I am," he sighed. "What a pity."

"Give yourself up," said Thorn.

"Give myself up?" Stinger laughed softly. "To be torn apart by your Great Herd? Tell me, clever Thorn, what would a trapped scorpion do? Would it surrender itself to be eaten by a hungry baboon?" He tilted his head. "Or would it raise its stinger and fight?"

Thorn stared at him, loathing in every bone of his body. "It would fight."

"Exactly."

Lightning flashed again, catching Stinger in a silhouette. And then he was on Thorn in the dazzling afterburn. Thorn managed to keep his grip and gave a high growl as he tore at Stinger's face, but the Crownleaf had the advantage of size, and he wrenched Thorn's arms away and twisted them viciously. Thorn's hind paws slithered on the sodden bark; he slipped, stumbled, and fell.

Lashing out in panic, Thorn caught hold of a slender branch with one paw, digging his claws in desperately. Above him, as he hung from a single hand, Stinger loomed. "I've already let you live too long," he sneered, and raised a foot, ready to stomp on Thorn's clinging fingers.

CHAPTER 25

Sky craned her head up, trying desperately to make out the fight through the rain that lashed her eyes. Fearless was on his hind legs, snarling as he clawed furiously at the trunk of the mahogany.

There seemed to be nothing she could do. That lightning strike must have been glancing, but the shock of it had drained her and she swayed where she stood, her head reeling with dizziness. Her heart pounding with frantic fear, she creased her eyes and peered up through the branches.

Above her, the dangling Thorn slipped again, his body jerking as he caught himself with little more than his claw-tips. Smiling, Stinger brought a foot down hard on Thorn's fingers. Sky gave a cry of terror. Somehow the younger baboon held on.

"We have to do something!" roared Fearless.

But what? Sky felt a stab of awful despair. In moments Thorn would fall—

Lightning blazed again, turning the sky and the lake to blinding silver, and Sky saw them: a flock of vultures sweeping on broad black wings through the storm. The birds dived toward the tree and through its branches, lashing at it with their wings, raking at the two baboons with savage beaks and talons.

"Thorn!" bellowed Sky. "Thorn, they'll kill you! Let go!"

"No!" Fearless cried. "Don't you see—they're not going for Thorn!"

It was true. Not a single beating wing touched the dangling Thorn; the vultures were attacking only Stinger, driving him back, sending him stumbling as he fought to protect his eyes. One vulture did seize Thorn's scruff with its talons, but only to support him as he dragged himself bit by bit up onto the wet branch.

"Is this you?" Fearless turned to stare in astonishment at Sky. "Are you using the Great Spirit to make them do this?"

Sky shook her head slowly.

Stinger was reeling back on his hind legs, forepaws raised protectively in front of his face as he snarled at the vultures. His back bumped into the mahogany's trunk and his eyes started open; another vulture slashed its claws, and Stinger dodged and slipped. He tumbled down through the branches to hit the sandy ground with a shrieking grunt of pain.

He was on his paws in an instant, but when he lurched along the edge of the steep bank, one back paw was trailing.

"Come on!" yelled Thorn. He was already jumping down from the lowest mahogany branches and racing after the fugitive. Sky and Fearless turned and ran after him.

Stinger glanced over his shoulder, his eyes brilliant with madness. He staggered to a halt at the point of the peninsula, where its banks plummeted down to meet the seething black water below. Glancing over the edge, Sky saw the sinister lurch and ripple of a crocodile's spine.

"Give yourself up," she called desperately to Stinger. "There's nowhere left to run."

He glared at her through the rain. Water streamed from his fur, mingled with the blood from the vultures' attack. The rest of the Justice baboons were catching up now, gathering behind Thorn, Sky, and Fearless to stare at the cornered baboon.

Stinger's gaze swerved past Sky, and his eyes widened. "Pear! Berry, my daughter! You'll help me, won't you? You both loved me once; isn't there just enough love left to save me?"

Sky watched as Pear bent her face into Berry's shoulder. Berry wrapped her arms around her mother, and they turned themselves away.

Fearless sprang forward, a silvery streak in the night, and pinned Stinger to the crumbling earth. He opened his jaws above Stinger's throat, and Stinger gave a strangled cry.

"Cub of the Stars!" he yelped. "Have you forgotten me? Have you forgotten all you owe me? I saved your life, Fearless—I saved it twice! I gave you a home and a family!" The baboon's eyes softened and darkened with warm emotion. "Nothing can change all that."

Fearless stared at him, tormented, his jaws slackening with doubt. In that moment, Stinger snatched up a rock and punched it straight into the lion's eye.

Rearing back, Fearless snarled with pain, pawing at his face. Stinger dragged himself clear and bolted.

Sky gasped as the Crownleaf lurched toward her, his face grim with malice and determination. He was stumbling between her and Berry, dodging through the narrow gap as baboons cried out in confusion. There was no time to worry about the Code, no time to ask what the Great Spirit wanted. Sky lashed out her trunk and seized Stinger's tail, swinging him up into the air.

Memories assaulted her like an ugly, solid darkness.

Bark's skull, crumpling as he slammed the rock down, again and again and again. Scorpion venom dribbling between her fingers as he squeezed it onto a dik-dik carcass.

Snatching up his infant daughter and running, filled with a bitter glee when he pictured the bereaved mother's grief.

Recoiling, touching the bleeding gash on his muzzle where that terrified monkey had lashed out with its claws. Oh, that would scar, but the creature would pay in its own blood. He kicked it back over the cliff onto the rocks below and reveled in its dying scream.

Oh, the delicious squealing of that baboon he loathed, the one who had insulted her, as the foaming river dragged him under! The excitement as he watched a petrified gazelle plead, hopelessly, for mercy!

How satisfying was the silent terror in Frog's eyes. Sky-Stinger smiled at his Strongbranches, admiring their ruthlessness as they strangled and smothered that silly, pious, inconvenient creature.

He reveled in the surge of triumph as he watched Thorn dragged away to be killed.

Now, at last, and best of all, the glorious joy of utter power and control as the herds bowed to him at the watering hole—

Sky staggered, gasping for air, dragging herself away from Stinger's horrifying life. The wind-torn darkness by the lake seemed bright in comparison. Stinger still dangled from her curled trunk, clawing at the air, screaming and shrieking, "You can't break the Code! Don't break it, you stupid brute! The Great Spirit will punish you!"

Sky shook herself violently, making Stinger bounce and thrash in the air. "It doesn't matter. Let the Great Spirit do as it must, Stinger Crownleaf. I know what Bravelands needs to survive!"

With a single deliberate pace, she was at the cliff, the lake gurgling and sucking far below. Drawing back her trunk, she hurled Stinger over the edge.

She watched his flailing limbs as he plunged toward the black water. A single furious shriek was swallowed as his head went below the surface, and then there was silence but for the rattle of rain and the eerie howl of the wind. Thorn, Fearless, and the Justice baboons rushed forward, gripping the edge of the cliff and craning to stare down.

Stinger's head surfaced once more, his features twisted by a warped grimace of hate and rage and terror. His paws thrashed for purchase as arrowing ripples formed in the water around him. The flashing sky lit up long, ridged backs as they rose, then submerged.

Then Stinger sank too. Foam churned, and thick-scaled tails lashed the air. Lightning blazed, and in a momentary light as clear as day, Sky saw the water turn red. Shudders rippled through her, and she felt a wrench of grief: not for Stinger, but for Great Mother, who had met the same awful death by his design.

The water calmed. Ripples spread out and broke in tiny waves on the shore.

Not a scrap of fur floated to the surface.

CHAPTER 26

How calm and still the lake is. Sky trembled on the promontory as morning light spilled from the eastern horizon.

The land's edges gleamed pale as the lilac sky lightened. A thin mist hung over the water's surface, and the glow of the rising sun sparked glints of gold on its gentle ripples. All that remained of the raging storm was a gentle breeze. As the Justice Troop baboons recovered from their stunned shock, the ominous silence was broken by whooping and cheering.

"The tyrant's dead!"

"Bravelands is free!"

Once again Berry flung her arms around her mother, and Thorn tried to embrace both of them at once.

A small brown shape crept past Sky and laid a tentative paw on Thorn's shoulder. Thorn twisted, startled.

"*Mud?*"

The little baboon did not get a chance to reply. Thorn flung his arms around him, hugging him and howling with delight. "Mud, you're back! You're alive! You're all right! Oh, Mud."

Sky could not hear Mud's mumbling reply; she only saw Thorn tighten his embrace, his eyes glowing with emotion. When Mud drew back a little from Thorn, his face was downcast with shame. "I'm sorry, Thorn. So sorry. I believed the worst of you, my oldest friend."

"It doesn't matter, Mud. We've saved Bravelands!" Thorn's eyes shone golden in the dawn's glow.

Fearless bowled into the two baboons, knocking them to the ground, and licked them till their fur was sodden all over again. Sky watched the three friends wrestle and roll and giggle in delight, but she herself felt detached, her heart heavy.

"Sky!" Thorn hooted, bounding over to her. "You're a hero! Don't look so worried."

Mud gave her trunk a brief hug that made her wince, and she flinched back as Fearless tried to rub his head against her leg. "Join the celebration, Sky," growled the lion. "You've earned it—if it hadn't been for you, Stinger might have gotten away."

"Oh, I'm happy. I am!" Sky forced herself to sound as if she meant it. She had to shake this awful hollowness, the deep unease and dread. "Well done, all of you. We did this together."

"We should get back to the rest of the animals," said Thorn. "Tell them the good news."

He called his new troop together, hugging them, slapping their backs, and accepting their congratulations in return. Together, with Thorn in the lead, the three friends and Justice Troop made their way back through the sun-dappled woodland of Baboon Island.

One or two baboons went racing away in terror at their approach. *The Strongbranches*, Sky realized. They were making their escape however they could, now that their bully of a leader was dead—and good luck to them. She doubted they'd find refuge with any baboon troop nearby.

Other baboons, though, crept from the trees, smiling and greeting them with delight. Thorn and Mud gave yelps of happy recognition.

"Moss! Petal Goodleaf! You're all right!"

"Lily! Is little Snail okay, and the baby?"

Their former troop-mates seemed just as glad to see Thorn and Mud, and Sky walked on in silence, letting them all enjoy their reunion. They seemed so full of plans for the future, she found herself envious.

"You have a new troop? Thorn, what about us? You won't forget us!"

"Let's join together! Brightforest and Crookedtree and Justice Troops, what do you think?"

"I *like* the name Justice Troop."

"So do I." Thorn laughed as he hugged yet another old friend. "But we have our justice now. Perhaps we should choose a new name for a new beginning."

Mud was grinning from ear to ear. Three little baboons were riding on Fearless's back, clutching his fur, their eyes starry with excitement.

As the other baboons jabbered and hooted with delight, Thorn slowed to walk with Stinger's daughter, Berry, at Sky's side. "Are you really all right, Berry?"

"It must have been painful for you," said Sky softly. "However bad Stinger was, he was your father."

Berry gave a sad sigh. "I'm sorry my father's dead, Sky Strider. I'm sorry it was necessary, that he turned into that baboon." She smiled at both of them. "But I'm happy Bravelands is free of him."

"We need a new Crownleaf," whooped a baboon nearby. "And I think it should be Thorn Highleaf."

Sky flapped her ears forward. Thorn stopped short, and Berry turned in surprise. "Thorn Highleaf?" she asked, creasing her brow.

"He's a Middleleaf, I'm afraid," called the baboon Sky knew was Petal Goodleaf.

"That's true." Petal's companion looked downcast.

"It *is* true," said Thorn awkwardly. He shot Sky a pleading glance, as if he was embarrassed, then gazed around at the baboons. "I'm sorry, Crookedtree, I misled you. Nut told you I was a Highleaf and I went along with it, but I'm just a Middleleaf." He lifted his apologetic gaze to take in all the troops. "You're all kind, and I'm flattered, but it's not possible."

"Nonsense," cried a voice, and Mud pushed through a cluster of baboons. "Bringing down Stinger is the greatest Feat there has ever been, and Thorn did it. I say he's a Highleaf. What does Sky Strider think?"

"Oh! I don't know much about baboon troops, and it's not my business," rumbled Sky in surprise, "but that sounds fair to me."

"I agree!" hooted Petal, brightening.

"And me!" enthused her friend.

"Thorn Highleaf!" yelled Moss.

Lily laughed, hugging her baby and Snail together. "Thorn Highleaf for Crownleaf!"

All around there was a chorus of agreement, the baboons whooping and cheering and pounding the earth with their paws. Thorn looked stunned. He glanced up at Sky, then back at his troop, and finally he turned to Berry.

"If you really mean it," he said softly, as the cheers hushed to an expectant quiet, "I thank you. Thank you, all! Not because of the Crownleaf thing—I mean, there would have to be a proper vote—but because it means . . ." He swallowed hard and took Berry's paws, gazing into her eyes. "It means we can be together. If . . . that is, if you still . . ."

"Of course I do!" Berry flung her arms around him.

Sky hadn't realized she'd been holding her breath. She sighed it out as a surge of warm delight went through her. She of all creatures knew how long Thorn had loved this golden-furred baboon—she'd seen Berry through Thorn's own eyes, after all. *He deserves this,* she thought, *so much!*

Berry drew away from Thorn and turned anxiously. "Mother? Are you—"

"I couldn't be happier." Pear's eyes shone as she bounded forward to embrace them both. "Let's go back to the camp to celebrate."

"Wait!" Thorn cried, hushing the cheers and hoots. "Wait, I can't leave Baboon Island yet. Where's Nut?"

Mud and Berry stared at him in astonishment. "Nut?" exclaimed Mud. "You're really friends with him now? I thought that must be another of Stinger's lies."

Thorn laughed and shook his head. "I can't quite believe it either, but Mud—he's changed. So much, you won't recognize him. He's been absolutely amazing."

"In that case," said Berry, taking his paw, "we'll help you find him."

She, Thorn, and Mud loped together into the trees, and Sky watched them go, rather wistfully. They seemed so content and purposeful.

Fearless was staring back toward the plain. It was quiet now, although Sky could make out the blurry shapes of animals milling around. "The battle has ended," Fearless murmured, "but did we win?" He looked anxiously at Sky, but she could give him no answer.

He sprang into a run and Sky followed.

As they emerged from the trees and raced up the shallow slope to the grassland, there was no sign of Titanpride. Of the lions, only Fearlesspride remained, on the far side of the plain, licking one another's wounds.

Fearless pulled up. "You did it!" he roared. "You drove Titanpride away!"

As Fearless bounded to his friends, Sky picked her way through the scene of the great fight, her insides aching. Titan-pride lions lay here, dead, but so did many other creatures, some from her own Great Herd. A zebra stallion was sprawled on his flank, glassy-eyed, his lips still drawn back in a rictus of fury; next to him lay two hyenas he had taken with him to the Spiritlands. Sky saw three dead wildebeests, a hippo, a cheetah with its throat torn out. And there at the edge of the churned earth lay Stamp the buffalo, his legs folded beneath him, his lifeless eyes set in a glower. At his head stood a grief-stricken meerkat, stroking his horns with its tiny paw.

"I was bringing a warning to Grimfoot," he told Sky miserably. "Some of Stinger's rhinos were organizing to ambush him. Those two lions"—he pointed—"they caught me, and they'd have killed me, but Stamp charged in and saved me."

Very gently, Sky blew at the meerkat's little head with the tip of her trunk. "You did well," she murmured. "And so did he. His spirit will find sweet grass, little meerkat."

He nodded mournfully and went back to stroking Stamp's horns. Sky trudged on, her heart heavy. Cheetahs sprinted through the milling survivors, carrying the news of Stinger's death, and Sky could hear cries of delight rising around her. *We've brought happiness back to Bravelands.* But thousands of flies rose in buzzing clouds, and vultures wheeled high overhead. . . .

With a great sigh, she glanced around for Fearless. He came bounding back toward her, his eyes distressed.

"I can see Keen and the others," he said, "and they look fine. But I can't find Loyal or Valor!"

"They can't be far away," Sky reassured him. "It's still chaos here, Fearless."

"Fearless!" A lioness's grunting roar made him turn, his ears flicking forward in delight.

"Valor!" He trotted a few paces as she loped toward him and butted his head into hers. "You're safe, thank the Great Spirit!"

Fearless's head was nuzzled into her neck, his eyes closed, but Valor's eyes met Sky's, and a bolt of dread went through the young elephant.

"What is it?" whispered Sky, and Fearless drew back sharply, staring at his sister.

"Fearless," croaked Valor. "I'm so sorry. It's Loyal. He . . ."

For a breathless moment, there was silence.

"No!" Fearless's roar of grief was heartbreaking; Sky could hardly bear it. "No, Valor, *how*?"

"Titan," she mumbled. "Loyal fought bravely, but Titan was too strong."

Fearless gave a yowling cry of distress and anger. "Titan? I'll kill him!"

"No, little Swiftbrother." Valor pressed her face to his. "Even if you were strong enough to do it, he's gone. He fled with his pride—or what's left of them."

Fearless gave a strangled snarl, and his tail lashed. Then he jerked up his head, and his eyes were glistening. "Where is my friend? Where's Loyal?"

His voice was choked. Sky reached out her trunk to stroke his back, not caring about the flashes of memory: a vision of two lions, sprawled happily together in the dusk on a lonely kopje.

"He died bravely, Fearless," she whispered.

"But he died," he said bleakly. "Take me to him, sister."

Valor turned and slunk away, her tail drooping.

Sky followed the two young lions to a patch of churned, bloodied earth. Loyal lay sprawled on his flank in the center of it, his eyes closed, his black-and-gold mane streaked with red, and his jaws slightly parted to show bloodstained fangs.

"He hurt Titan before he died," growled Fearless shakily as he touched his nose to Loyal's. "I'm glad for that at least."

"With luck Titan won't last long," growled Valor. "Loyal wounded him badly."

However violent his death, thought Sky, there was something very peaceful in Loyal's face. The rest of Fearlesspride was approaching, padding silently toward their leader, their triumphant faces now subdued and sad. Fearless crouched over his friend, his face buried in Loyal's bloodied mane.

Oh, poor Fearless. And poor Loyal. But the great lion had died fighting for his friend, the cub he had cared about so much; perhaps that was why he looked so calm in death. Gently Sky reached out to stroke Loyal's forehead—

And the open sky was gone, the sunlight extinguished.

Yes, he was happy in the shady coolness of this den, happier than he'd ever been. He no longer cared about being Loyal Prideless, not when Fearless curled there, sleeping in safety under his protection. No harm would ever come to him, Loyal thought fiercely, not so long as he was there to watch over him. And when the time was right—only then—he would tell him the truth. Oh, he longed for that day. It would be hard, it would be painful, but Fearless had to know. He deserved it. And he needed him to know it. Because he loved him.

Until that day, Titan would not lay a claw on his son.

With a gasp, Sky broke the connection. Panting and trembling, she stood there, staring down at Loyal Prideless, and at the cub who mourned his death without knowing how much he had to mourn.

"Sky?" Valor was eyeing her with a furrowed brow.

She swallowed hard. Suddenly that other vision made sense, the one she'd seen when she touched Fearless's unconscious body in the forest: Gallant's gentle words as he stood over his mate and infant son.

Yes, I love you both. This Swiftcub of ours is my heir. Any lion who denies it will have to fight me. Gallant had loved the cub as his own, but he'd always known he wasn't.

Sky reached out and touched Loyal's warm flank once more, just to be sure. And as the memories—with all their warmth and love and pride—washed over her, she knew there could be no doubt.

Loyal always planned to tell Fearless the truth. And now he'll never get the chance. It's up to me.

She took a deep breath.

"Fearless, I have something to tell you," she said. "This lion—Loyal—he was your father."

Fearless swung his gaze toward her. "What?"

"Gallant raised you with Swift," Sky whispered. "But he knew it too."

Fearless turned back to Loyal's corpse. He didn't look angry, only desolate. "But . . . it doesn't make sense." He glanced at Valor, who was gaping at him and at Sky. The other cubs had shrunk back, bewildered, exchanging shocked glances.

Sky gave him a pleading look. "Yet it's true."

"Are you *sure*?" Valor took a trembling pace forward.

"Yes. I'm absolutely sure." Sky stirred the dust with her trunk. "There's no doubt."

"I . . ." Fearless lapsed into silence.

Sky wanted desperately to comfort him, to offer some explanation, but what could she do? As Valor nestled at Fearless's side, rasping her tongue comfortingly across his jaw, Sky backed a few paces and turned away. He would need time, she thought: perhaps a lot of time. And Fearlesspride would be there for him. . . .

Rock was striding to meet her across the plain, and Sky trudged forward to meet him. His flank held channels of drying blood from several cuts, but he was otherwise unharmed. When she was in touching distance he reached out his trunk before drawing it back, though there was longing in his dark eyes.

"You're alive," he murmured. "You made the Great Spirit proud, Sky. Bravelands is safe, thanks to you."

"I'm glad we could do it," croaked Sky. "But I wish animals hadn't had to die."

"Their deaths are Stinger's doing, not yours. You're the one who gave them justice, Sky." He was gazing at her in wonder. "Surely you really are our Great Mother."

She drew away, shaking her head. "I've never been so sure that I'm *not*," she told him. "By killing Stinger, I broke the Code—after everything I said about keeping to it. No Great Parent could do such a thing." *And it's left me as empty as a hollowed-out tree*, she wanted to tell him, but she couldn't get the words out of her choked throat.

"Look." He gestured with his tusks across the plain. "Your family, Sky. The Striders have come home."

Her heart lifted a little, and she gasped. He was right. They came striding ponderously across the grassland toward the watering hole, great gray bodies blurred a little in the hazy sunlight.

"Everything will be all right now," Rock told her.

She tilted her head to him. "Will you go back to your herd?" she asked quietly.

"No." He shook his great head. "No, I don't think I will, not yet. I want to stay with you, Sky."

Touched, she blew a gentle breath at his strong chest, wishing she dared to embrace him with her trunk. Her family was on the shore now, lifting their trunks to scent the fresh morning air. It was a beautiful sight, but something held her back from running to them.

"I think . . . Rock, I'd like to be by myself for a little while." She managed to give him a reassuring smile. "I'll join you and my aunts at the watering hole a little later, all right?"

He nodded, watching her sadly as she turned and walked away.

She strode on past the blood and spattered mud of the

battlefield and onto the fresh green grass of the savannah beyond. Dewy mist still hung over the plain, softening the horizon and making the grass blades sparkle. The dampness on her tired feet was blissfully cool, and she walked on dreamily, the sounds of the herds fading behind her. At last, when she glanced over her shoulder, she could no longer even see them.

With a deep sigh she stood for a moment, letting the peace and silence flow over her. How tired she was. When she opened her eyes, she thought she saw the mist swirl and coil before her.

Sky tensed, blinking. There *was* movement in the white mist, and now it seemed to be coalescing. It drifted into an outline, as if something solid and real was carved in it: a familiar, well-loved shape.

Sky gave a gasping cry. "Great Mother!"

The shape of mist moved, drawing closer, and its ghostly trunk curled around her, comforting. She felt it not on her skin, but with her very essence. "Oh, Sky." The voice was as soft as a bird's wing, light but resonant, as if the mist itself was speaking to her. "You have served the Great Spirit so well."

"Have I?" Sky's voice trembled, hoarse in contrast to that gentle breath at her ear.

"You have, little one, but now your task is done. You carried the Great Spirit safely and passed it to the new Great Parent."

Sky sucked in a breath. "I did? Oh, Great Mother. So that's why—"

"What, little one?"

"It's why I feel so empty," she whispered. "I thought it was because of what I did to Stinger. . . . But it's because the Great Spirit isn't inside me anymore."

"That's right, Sky, and the feeling will pass. I promise you." The mist-trunk caressed her neck.

"Who . . . Great Mother, who is it? The new Great Parent. I never felt it happen! Will you tell me?"

There was a laugh like a breeze through new leaves. "Oh, child. You did feel it. And you'll know the Great Parent, in good time. The troubles of Bravelands are not over, but now its creatures have a Parent to guide them. And they'll need you too, Sky, for a long time yet."

The mist was dissipating, leaving sparkling dew on the grass blades. Sky reached for Great Mother, touching her trunk with her own.

Then the beloved form was gone, dissolved in the morning sun. The voice murmured again, but it was all around her, in the air and in the sky and in the earth beneath her feet.

"Well done, granddaughter. Well done."

EPILOGUE

The great vulture Windrider soared on the currents, letting them carry her higher in the crystal-blue sky. Behind her, her flock twitched their wingtips, following her lead as they gazed down on the great expanse of the savannah. Tiny herds crossed the sea of yellow grass on age-old tracks; in the bright blue patch of the watering hole, the blobs of darkness were hippos, wallowing in the shallows. Three giraffes browsed the edge of a forest, and a cheetah perched on a hillock nearby, scanning the plain for prey as her tiny, fluff-headed cubs capered heedlessly at her paws.

Blackwing angled closer to Windrider. "Everything seems to have returned to normal," he remarked in their rasping Skytongue.

"And yet it cannot have," murmured Windrider. "Too much has changed, Blackwing. Now fly with me, my flock, down to the Lightning Tree."

Twitching the tips of their broad black wings, they wheeled and stooped downward, jutting out their talons to catch the charred branches, flapping and stretching as they settled. One by one they hunched and folded their wings, and Windrider dipped her head to rub her long hooked beak against the blackened wood.

"Look, my flock," she told them. "The tree was struck again during the recent storms. Yet now—this."

Her companions peered down, their beady eyes widening as they studied the charred boughs. "Green shoots," murmured Blackwing, scraping gently at one with a talon.

"What does it mean, Windrider?" A younger vulture cocked her bald head.

"Rebirth," said Windrider. "Now all is as it should be, Longfeather. The Great Spirit has been appeased. New life means new hope. As you can all see." She nodded toward the distant tree line, and the flock followed her gaze.

A baboon emerged from its shadows, bounding across the long stretch of grassland and slowing respectfully as he drew close to the Lightning Tree. When he stopped beneath the vultures, he dipped his head. The flock watched him, hunched and intent.

"It's him," rasped Longfeather in awe.

"Yes," said Windrider. "It is." Old and experienced as she was, excitement coursed through her bones and blood.

The baboon cleared his throat, a little awkwardly, and gazed up at the birds. "I just—you can't understand me, and I know this seems odd, but I wanted to thank you. I'd have died if not for you. In that tree by the lake—Stinger would have killed me." His eyes flicked from bird to bird. "I'll never know why you did it, but I'll always be grateful. I'll never forget you, and I wanted to tell you that. If there was a way of speaking your language, I would. I wish you knew what I was saying. But *thank you*."

His gaze lingered on them, intent and piercing, as if he could convey his meaning with his eyes.

Windrider stretched her wings, tested the air, and took off. Around her the flock rose with her, and together they circled the Lightning Tree, wheeling over the baboon's head. He watched them, fascinated and a little nervous, his forepaws clenched on the ground.

Strange indeed, thought Windrider, but with every fiber of her being she knew it was true.

She dipped to the left, letting her wingtips brush his furred head, and he started. As one, the flock bowed their heads toward him.

"But we do understand you," rasped Windrider. The baboon froze, his eyes wide with shock as they locked on hers. "And you understand us," she told him. "Great Father."

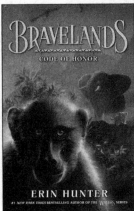
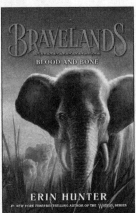